– ROCKING THE BOAT –

John said, 'That's the one, baby, that's the one!' Then laughed rather loudly at the sudden glances in his direction. He took a big pull at his drink. I looked over at Daddy to see if we were indeed at last on the same wavelength. His face had become inscrutable. Liam flashed a withering look at John, then went back to work.

'A small survey conducted on the south coast . . . listen to this . . . a small survey on the south coast' – Liam started to sift papers about like tarot cards; he was in the deep end now and he knew he must swim or sink – 'has revealed' – he looked up with magic-circle eyes, the stabbing finger cutting the air like a conjuror's wand – 'that if a *ship*' – my father shifted imperceptibly at this – 'were *moored* there, three miles out in *international waters*, equipped . . . are you ready for this, Jimmy?' – my father nodded testily – '. . . with a radio transmitter of *fifty thousand watts*, you could cover the whole country with music and it'd all be *completely legal*. A licence to print money.' Liam paused dramatically in the pregnant hush.

My father dropped words like pebbles into a well: 'What exactly did the survey reveal?'

Liam was ready. 'Why, that every able-bodied person with ears and a radio would tune in and turn on.'

– IAN ROSS –

Rocking the Boat

Mandarin

A Mandarin Paperback

ROCKING THE BOAT

First published 1990 by William Heinemann Ltd
This edition published 1991 by Mandarin Paperbacks
Michelin House, 81 Fulham Road, London SW3 6RB

Mandarin is an imprint of the Octopus Publishing Group

Copyright © Ian Ross 1990

A CIP catalogue record for this book
is available from the British Library
ISBN 0 7493 0462 6

Printed in Great Britain
by Cox and Wyman Ltd, Reading, Berks

'Around & Around' by Chuck Berry © 1958 Arc Music Corp.
Reproduced by permission of Jewel Music Publ. Ltd
'Boom Boom' by John Lee Hooker © Tristan Music Ltd
'Crying' (Roy Orbison/Joe Melson) © Acuff Rose Publications Inc.
Reproduced by permission of Acuff Rose Opryland Music Ltd
'I Got News For You' (T. Osborne/G. King) © 1963.
Reproduced by permission of Ardmore & Beechwood Ltd,
London WC2H 0EA
'I Put a Spell on You' (J. Hawkins) © 1956.
Reproduced by permission of Screen Gems-EMI Music Ltd,
London WC2H 0EA
'The Night Time is the Right Time' (Louis Van Dyke) © 1955,
Screen Gems-EMI Music Inc., USA.
Reproduced by permission of Screen Gems-EMI Music Ltd,
London WC2H 0EA

This book is dedicated to
Ian Kennedy Martin

You never know what is enough unless you know what is more than enough.

The road of excess leads to the palace of wisdom.

The Marriage of Heaven and Hell
Proverbs of Hell
William Blake

– One –

The call from John made a welcome dent in the monotony of the carwash on Richmond Road.

'Can you get away at lunchtime, lad? Something might be happening.'

I craned around warily at my half-brother Melville, who was making theatrical noises on the other line. 'No, darling, you were marvellous. No, no really. Simply bloody marvellous . . .'

'Well . . . Yeah, why not.'

A couple of years back I'd been plucked with all my music still within me from my school. A quango of parents and beaks had concluded enough was enough. The question of my future loomed large and mysterious until a business trip to America made Daddy see the light. Of course! What the boy needed was to travel to the mountaintop! The cities of the plain would learn him more than any amount of Latin!

We stayed at the Beverly Hilton Hotel, Beverly Hills. I conferred with platoons of room-service personnel, who gave me stiff slips of paper in exchange for everything under the sun, and were unanimous in urging me to have a nice day.

Daddy didn't slip so easily into West Coast culture. One nice day he presented me with my room-service bill. His manner was far from laid back.

'Nobody eats this much breakfast before eating this much lunch! Is that all you do all day? Don't you ever go out?'

'Well, Daddy . . .' It didn't seem worth mentioning my diet of TV.

'Right, well that's it, then. We'll see about this bloody nonsense.' And I was turned out daily on to the bland, sunbaked sidewalks.

It wasn't so bad. 1959 was the heyday and the swansong of US Autostyle. Detroit cranked out the last of its Great Cars and the first of its Great Sounds at almost the same moment. General Motors had started sinking as Berry Gordy Jr started rising, but we weren't to know that yet in Sunny Southern California, land of Jan and Dean. The finny fantasies drifted by, red and white on the rich black tarmac, manned by girls in pink with ponytails. When they spoke in their cheerleader voices, it was to say warm, encouraging things like 'Hey! Wheredya get that cute accent?' A good place to go and get acquainted, I discovered, was an automatic carwash on Santa Monica Boulevard. Here hamburgers and malts were served by girls on rollerskates. I would hang over a rail, full and vacant, and watch. It was every bit as entertaining as TV.

Giant brushes of multicoloured nylon throbbed and squirted waxy soap over the already gleaming autos, which wound along on a chain with wonderful monotony. There is a deep and meaningful pleasure to be derived from observing the same process repeated over and over again. Every so often the warm gale from a heavy-duty dryer would get up the circle skirt of a surfer-girl and give us all a look at more than just her bobbysox.

The lean, crewcut carwash guys wore bowling shirts with embroidered names, Steve and Dean and Chet. They acted, like all Californians, as if someone with a clapper-board has just said 'Take three.' With on-camera smiles they handed back the cars, all teeth and tans and tips. 'Have a nice day!'

After a few happy days of this it dawned on me that there might be a way to make it last for ever. I strolled thoughtfully back to Wilshire Boulevard as Happy Hour approached. I eased into the artificial sleaziness of Trader Vic's, trying hard to look over twenty-one. Sliding into a slippery booth I was received into the bosom of my family.

'Where the hell have you been?' my father growled.

'I went to an automatic carwash today,' I announced.

'An automatic carwash? What's that?'

'Well it's this big, you know, sort of garage place, where everyone takes their cars to get them washed.'

'How much do they charge?' my father demanded.

'Erm . . .' I had missed the most important point of all, of course.

My mother said, 'They don't have those in England, do they Jim?'

'No, they don't.' A speculative glint in his pale blue eye. 'Where is this place?'

Two years later Shaw Autowash Limited opened its doors to the unsuspecting British Motorist in the London suburb of Richmond. My future was assured. 'Paul's Bright Idea' had set me up for life. 'America did him a power of good, just as we said it would.'

Privately, though, the reservations rankled. I couldn't help missing the sunshine, the giant, low-revving gas-guzzlers, the bare-shouldered, warm-skinned girls . . .

As it was we had imported, under circumstances of considerable expense and delay, every piece of the latest gargantuan equipment that Chem Therm of California could muster. The tempestuous, gale-force dryers were there, and the colossal structures of multi-coloured nylon that would throb, roar and squirt soap all over your Morris Minor, with or without wax. The British Motorist jammed the place at first, curious and complaining in their Vauxhalls and Rovers. They huddled about the damp, steaming installation that seemed so much smaller than in the spacious hinterlands of America. The equipment itself was big enough, looked larger than ever, grotesquely dwarfing the penny-pinching cars. Whereas the Whales and Sharks had rolled and whirled off into the hot blue Pacific afternoon, shaking themselves clear of drips with bright rainbow sparkles, in Richmond it was different. Pinchfaced and testy the motorists scrutinised the drips like petty officers, muttering about rust, pulling out reluctant coins with clenched gloved hands, inching off finally into the grimy, drizzling street. Our carwash was one long dismal traffic jam at best, that subsided during most weekdays into a ghost-town of disgruntled casual labour. It was remarkable for an almost total absence of rag-top Cadillacs and golden-skinned girls.

The caff across the road sold dark, sinister tea or Camp coffee. Both tasted approximately the same with evaporated milk. At lunchtime they offered a variety of meats, darkly veiled in tepid, gelatinous gravy, each cooked to the same solid grey consistency, accompanied by wet mounds of yellowish cabbage. Hamburgers were not a feature in their repertoire, and the one elderly and unhygienic waitress, had it even been possible to mount her on rollerskates, could have made only the most doubtful progress through the persistent traffic jam on Richmond Road.

Our labour force consisted of taciturn tribesmen from Pakistan. They did not wear bowling shirts, and while it's true that if they had smiled they could've looked Californian, none of them ever did. They appeared and disappeared on an irregular basis from the local labour exchange. The only permanent rag basher was me. The responsibility for this abysmal twist in the tale can be laid firmly at the nattily shod feet of my older brother, Melville, a chap with wavy hair and a strong taste for blazers.

He had been to Elphinstone's before me and to say that his career there was distinguished would be to err catastrophically into understatement. From my first day my wretchedness was heightened to despair by the endless repetition of his glorious name. 'Your Brother was the Only Boy in the History of the School to be Captain of Football while he was still a Fag.'

Melville passed from these rich fields to even greater glory in the Grenadier Guards. One Christmas during a spot of duty on the post-war Rhine, the rank and file seeming in need of a boost to their morale, Second Lieutenant Shaw was called upon to organise the Battalion 'Smoker' – a harmless and uplifting entertainment for the troops.

But the rousing calls and repeated cries of 'encore' were too much for my brother. They went to his head like Liebfraumilch. He resigned his commission without delay, passed in and out of RADA with his usual ease, and the next thing we knew we were all sitting in the stalls of some theatre watching in awe as he kicked his legs in the chorusline of *Airs On A Shoestring* to a mixed reception from friends and relatives and brother officers alike.

One blood-relation to view Melville's progress with a certain amount of restraint was Daddy. A man not without imagination, he had a shrewdish inkling of the way things were headed. Tantalised by the memory of roars of acclaim from the BAOR, Melville soon decided that auditioning for bit parts could be an awfully tedious waste of his valuable time, which might be better spent venting thespian extravaganzas of his own on the cash customers of the West End.

Life was soon a playbill and a large cigar. Footlit, greasepainted faces of the charming light baritones, salad days and 400 Club nights, this became Melville's timewarp. However the public and critics might behave, Melville was a backs-to-the-wall believer in revue. His were the thin red lines of innocent dittydom, and how we all hated Bernard Levin. 'It's a personal bloody vendetta, that's what it is.' We all agreed, of course, in the chill drizzle of post mortems over midnight first editions; cold burgundy sour as a critic's curse. The shows opened and closed, often without a second night. Daddy, a reluctant angel indeed, reached into the nether regions of his pocket with ever deeper gloom.

Paul's Bright Idea when it came along in the nick of time was a gift horse not to be looked in the mouth by Daddy. It didn't take him long to convince my brother that it had been Melville's Bright Idea all along. So Melville got to put his feet up in the warm office with 'Manager' on the door, with nothing more arduous to do between phone calls than boss me around.

He encouraged me to reach down beneath wheel-arches and bumpers where stubborn grime might transfer itself to fingers that could have been more profitably employed unbuttoning the blouses of girls and fumbling with their bra-straps.

'I have to go now, Melville.'

A moment of bemusement as he glanced up from the telephone with the same curtain-call smile – 'Hold on a moment, darling . . .' – now slightly quizzical about the corners, as with a heckler. 'Go? Go where?'

'A matter of some urgency in town.'

I listened with only half an ear and sipped my pint distractedly as Henry Pelham described in pitiless detail his recent progress round a certain bend at Silverstone. It was gripping stuff all right, but failed to bind me fully in its spell since my attention kept wandering to the door and the vexed question of John. Valuable feeding time was passing and there was no sign of him. The possibility of a no-show could not be ruled out since strictly speaking the Admiral Rodney, with its hale and hearty clientele, was off-limits to John, beyond the pale in the tight geography of places that were cool. It was a measure of his elaborately camouflaged anxiety that he'd agreed to meet me there at all.

I'd met Johnny Meadows only a few brief weeks before when Henry, because he was a viscount, got enrolled on the roster of London's most desirable new nightspot, Pandora's Box. My name had been omitted from the list. Henry was quick to spot the silver lining in this cloud. He could get me in and I could pay the bill.

Once safely inside this hallowed hole I felt I'd arrived at last. Even Henry was a bit out of his depth here where one was pushed and shoved at every turn against the famous. The music pounded, the tough model girls danced, and the waiters charged like the Light Brigade.

I nursed my hard-on and watched with hazy lust as the models writhed and boogied with the Caines and Stamps and Finneys. That's when I noticed how much action surrounded the DJ. He seemed to be the centre of a surging sea of models and laughing, carefree hairdressers. That's it! If I couldn't get at it direct I could get at it through him. Like lightning I formulated my plan. DJs play requests, don't they? At least they did at all the parties around Haslemere, and this process requires the personal touch, a dash perhaps of the old charm. At public school they teach you how to deal with people in every walk of life, and bend them to your will without them knowing. I felt brashly confident of pulling it off in my carefully selected nightclub kit: tight jeans of some dull gold material, loud striped shirt, old school tie, brown suede shoes, hair quiffed in irresistible imitation of Elvis and Billy Fury. At school I was handicapped by, among other things, having a face like a monkey. But the tables were turning now. Everything I had seen of groups in the pubs and clubs of London suggested an encouraging reaction from girls to boys of anthropoid appearance. How could I fail as I swaggered across the floor, dry-mouthed, lip curled in Presleyesque disdain.

'I'd like to listen to a Billy Fury record, if you don't mind,' I ventured with some heartiness.

At first I didn't think he'd heard me, so I repeated my request, this time a bit louder. Now, very slowly, he turned and took me in with dark and world-weary eyes.

'Would you now?' He considered me intently. 'Yes,' he concluded, 'I believe you would,' and turned away again, apparently exhausted by the experience. I shifted from foot to foot.

'Well, could you play one, please?'

'No, I couldn't.'

'Why, don't you have any?'

'Not exactly.'

'How do you mean, not exactly?'

'You're very persistent, aren't you?'

'Well, I . . .'

'Look, man, what I mean is, no I won't play any Billy Fury record, even if I did have one, which I don't, OK? I mean, I just don't play requests, that's all. That's not very difficult to understand, is it?' He had become quite animated, had removed the cigarette from his finely chiselled lips with two long fingers and was making small, delicate gestures, like someone defining the shape of a narrow, oblong box, with his hands. I hung irresolutely on, dumbfounded and temporarily unmanned, while the Searchers sang 'Needles and Pins'. My continued persistence caused John to stir uneasily, and make minuscule adjustments to his pose. A few moments of agony later I was struck with a possible solution, the same one I had used not long ago to scrape an acquaintance with Henry.

'I say . . .'

John's eyes flicked up, amazed and wary.

'. . . would you like me to buy you a drink?'

He treated me to a long, penetrating stare, one which in the subsequent months of my coolness training I would try so hard to emulate, one which, with a certain sultry infusion, made mush of the emotions of girls.

'Not if it means I have to listen to Billy Fury all night.'

Like a chalk and cheese sandwich we became friends. John was cool. I was not. In those days, when Chelsea was still Chelsea and the King's Road Cowboys reigned supreme, it was important to be cool. With infinite patience John undertook the task of showing me how.

John's head appeared around the saloon bar door, one hand minutely adjusting a dark flip of hair. The Castrol 'R' Crowd were letting off steam by the pint. His height enabled him to search over most of their heads. By climbing on my chair I caught a cautious eye. 'Hi! Over here!' I saw him flinch. He replaced his shades. Stooping slightly he sidled through the throng, white hands fending hairy tweed off the tailored darkness of his frame.

'Hi, John, what's happening?' I couldn't wait to know.

'Nothing much. We have to go.'

In the car I raised my mild objections to his cavalier approach, '. . . not to mention lunch.'

'We can have lunch in the Kenya.'

'In the Kenya?'

'Why not? Other people do.'

'Yes, but I still don't understand the reason.'

'Does there always have to be a reason for everything you fucking do?'

'I just wondered, you know.' Most things we said included – sometimes even consisted entirely of – the words 'you know' and 'I mean'.

'I mean, God! As a matter of fact there is someone you ought to meet, who might be there.'

So this was it at last. This undoubtedly was a set-up and I was the mark. I prayed the kind of moody we were getting into would be heavy.

We pushed carefully into the warm and steamy fragrance of the Kenya Coffee Bar, the last stop on the King's Road for any self-respecting face, before Sloane Square and the Belgravia straights. The hustlers looked up warily as we entered, then quickly down again, avoiding painful eyeball-contact. They lounged with affected nonchalance over their Pentaxes and Hasselblads, toying with cappuccinos and keeping a weather eye on the King's Road and each other, for prey or the slightest sign of weakness.

We found a lonely enough table but sat in silence anyway, precluded by the rules of cool from speech. We waited and waited and stared off into anywhere but each other, while the electric wall-clock swept time interminably away, until I could stand it no longer.

'Is this guy definitely coming?' I said guy now instead of chap. My voice was tainted with a slight mid-atlantic accent not unlike John's, though he could at least claim American birth and domicile until the age of two. He couldn't answer, of course. Moments later I heard him grunt, 'Aha.' Looking up, I caught him in surreptitious scrutiny of the door. I followed his furtive eye.

The small and smiling figure making its way towards us struck a sense of excitement straight into my heart. He beamed in on every shifting eye in the place like a charismatic searchlight, piercing their defences, sussing out their secrets.

'Hi. Howareya? What's happenin'? Howsitgoin'?' The uncoolness confused me, the nondescript clothing too. Later I learned that he was so cool that clothing didn't count. Paradoxical were the dilemmas for the novice in those days. Liam O'Mahoney sat down and I was introduced as an afterthought by nonchalant, nervous John. 'Howareya?' He held out a thin, white, fragile hand and his wide grey eyes pierced my soul.

O'Mahoney had the power of a Svengali. His values were all upside-down from mine. I was a bumpkin in his presence. Anything I might have learned from John seemed desperately superficial now. The grandson of a Hero of the Revolution who died at Dublin post office in 1916, he was a champion of impossible dreams, what he called the 'nineteen-sixteen thinking', a wolfish idealist who if asked at parties what he 'did' would smile terribly and say he was in the why-not business.

The Kenya meeting was purely exploratory, to 'check me out', to determine if I was a worthy recipient of this pitch of pitches. To see if I could dig it.

'How does the idea of making millions of pounds grab ya, baby? Literally millions!'

What could I say? No one had ever called me 'baby' before.

'You interested?'

'Absolutely!'

We were three up in my MG. Liam was at the wheel. John had long legs, so I was huddled behind the front seats navigating and wondering at the performance of my car in the bony, white-knuckled hands of O'Mahoney. The wet weather had cleared and a washed late sky shone blue on the shiny highway to Haslemere and my father.

Daddy had found his slab of wilderness somewhere in the no man's land between Hindhead and Haslemere, a hundred acres of stubborn unpromising scrub, and had set feverishly about converting it into his idea of Paradise. I suppose it was something in the blood of his forebears, who had settled in New Zealand and behaved in much the same way. The house was on top of a hill which became impassable most winters, a fact that suited him, and only him, down to the ground. Colonial pioneers like nothing better than a good battle with the elements. Remote, bleak and deeply unsociable – somehow the chained wheels of his Rolls Royce would always get him up, past the stranded sideways people who littered the snowy ditches. Apart from this obvious plus, and the fact that he knew nobody in the district and didn't want to know them, it was never fully understood why he had stuck his pin in this precise spot on the map. Particularly by my mother. She had been uprooted from the genteel pleasantries of Weybridge and a whole fragile eco-system of friends, and the nice butcher, and Fuller's in the High Street, and once a week to the Odeon, Walton-on-Thames. Haslemere was not her scene at all, where quasi-county ladies, mostly in tweeds and some of them Hons, snubbed her.

As Liam hurled the MG down the drive I caught a glimpse of the old frontiersman through the pines where he was wrestling to create a clearing with his Massey Ferguson tractor and chain. No amount of blows to his own shin, nor gut-rending mechanical setbacks could deflect him from the challenge of the endless task.

We pulled up in front of the house which had once been modest, small and square, but now had sprouted Spanish wings. The swimming-pool glittered in the fading rays through incongruous wrought-iron arches, beyond the crazy-paved expanse of patio.

'You chaps wait here.' I swung stiffly out on to the familiar ground, my heart sinking slightly. 'I'll see if I can get the old man to come and talk.'

Liam gave me a quick boost. 'That's the scene, baby! Remember' – he paused until I got into my stride – 'heavy heavy bread!'

'Relax, man, just relax.' John was looking extra languid, his heavy eyelids drooping with disdain.

I stumbled through the undergrowth, heading for the crackling racket that marked my father's battleground. I got quite close and yelled unheeded for a while. Then he glanced up with the slightly cornered look of some animal that feels both hunted and disappointed by what it sees approaching. Things had not been easy between us for some time.

'Daddy' – his power saw stalled abruptly – 'I've brought some people to see you.' My voice bellowing in the sudden silence.

'People? What people?' His wet face boiled under a fine patina of pulverised undergrowth, pale eyes vivid as they focused on me briefly, before returning to the more wholesome problem of a sticking carburettor.

'Friends of mine.' He kept his head down for a while, tinkering, in the faint hope that I might go away. I waited on and tried another tack.

'It all seems to be coming along pretty nicely . . . doesn't it?'

'What do they want?'

'They just want to talk to you.'

'What about?'

'Well, er . . . something pretty interesting, actually.'

Liam had instructed me under no circumstances to broach the proposal myself. 'Leave all the moody to me. You don't want to blow it.' With all my thumping heart I did not.

My father said, 'Hmmm,' and started giving what looked like the kiss of life to the machine until I thought the whole thing might've slipped his mind. I cleared my throat. He spat out some petrol and said, 'Do you think they'll want to stay to dinner? You'd better tell your mother.'

'Absolutely!' And I strode purposefully away.

'This is a fantastic set-up you have here, Jimmy. Absolutely fantastic.' He called him Jimmy. He even refused a drink.

We were sitting in what my mother called the drawing-room and my father called the lounge. Liam had brought an impressive stack of papers and sat poised above them like a falcon. My father relaxed in his usual chair by the window with his drink, seemingly lost in reverie. John and I sipped in silence. The clock ticked. My father's eyes slid back into focus to find Liam watching him intently, a slow, wicked smile spreading over his face, one sharp finger stabbing down at the documents.

My father, trapped in his gaze, smiled too, and shifted in his chair. He cleared his throat expectantly.

'This is the one, Jimmy, this is the one. This is the big one!'

'You'd be surprised how many times I've been told that.'

'No, I wouldn't. A cat like you. You've heard 'em all. But this one you will know. Jimmy, I'm tellin' ya, when ya hear this one you will know!' Liam leaned forward, emphasising through a dog-face grin. I watched, mesmerised, while the orderly glue around my life began to come apart.

'You're not into sounds now, are you, Jimmy?'

This I could confirm. Daddy's views on pop music had always been expressed very clearly.

'Paul here keeps me in touch.' I couldn't believe it. I writhed and grinned like a performing worm.

'I think I know what's going on.'

'Do you now, do you now? Yes, I believe you would.' Liam coiled like a cobra and his eyes glittered. 'But do you know what's going on underneath? In the little clubs and pubs the world can't see there's a whole revolution brewin'!' – liam paused for emphasis – 'And a fortune just waitin' to be made!'

My father raised his eyebrows slightly, and scratched his ear.

'And do you know what the key to that fortune's going to be?'

My father leaned forward a little in his chair. 'Why don't you go ahead and tell me?'

Liam sat back and made a single cut with his hand. 'COMMUNICATION!'

The word broke out like a cannonshot. We all started back slightly in our chairs. I beat my fist slowly on the velour arm of mine, and smiled the tight smile of one who knows.

John said, 'That's the one, baby, that's the one!' Then laughed rather loudly at the sudden glances in his direction. He took a big pull at his drink. I looked over at Daddy to see if we were indeed at last on the same wavelength. His face had become inscrutable. Liam flashed a withering look at John, then went back to work.

'A small survey conducted on the south coast . . . listen to this . . . a small survey on the south coast' – Liam started to sift papers about like tarot cards; he was in the deep end now and he knew he must swim or sink – 'has revealed' – he looked up with magic-circle eyes, the stabbing finger cutting the air like a conjuror's wand – 'that if a *ship*' – my father shifted imperceptibly at this – 'were *moored* there, three miles out in *international waters*, equipped . . . are you ready for this, Jimmy?' – my father nodded testily – '. . . with a radio transmitter of *fifty thousand watts*, you could cover the whole country with music and it'd all be *completely legal*. A licence to print money.' Liam paused dramatically in the pregnant hush.

My father dropped words like pebbles into a well: 'What exactly did the survey reveal?'

Liam was ready. 'Why, that every able-bodied person with ears and a radio would tune in and turn on.'

He attacked his papers now with gusto, and read out extracts from the tightly printed sheets. 'The signal carried by water will be greatly strengthened. The three-mile limit will actually help us in that way. With a fifty kilowatt transmitter and a hundred-foot mast we'll cover the whole south of England including Greater London and probably Birmingham and Bristol. That's twenty million people at least. According to our projections, at least seven million are in a category that'll tune in once or more every twenty-four hours. In advertisin' terms that's major, and I personally reckon it'll be much more. There's nothin' like this happenin', Jimmy, nothin'. It'll be like water in a desert. The hottest thing the poor fuckers've got right now is Godfrey Winn!'

My father nodded in slow, sage silence.

Liam proceeded after a quick intake of breath: 'Supposin' we sell only six minutes in every hour of commercials – these cash projections are based on six minutes only – against the comparatively tiny cost of operation . . .'

'Tell me a bit about cost,' my father interrupted, 'never mind the overheads for the moment. What do you reckon it would cost to set it up?'

This was the question Liam had been waiting for. His voice was tense but precise.

'The ship, say twenty grand.'

'That's not too bad.'

'Then there's all the equipment and the cost of fitting her out. First we have to ship everything over from the States.'

'Why?'

'America's the place where offshore radio started. All those revolutions they stir up round the world with the Voice of America? That stuff's on ships. It comes from Galveston, Texas. Some of it's pretty expensive.'

'What do you call expensive?'

'The transmitter's fifty grand. And the mast. The mast isn't cheap either.'

'So what do you think for everything? Could it be done for under a hundred thousand pounds?'

Liam shook his head. 'A hundred and fifty.'

My father puffed out his cheeks dubiously. 'I don't see how or where the hell all this could be done, quite apart from the cost!'

Liam was ready for this. This was his ace in the hole. 'Aha. That's the easy part. Don't worry about that part at all. The whole operation will be done in total secrecy at my father's private port on the Irish coast.'

'I see. That could be useful.' My father was pensive. 'Just how illegal is all this?'

'It isn't illegal at all. That's the whole point. But if the British government got wind of it and could stop us before we were on the air, they would. Afterwards it'll be too late. It's essential that we hit them with a *fait accompli*. This is how it works under international law. A Dutch team will help us set it all up. Legally the ship will be owned by a company in Liechtenstein, completely secret, then leased to another company in Panama, where the government will give us a flag of convenience. The Panamanian company licenses an Irish company to sell advertising and collect money in the UK. The Irish company just bungs the one in Panama enough cash to pass to the right guy in the government, who tears up all the diplomatic bullshit from HMG! The Irish company operates here without any problems. We don't have to pay English tax. The radio station is on Panamanian soil, three miles off the English coast, and there's not a damn thing anyone can do about it. A beautiful set-up!'

'What about the ship? What about the sea-crew?'

'The Dutch team take care of all that.'

My father stared out of the window at the gathering darkness for a long time. At last he broke the silence with a sigh. 'In the event that all this could be organised, how much profit are you projecting it would make?'

Liam sat up in his chair until the air in the room became completely still again.

'A million pounds a month.'

In the cosy dining-room candles twinkled in cut glass. My mother chatted to John about fashion and the startling rise in hems.

Liam concentrated his spell on me, boggling my mind with tales of his Soho nightspot, the Happening. My father listened like a grim sponge, taking it all in, chewing silently. Without warning he rose to his feet and made for the door, throwing his napkin on to his plate. My mother's feathers fluttered.

'Wherever are you going, Jim, in the middle of dinner?'

'I just need to ring a few people up.'

'They'll probably be eating too, dear. Who were you thinking of?'

'Never mind who.' He was getting testy now, more his old self. 'Just Jeremy Hammond and one or two others.'

'But won't it wait?'

'It won't bloody wait!' My mother flinched. 'This boy here wants a radio ship. Paul wants a job. Washing cars apparently isn't good enough for him any more. Now he has to start a pop revolution! I need some partners.' He slammed out of the room.

In the shaken silence that followed, conversation never really got going again, in spite of brave attempts. Wine glasses drained away and food grew cold. Minutes crawled like snails. Liam was strangely silent.

When the door opened at last it was abrupt and shocking. We all looked up. My father's face was grim. He shook his head. 'Well, Liam, I'm afraid . . .' I felt my face drain into my heart. Liam looked like a death's head. John stared intently into his empty glass. '. . . you're going to have to break the habit of a lifetime and have a drink with me now. I've got your money for you.'

– Two –

We got the money in cash. First there was a cheque for the full amount: £210,000. John and Liam and I went to the bank. With toe-curling loudness Liam engaged the lady clerks in intimate conversation: how did they like workin' in a bank? How regularly did they get laid?

He disappeared through a door marked 'Private', filling us all with apprehension and temporary relief, soon to re-emerge, expressive gestures all but covering up the discreet bum's rush, rapping wild political gibberish to a patient-faced man in a grey tie.

'Private's just a state of mind, baby, believe me. Take JFK, for instance. He's the fuckin' president of the United States . . .'

'I'm sure you're right, sir. If you'll just take a seat over there. We won't be long.'

Liam's face was excited as he sat down. 'They can't wait to get us out of here.' It wasn't real. It didn't feel real. I said so. 'Forget about reality. It's only real when we see the green foldin' stuff.'

'Reality is for people who don't have a dream,' said John mysteriously.

'Yes, but' – thinking of my father, whose signature was scrawled offhandedly on the bottom of the cheque – 'won't people think it odd? I mean, drawing it all out at once in cash?'

'Faith, baby, faith. Walkin' on water, that's what this scene's all about.'

John patiently explained, 'If the cheque goes through it means they're really with us all the way. If it doesn't, well . . . it's been a waste of fuckin' time.' He finished heavily, then grinned a tense, sloppy grin.

'It will.' Liam's eyes were bright.

It did. Suddenly there it was, stacked like packs of playing cards in the black case which Liam had provided for the convenience of the bank. The patient grey man handed over the swag.

'Do you have a car waiting?'

'No.' Today we would travel by bus.

'Well, cheerio.'

'Nice doing business with you,' said John. At the last moment Liam paused, framed against the plate-glass exit, faced the massed ranks of clerks and typists, black bag held high. 'Kick out yer jams!'

Our first corporate investment turned out to be the complete refurbishment of my flat. We went straight there from the bank.

My London home was in a peeling Georgian terrace, somewhere in the maze of streets between South Ken and Sloane Square. The tall houses, with their jutting porches and railing-bound basements, were all vaguely cream, anywhere between dirty English snow and Nanny's egg custard. Seediest of the lot, by far, was No. 28, whose grimy façade was patchiest, whose window-frames were the rottenest on the block. The owner/operator was a Mrs Flowers, a widowed charlady of the old school. After the untimely death of her Albert, a king among husbands, during the blitz, Mrs Flowers had been obliged by reduced circumstances, and some mix-up over Albert's life insurance, to take in lodgers. The ad had read 'furnished', and this proved to be a considerable understatement. No space or surface had been spared. 'That's Albert's mother – Mrs Dawkins that was – passed over now. You can blame 'er for all this stuff, if you don't like it.'

We took the stairs two at a time like boys returning from a really whopping dare, and fell breathless into the heavy horsehair chairs in the sitting-room.

'Fuckin' unbelievable!'

'Too much.'

'Let's have a look!'

The case lay on the floor between us. Liam opened the lid and we gawped at the contents, awed into silence. Liam was the first to recover. He got up, went over to the mantelpiece and stood there, resting his elbow, looking vacantly at the reflection of the room in the mirror. In keeping with the general decorative scheme the shelf was densely over-populated with china figurines, glass Bambis, and mementoes from seaside resorts.

Liam's fingers toyed absently with a terracotta statuette of the Infant Samuel at Prayer. Then, more deliberately, he picked it up. As he caught me watching in the mirror the intentions of the little green demon inside him gathered on his face. They became apparent in the same moment to both of us. Liam and I were locked together into something inevitable, inexplicable. He smiled with bared teeth and ray-gun eyes. John was outside the circle. He swung round from the mirror with the doomed ornament raised high, like a sacrifice. He brought it down hard, at the same time executing a little stamping jump with his feet. All the while his eyes burnt into mine. The coloured clay exploded on the hearth. I smiled back with the same smile, like a mirror.

John jumped out of his fiscal reveries and yelped, 'What the fuck . . . ?' I rose and moved over to the killing ground, like a zombie, still smiling. I picked up a white china shepherdess, complete with lambs, and hurled it to destruction. My blood roared in my brain. Liam picked up two things and smashed them both at once, this time letting out a sound that started somewhere at the dawn of time.

'Yes,' I cried. 'Yes! Come on, John!' I made a clean sweep of the mantelpiece and we all three started stamping and caterwauling like Sioux. Nothing was spared. After the destruction of every ornament we moved on to the many possibilities presented by the kitchen.

Every Thursday six pounds' rent became due and payable to Mrs Flowers. This transaction was difficult to avoid because her lair lay between the flat and the only point of egress to the outside world. On Thursdays Mrs Flowers lay in wait there, like a troll under a bridge. Embraced by this sum was a kitchen full to overflowing with crockery of every kind. Plates, chipped but serviceable, almost every one a different colour and size, were piled up high. Cups, saucers, mugs, bowls, dishes and tureens; glasses for wine, whiskey, water, beer, highballs, snifters, shots. We smashed the lot.

When at last we fell into an exhausted lull we heard the agitated pounding at the door. Then and only then did the magnitude of our actions seep through the fever and dawn. With terrible clarity I awoke to the devastation all around. Something inside me felt like a descending lift.

'Whatever's going on! Whatever's going on!! Open up at once or I'm calling the police!'

'It's all right, Mrs Flowers. Just coming.'

The front door to the flat opened inwards onto a tiny half-landing at the bottom of a short flight of stairs. Beyond this point, it seemed to me, Mrs Flowers must somehow be prevented from advancing. But how? In slow motion I approached the front door.

'For God's sake keep the old bag from coming up!' Hoarse words of warning from John only panicked me more. Recently he had been toying with the idea of hanging up his own hat in my 'pad', and premature spasms of droit de seigneur were now causing him obvious anxiety.

'Yes, yes, OK, Mrs F.' I gingerly opened up a crack of communication. 'Now, what seems to be the trouble?'

'Mrs Flowers, is that you now?' We had been reckoning without the power of Liam's blarney.

'It most certainly is!'

'Come up and join us, why don't you?'

'I most certainly shall!' Mrs Flowers suited action to these words. 'And who might you be?'

Liam stood at the top of the stairs, ready to receive her, for all the world the King of Courtesy embracing an honoured guest into his heart and home. He held out the hand of friendship, at the same time standing aside with a flourish to let her pass. 'Howareya? Yer lookin' good. Paul here's told me all about you.' Mrs Flowers, a bit puffed, began to melt a little. 'Funny, though, he always gave me the impression you'd be much older than you are!' Not wholly impervious to this gallantry, she was showing definite signs of calming down when her forward momentum brought her level with the open kitchen door. Large, sheepish John hulking nonchalantly over most of it failed completely as a cover-up. The only thing holding Mrs Flowers back over the next few seconds was stunned disbelief. She seemed more awed than angry. Nothing her imagination could have stretched to could have readied her for this.

'Lor luv a duck, Mr Shaw. What ever . . .' Words failed her.

'We thought it was time for a bit of a clear-out.' Such was the enthusiasm of Liam's delivery that this monstrous act of destruction seemed for a moment like a frightfully good idea.

'A new broom sweeps clean, don't you know!' John had a fondness for old English adages and Regency banter.

Mrs Flowers picked her way like a stick insect into the debris of the sitting-room. Even Liam was spellbound into silence by the scene. She sat down slowly with her back to us, like a theatre-goer taking her seat in the front row of the stalls. Her shoulders started shaking, and, after some moments, sharp, sobbing cries rent the air in the wrecked room, stabbing our consciences so that we shot each other guilty glances, and made furtive, irresolute movements with our hands and feet.

John cleared his throat, and made as if to place a comforting hand on the poor, convulsed creature. She let out a hair-raising howl and turned her tear-stained face in our direction. Her breath came in great, drowning gulps as she fought to form words. Liam stared at me with wonder, then leaned over the landlady with a grin of rapture.

'Tell us in the name of Jaysus, what's the joke?'

Mrs Flowers shook her head helplessly. 'I can't, I can't . . .'

The penny dropped on me and John.

'I can't stop thinkin' of my mother-in-law!' Mrs Flowers was at last able to gasp, before whinnying off again into a new fit which in the end only brandy, straight from the bottle, could relieve. 'Whatever would she say!'

In those days in pre-swinging London things tended to happen in cellars, where black culture manifested itself aromatically on the bluesy air. At first I had thought myself extremely cool, when, with Henry Pelham, I made the descent into Pandora's Box. The place was, after all, underground. John and Liam soon set me straight. With them I would listen to Sonny Boy Williamson and Ray Charles, and for the first time partook, with some anxiety, of the dreaded reefer. Where I came from, in the Home Counties, this sort of thing could still turn a decent white boy into a human wreck overnight.

Liam was heavily involved in the Club and Music scene in London. His club, the Happening, was definitely below ground level and opened my eyes to just how sheltered my life had previously been. In the hellish darkness 'heavies' kept anything that might be going on there under tight control. Heavies were patient-seeming men, of few words, about seven feet tall, with torsos like Victorian chests-of-drawers. They wore tight-fitting dinner jackets, and, at the Happening, kept their hatchets on a convenient shelf above the inside of the door.

The prevailing ambience was of sweat, urine and stale marijuana. Light-bulbs were hand-painted red. The only other illumination came from occasional violet neon strips which stittered balefully, showing up the stamp on the back of one's hand. Imported rhythm and blues records wailed over the dense throng, played by a black DJ called Needles, on a sound system that was primitive but loud.

'That fellow seems pretty hip!' I pointed out excitedly to John on my first visit. His pained look was just visible in the gloom.

'You don't know the meaning of that word, sweetheart.' And, as an afterthought, 'Neither does he.'

Musicians with whom Liam was 'thinkin' of gettin' somethin' together' would occasionally play there live.

One late morning in early May 1963, John and I were loafing about the flat, thinking about lunch, and mulling over the money we were soon going to make with our radio ship. The place had been much improved by purchases from Habitat in Sloane Avenue, which marked, I think, the turning point in Terence Conran's career. Liam had entered the shop, opened our money bag, ripped off wrappers, thrown up high-denomination notes until they filled the air. So heartily did John approve of the fittings he had selected for me when he saw them *in situ*, that he felt able at last to change his address to mine. He arrived with a wide selection of identical shirts, strides, jackets and shoes, all of which could only be reasonably expected to fit into the bigger of our two bedrooms, the one with the decent view.

Because of his extensive record collection we had thought it advisable to replace my gramophone with the best possible stereo system money could buy. This was throbbing away groovily that morning to the sounds of Muddy Waters, when Mrs Flowers announced the unscheduled arrival of Mr O'Mahoney.

'Greetings, Palefaces!' Liam flung himself down on something beige and modular near the window. He wore brightly embroidered cowboy-boots, a stetson, and a thonged garment in fawn leather which might well have been fashioned for Davy Crockett by Jim Bowie with his world-famous knife.

'I hope your horse isn't shitting on our doorstep,' said John.

Liam gave him a long, glittering smile. 'Nice one, baby.'

'What on earth image are you trying to project, if one may be so bold?' John asked.

Liam simply glittered more and switched to me. 'Galveston, baby, G-A-L-V-E-S-T-U-N!'

'T-O-N, isn't it? I think.' I smiled helpfully. John laughed.

'Huh?' Liam wasn't with it.

'The spelling of Galveston . . .'

The thing dawned on him and was dismissed all in the same instant. 'Never mind about that. The point is I'm off there. Today!'

'Wow!' I obliged. 'What does that mean to us all exactly?'

Liam's glitter became more of a shine. 'What it means,' he paused to shine on John, 'what it means, is very fuckin' simple. It means we're in business!'

Liam had been rapping with the Texan cats all night long by phone. It was all settled. Any anomalies of price or international treaty had been ironed out. Jimmy and the rest of his City team were impressed out of their fuckin' minds. Everything in the way of the very latest American equipment that the would-be radio pirate might possibly need for an airwave coup was in the bag.

Liam would be gone for a few days. 'There's somethin' I need you both to handle while I'm away, OK? A group playing in Richmond I want you to check out.' We wanted to know where, when and why.

'We should start signing acts right away,' he said. 'There's no point us gettin' all this radio madness together just so everybody else can make a fuckin' fortune.'

I said, 'I thought we made our money through advertising?'

'That's right, baby; you're absolutely right.' Liam turned to me with patient care, 'But there's a little bit more to it than that.' His eyes flickered warily at John.

'Oh,' I said.

John said, 'Don't worry about Paul. He'll figure it out.'

'Look, it doesn't do the shareholders any harm' – Liam got me right between the eyes. 'It's positive for everyone, this move. People have to have a reason to turn on in the first fuckin' place, before you can begin to sell them any fuckin' advertising.'

'Absolutely.'

'Right. So there's nothin' to stop us signin' a few acts and cuttin' a few discs. This group I'm talkin' about's called the Rollin' Stones. Great R&B. They do a residency out at Georgio's place.'

'Gomalsky?'

'Yeah. You know Georgio?'

'Sure.' John knew Georgio.

'You think you can make it down the Crawdaddy on Sunday afternoon? It's in the Station Hotel.'

'Paul knows Richmond like the back of his hand.'

'And if they're any fuckin' good at all, sign 'em up!'

Later on, after a good lunch and lots of kümmel, John said, 'Selling advertising does sound pretty fucking boring. If you make hit records lots of dollybirds want to suck your dick.'

I said, 'Absolutely!'

Richmond is notable for a park, an ice-rink, an impenetrable one-way system and, in 1963, England's first fully automatic carwash. I knew my way to the latter through the former, and how to get out again and back to the Admiral Rodney in under twenty minutes flat, even in rush-hour. How was I to know the hottest spot in Greater London was a mere stone's throw from what I now considered the coldest – Messrs Shaw Autowash Ltd? Until that moment the important names of Georgio Gomalsky and the Crawdaddy Club were unknown to me. Nor did I ever remember seeing the Station Hotel on my travels, but I was unwilling to admit it at a critical juncture like this, when just such special knowledge seemed to fit me indispensably for the bill at hand.

I drove forth in the MG with John on the damp, grey Sunday following Liam's visit. We were well and truly stoned. This, said John, was essential, considering the nature of our mission. I hadn't liked to disagree. 'If they're good they'll sound great and if they're bad they'll give us the fuckin' horrors.' I had a bad dose of the horrors anyway by the outskirts of Richmond. Hash makes driving weird. The most familiar terrain can suddenly appear paranormal. Today, under a vacant Sunday sky, the shut shops and wet, empty streets were terrifyingly extra-terrestrial. My recall was down to about one and a half seconds, so I couldn't tell how many times we'd been around the one-way system in search of the Station Hotel.

'I could've sworn . . .' I banged the wheel with the heel of my hand.

John said, 'Maybe it's somewhere near the station. Is there a station?' The question filled me with the deepest anxiety.

'Half a minute! Look! Over there!' John pointed to an oddly stunted creature, crouched at the kerbside, staring fixedly into the open engine flap of an immobilised Lambretta. Whatever-it-was wore a parka. The scooter flew a triangular pennant, like a burgee, from the top of a tall tail aerial. It was embroidered with the word 'Brighton', in orange on a field of brown.

'Oi,' John called out.

The creature turned its head. The face was an identikit of Lionel Bart, miniaturised, squashed up against thick glasses. The body, as he rose defensively to face us, was a twisted mimic of Richard the Third. The voice was that of a costermonger.

'Sumfink I can do you for, my friend?'

Inside the safety of the car John said, 'Jesus!' Then, through the window, 'We're looking for the Station Hotel.'

Our new discovery made his way across to us. Beneath the parka, I noticed, he wore a suit of fluorescent orange. The face, on arrival, came about level with the car window. 'C'mon ven. Shuvover.'

Emmanuel, King of the Mods, was headed for the same venue as ourselves, as John had accurately surmised. He hopped in the back and was instantly at ease. John said, 'You must introduce me to your tailor some time.' It was hard not to notice the suit. On closer inspection it appeared to be manufactured from some porous material, like foam rubber, which in the warm car gave off visible clouds of steam.

'Yeah, but you'll never get no more cloff like this, though. Copied it straight off me mate. E's the drummer wiv me local group.'

'Oh, yeah?' John enquired with mild professional patronage. 'And what are all the kids digging down in Brighton these days?'

'Brighton?'

'It says it on your scooter.'

The King of the Mods guffawed. 'Vat fuckin' fing's not mine! I 'alf-inched vat ter get me 'ere.' He paused reflectively, considering his crime. 'Might just's well not've bovvered.'

John resumed his musical interrogations. 'What local group do you mean, then?'

'The Detours. From Shepherd's Bush.'

'Any good?'

'Any good?' Emmanuel was thunderstruck. He scratched his blue-black curls vigorously, creating powerful emissions of violet steam 'You gotta be fuckin' jokin' mate. Any good? Yore talkin' bout the fuckin' greatest group in the wewld!'

'Better than this group today?' John stroked his nose and gave me an intensely careful look, as if to say don't say a fucking word. We were getting unexpectedly well tuned in at grassroots level now, and he didn't want me to blow it.

'I should fuckin' say so!'

'So the Rolling whatsitsnames aren't any good, is that it?' I had to have my say. I was in the management game too, after all.

'The Rollin' Stones is fuckin' brilliant, mate.' My passenger's loathsome face, as he caught my eye in the driving mirror, was a mask of contempt. 'Just nowhere near as good as the Detours, that's all!'

The Station Hotel was a redbrick pub separated from the road by a tarmac forecourt. This zone was dense with mainly mod and beatnik humanity, and they all had one thing to say: 'We want the Stones!'

Two heavies guarded the double wooden doors with folded arms and impassive faces. They wore camelhair coats over their DJs. My suede winkle-pickers hit the tarmac. The air was like pure oxygen after the multifarious fragrances of the King of the Mods. Before he left us to mingle with his subjects, I asked him if and when this performance was likely to commence. I had thought we were late, but nothing seemed to be happening.

'We ain't on military manoeuvres now, old boy. Got to get the crowd worked up.'

Evidence of the wisdom of this tactic was breaking out all around our rather noticeable group. John unfolded languidly from the car, followed closely by Emmanuel. In the upright position he came somewhere around John's upper leg. He seemed to have formed a strong attachment to his lofty new chum, which he displayed with suggestive rabbit punches to John's elegantly tailored thigh. 'Gotta get them gewls' knickers nice and creamy, eh, John?' John looked down with hooded eyes and patted his pockets for his Rothmans.

''Ere, John, John. 'Ere, John!' – the little, intimate punches hammered insistently home – 'You cin call me Manny if you like.'

'I'll call you anything I fucking want, you horrible little runt.'

'Oh, John, John. Don't be like that.' Manny the mod stretched all the way up from his toes with his Zippo. John bent condescendingly down into the proffered flame.

'Listen, Manny.'

'Yes, John.'

'How would you like to be very, very helpful?'

'I don't know, John. Never tried it.'

'I want to make contact with someone in this group.'

'Who?'

'I don't know who. That's the whole point. If I knew who I wouldn't need you. We need to speak to one of them, any one at first, to get something going.'

Manny tapped one forefinger against his nose and broke into a hideous leer. 'Leave it ter me, John. So 'appens one of 'em's me mate!'

'Why didn't you say so?'

Manny's leer intensified. 'Din't know what the game was, did I?'

'Don't kid yourself. You still don't.'

'Oh yes I do, John. Oh yes I do.'

John closed his eyes and slowly shook his head. 'After the show, Manny, OK?'

'After the show? You gotter be jokin'! After the show my mate Brian's gonner be gittin' inter sumfink a bit more tasty van talkin' business wiv you two blokes.' Manny leered suggestively at an eager knot of nubiles nearby. 'It's now or never.'

'Now? What about the show?'

'Round the back. Vere's a door sez Private Bar. Wait for me vere.' Manny disappeared.

John and I sloped cautiously around the corner of the building and found the door. It was locked. Time passed. I had just become prey to some grave doubts about where I was and why, when a rattle of bolts jolted me back, and there was Manny's horrible face.

'Come on in, gents. It's all fixed!'

Inside the room was dark, and small, and musty with stale bevvys. In one corner was an open hatch and a ledge for the convenience of private patrons. A small iron grate stood empty and cold beneath a print of Stevenson's rocket. Beside it, in another corner by a grimy window, was a table. At the table sat Brian Jones. He was about my age, pink-faced and chirpy looking, with a thick mop of hair. His fringe fell girlishly over his eyes. He was natty in a herring-bone jacket and a knitted tie. Manny did the honours.

'Two mates ter meetcher, Bri. They wanner buy you a drink before the show.' Brian nodded his head up and down rapidly, as if to indicate that he quite understood.

'This 'ere is John, and this, er . . .'

'Paul.'

'This is Paul. This is Brian.'

'Right,' said John, 'right. Manny, my friend, could you rustle us up some drinks?'

'I think so, John. I think that could be arranged.'

'Good!' John rubbed his hands, 'Brian, what'll it be?'

Brian glanced at the empty balloon glass before him. 'Same again, all right?'

I gave Manny some money and he bustled off. John and I sat down. After examining a beer mat with considerable thoroughness, front and back, John said, 'So, Brian. There's no business like show business, eh?'

Brian smiled. 'What is your business?'

I cleared my throat. John glanced at me, and said, 'Not all that different from yours.'

Brian said, 'Oh?'

'I mean, rock 'n' roll!' John held up his hand in a brave gesture.

'We're more into rhythm and blues.'

'Well . . . same thing really.'

'Is it?'

'Look, man, I agree with you. I like Sonny Boy and Muddy Waters and all those guys, but from a management point of view . . .'

'So you're managers. Why didn't you say?' Brian Jones looked across at us in a hard-eyed way that made me feel uncomfortably bogus. 'You don't look like managers.'

At this point Manny returned bearing refreshments.

'You never told me they were managers!' Brian took his brandy accusingly from Manny and swigged most of it down.

'Stone me, Bri, I never knew!'

I took a good pull at my gin-and-tonic. 'So what's wrong with managers?'

'Managers are parasitical turds!' Brian declared. 'We've seen every manager in England in the last month, so I should know. You blokes are a bit late. We got a contract last week from one old ponce called Eric Easton. Looks like we're gonna do it.'

John said, 'What's this geezer like?'

'Poxy old turd from the North. An old pro.'

'Well, there you are then' – John was being unexpectedly tenacious – 'sounds like the perfect time for a change!'

Manny broke out with his horrible laugh.

'Who do you manage right now?' Brain wanted to know.

'Well, there's lots of stuff sort of in the melting pot, you know. You see, we're just about to . . .' John was just getting going when Brian stopped him.

'Look, it's all pretty well settled with this bloke and I've got to go. But if you're really interested come down the Flamingo tomorrow night. I'll see if I can get the others to have a quick word.'

Ice-breaking crashes from a drum-kit and wild, disjointed forays on electric guitar produced an eruption that made our empty glasses rattle. An angry voice shouted, 'Where the fuck is Brian?' The crowd instantly responded: 'We want Brian. We want Brian. We want Brian!' Brian rose modestly to his feet. 'Thanks for the drink, ladss' and was gone. Moments later the joint was rockin', goin' round and round,

> Oh, reelin' and rockin', it was a crazy sound
> An' they never stopped rockin' till the moon went down.

In the car on the way home we talked over our first sortie into management, and concluded it had been an unqualified success.

'I'm not too sure about this other chap, though, this fellow Easton,' I wavered for a moment. 'Couldn't he be a bit of a problem?'

'He probably doesn't exist.'

'How do you mean?'

John spoke patiently. 'If you were that fellow Brian, what would you say? You're not going to tell a couple of lads like us no one else is even interested, are you?'

After our meeting we hadn't stayed long. I had thought we ought to hang on and see what the group was like.

'I mean, if we're going to manage them, and all that.'

'We can get a pretty good idea from back here, don't you think?'

As the motor of the MG burbled at last into Chelsea, I felt tired and comfortable and happy to be home.

'Let's go straight to the Kenya and have tea,' John suggested.

'Absolutely,' I responded.

When the Kenco cappuccinos and the buttered teacakes and the chocolate eclairs were on the table I said, 'What did you think of the Rolling Stones? You know. When Liam asks. I mean, really?'

John savoured the question slowly. 'I dunno. There's a bunch of spades in the Mississippi delta who do the same thing a whole lot better. Let the little fucker see for himself, anyway. He'll be back tomorrow and we can all go down the Flamingo.'

The Flamingo was a spade club, devoted to the blues. Exotic drugs could be obtained for consumption on or off the premises. You got stoned just breathing at the Flamingo. Spades looked upon the place as their territory. White folks who wanted to make the scene there did so taking their lives in their hands. Spade chicks, who reputedly performed with a difference almost impossible to imagine, compared to the colonel's daughters of Haslemere (who mostly didn't perform at all), could be met there and possibly 'pulled'. In any event, going down there was cool, and being scared shitless about it, or at least being seen to be, was uncool in the extreme.

When Liam arrived at the Flamingo he was two hours late and still wearing the stetson. In addition, beneath the now familiar thongs, the subdued lighting of the club flickered and blazed with the reflections of a thousand rhinestones. Some of the brothers, I felt, might've had something to say, or even do, about this intrusion into their midst from the Lone Star State, but Liam cut a swathe through their misgivings, put them at their ease with the same reassuring camaraderie he had displayed in the Kenya at our first meeting. 'Howareya? Howsitgoin', baby? Yer lookin' well!'

When he reached our inconspicuous corner he grinned and put his hat and feet on the table. Ray Charles was singing 'The night-time is the right time'. Liam's boots, I noticed, were new and even gaudier than the last pair.

'Howdy pardners! When're they on?'

John said, 'I like the shirt.'

I said, 'They've been on. You've missed them.'

'Not to worry. We've all missed them, as it turns out.' Liam seemed unconcerned.

'How d'you mean?' My voice was querulous.

'Didn't you speak to Georgio when you went out to Richmond?'

'We didn't think it would be cool. We didn't want anyone to know we were interested.'

'I had 'im on the blower just this evening. The group was signed last week.'

'Who by?'

'Some cat called Eric Easton. It doesn't matter though – much more important things are happenin'.' Liam's features were a soliloquy of eagerness as he leaned towards us through the dense air. 'Listen . . .' I exchanged glances with John. So Eric Easton did exist after all. On reflection I decided not to mention that we'd ever doubted it. 'Listen! I found a ship! I think it'll be ideal. We need to check it out right away.'

And the next thing I knew I was smearing marmalade on a British Rail kipper, while the Pullman sped us to Liverpool.

– Three –

'But what sort of ship, Liam?' The Hon. Jeremy Hammond slapped the leather surface of his wide, empty desk. 'Apart from being a bargain at thirty thousand pounds of my money!'

We were sitting around among the rubber plants and glossy magazines in Jeremy's office at J. W. Hammond and Partners, Advertising Agents. There were, in fact, no partners. Jeremy had a preference for autocracy. 'When I redecorate my office,' he would say, 'the design will be much simpler. One throne and two kneeling-stools!'

'It's a ferkin' beautiful ship!'

'Yes, but what's it been doing up to now?'

Liam glanced at John, who cleared his throat elaborately. 'It used to be a ferry-boat, Jeremy,' – his deep voice oozed reassurance – 'in Holland.'

'In Holland? Where in Holland? From where to where did it go?'

Liam made an inspired comeback. 'There's a lot of inland waterways in Holland.'

He had never fully mastered the nautical minutiae. In the train to Liverpool the speeding countryside had whipped him into a gale of enthusiasm. 'We can sail straight from there to Ireland. The stuff from Texas will be there any day now.'

John, lounging over his fifth coffee and tenth cigarette, was more sanguine. 'What makes you so certain we'll end up buying this tub?'

'We're holding the bread, aren't we?' This was true. A case of it joggled gently under John's feet. A pathological love of secrecy drove Liam into cash transactions only. Apart from the psychological effect, 'When people see the folding stuff it gets them at it!'

'That's not the point, Liam, is it?' John was able to be patronising. Unlike me he had a past. Part of it had been spent in the purser's mess of a cruise liner. This brief experience qualified him, we felt, for command of matters nautical as well as musical. 'There's a lot can be wrong with a ship this size. We could be looking at seven hundred tons of trouble.'

'Absolutely!' I could second this. My father was a Navy man and a member of the Royal Thames Yacht Club. In the days of our large yacht and my small dinghy I had been admitted to this exclusive organisation for a nominal fee. I had something to say about ships.

Liam said, rather sourly, 'The Dutch cats've been to a load of trouble findin' this fuckin' boat. They say she's the greatest.'

'That's what bothers me,' muttered John, equally sour.

From Lime Street Station onwards everyone looked and sounded like the Beatles. The ticket-collector. The cab driver. Even the clerk at the Adelphi Hotel. His act was modelled closely on John Lennon.

'Sumthin' I can do fer you gents?'

'You can check these bags for a start.' John had him covered.

'Not this one.' Liam's knuckles white on the black bag.

We had booked their most impressive suite for the benefit of the Dutch. Paying for the ship wasn't the whole story, Liam explained. We needed to convince them we could handle all the services, like sea-crew, insurance and so forth.

'As far as they're concerned we're heavy duty.'

John and I were happy with this. So, it turned out, was Captain Vig Moller. He was already in our suite. We were ushered by the bellhop into an atmosphere thick with the smoke of small Dutch cigars. The ashtrays were full. The captain was engrossed in an international phone call. He waved us down absently between puffs and guttural observations. We made ourselves at home in the pink gilded splendour, and waited for him to finish.

He replaced the receiver with a flourish. When he rose to his feet we saw how truly huge he was.

'Vig Moller!' he announced, brushing ash grandiosely from his double-breasted jacket. 'Let us haf lunch before we go. The French restaurant in this hotel is reputed to be eggsellent!'

The captain sailed down carpeted corridors with us in his wake. We arrived at the arched entrance to the French Room.

'Show us to your very best table!' The captain had a way of clipping words to make his message clear. The *maître d'* bowed and described a grovelling gesture with his arm for us to follow.

Throughout the meal the captain puffed smoke and scattered ash.

I didn't know whether to call him Vig, or what. He cleared this up for us.

'You may all call me "Captain". It is simple, ya?'

He recommended dishes from his wide experience in the capitals of Europe, complete with gastronomic anecdotes. He thought we might enjoy a little wine with the meal. We thought so too. He fixed a pair of steel-rimmed glasses on to his fleshy nose and studied the wine list as though charting a course through reef-infested seas. 'Let me see, now. Let me see. Ah! Ya, ya. I think this one will do.' He laid down the list, removed his spectacles and faced us triumphantly. 'I think this will do *very* nicely!'

I was rolling and pitching pretty freely even before we hit the deck of the tender. It was built like a small trawler, big in the beam with a high bridge-house and a hold which had been converted to an uncomfortable passenger tank, like a floating railway waiting-room, with hard, narrow benches round the walls, reached by a steep ladder. I stood alone in the bows with the west wind blowing hard on my Remy Martin afterglow. The meal had ended with us being sold on everything the captain had to suggest, from ships to liqueur brandy. He had raised his glass in a conclusive toast:

'A fine wessel! A wessel to be proud off!'

Liam had raised his too, and looked around the table brilliantly. 'Didn't I tellya?'

John smirked. 'Down the hatch!'

'Yo ho ho!' said I, draining my glass. It had seemed amusing at the time.

I clasped my hands behind my back and surveyed the bleak horizon. With my RTYC yachting cap I was Horatio Hornblower from stem to stern. On splayed feet I strolled stiffly aft. John's head appeared above the hatch-combing.

'Anything to report, number one?' My legs were braced firmly against the corkscrew rolls.

'The quare fellow's turned green, skipper, I'm afraid.'

International law and the obsession with secrecy which seemed to grip the captain as much as it did Liam meant that our prize was anchored more than twelve miles out, beyond territorial limits and prying eyes. Liam, I could see, was beginning to regret this. Twelve miles doesn't sound far, but in small boats on big seas most of the time is spent going up and down instead of forward. Progress is sluggish. Liam's equilibrium, overdosed by Irish Mist, had obviously weirded out. The air in the hold shuddered monotonously. It smelt of old fish and foul engine. Liam was propped up in one lurching corner, like a scarecrow toppled over by a storm.

'I shouldn't stay down here, old chap.' I spoke bracingly. 'Come on up into the fresh air!'

He turned a phosphorescent death's head towards me. The lips pulled back in a parody of his old grin. One hand flapped feebly. Go away.

On a shelf above Liam's head stood a group of tins and jars: cocoa, Coffeemate, Camp. At this moment the boat gave a particularly vicious twist. A can of Nescafé performed a slow and magical arc, from the edge of the shelf to the top of Liam's head. The lid sprang off and the grains poured forth in a brown avalanche, cascading down the pallid contours. He remained inert. He never even flickered.

I pulled my head out of the hatch. John climbed out. He shrugged and grinned. We stood at the taffrail and let the wind blow.

The swell heaved and we bumped hard against the side of the ship. A real ship. Black riveted plates, streaked with rust, towered up. White superstructure above. Lifeboats on davits. High overhead crossbeam masts swung in dizzy arcs across the sky.

The crew laughed encouragement over the side above a dangling ladder of rickety wooden slats tied unevenly between slippery ropes. There was no mistaking the challenge on their foreign faces. I waited for the next wave going up and thought of England. Nelson, one arm and one eye shot away, would not have flinched. On the way up, hanging and clinging, I was glad of both my arms and could've done with a few more. At the top I was pulled aboard head-first by a lot of raucous Dutchmen.

I looked down in triumph for John, but he was already swarming up towards me with irritating ease.

Nothing Captain Vig Moller had said about the ship could possibly match the fierce excitement I felt standing on her deck. I had suddenly come alive in the middle of a book by C. S. Forester. Adventures without limit stretched away before me from stem to distant stern; from the rhythmic squirting of bilge to the soaring funnel.

Below the funnel, above a series of metal companionways, was the bridge. I could see Vig Moller talking with gestures to a man in yellow oilskins and an officer's jacket. He pointed to the tender. The officer nodded.

John and I ducked into a doorway and went exploring. When we re-emerged, something had been rigged up from a spar and was being lowered towards the pitching tender.

'What's that?' I appealed to John the mariner.

'Bosun's chair.'

A rope was passed from the boat above to the boat below. The bosun's chair, a sling on a pulley, is very much like a thing we had at school called a Davey Escape. Fire practices at Elphinstone's had entailed desperate journeys in it from which the wise man excused himself with every means at his disposal. And that was fixed to terra firma.

The cargo on this occasion was Liam. His supine frame at least appeared to possess the advantage of unconsciousness. John and I hurried over to the section of deck where he should touch down if all went well. Bits of him flapped madly in the wind as he swayed down at last. The corpse-like features gave rise in us to the highest anxiety.

'Liam! Liam! Speak to me!'

The eyes clicked open like a Hammer Productions Dracula. The teeth bared.

'How do you feel?' We were both bent low with solicitude.

'Fuckin' fantastic!'

The careful study I had made over the years of the career of Horatio Hornblower had led me to believe that the most important person on a ship is the captain. An early lesson I learnt on board the MV *Anastassia*, soon to be renamed, put me straight on one reality of seafaring life. The most important person on a ship is the cook. The captain might be a hopeless drunk who can't splice a mainbrace to save his life, but the cook must be a master. Sailors don't care much where they sail, so long as the long days and nights are broken up at regular intervals with exquisite cuisine. If anything happens to the cook they make for the nearest port at full steam. And woe betide the cook who loses form. The cook employed on the MV *Anastassia*, Captain Vig Moller assured us, was an artist without peer throughout the seven seas. We were ushered with much ceremony into a large saloon in which, it soon became clear, a feast was to be prepared.

The captain and assorted seafarers, all with names similar to Vig Moller's, all speaking non-stop Dutch, were introduced. They treated us with great enthusiasm, nodding all the time, ya, ya, ya. They told unintelligible stories and laughed uproariously, passing round bottles of aquavit. Language barriers soon became blurred. John and I found ourselves nodding away with the best of them.

Liam had recovered enough to join the party. He sat with the captain, talking intently, looking pale. We looked over at him and raised our glasses.

'This is the life!'

'A life on the ocean wave!'

This was all right with us, radio station or no radio station. Liam glanced at us with a brief smile that flickered on to his face like a freeze-frame and was gone. He raised his glass mechanically, but I noticed that he lowered it again without drinking. His eyes slid back to Vig Moller. The moment left me feeling strangely voided, like I'd interrupted Daddy when he was busy. I turned to John for reassurance. Surely everything was OK? We were all for one and one for all, were we not?

'What's that?' John shifted his attention with an effort. He couldn't hear above the din. What had I said anyway? I didn't know. It was just a feeling. The aquavit was closing in around my eyes and darkening my mind. I opened my mouth, determined to make some sort of definitive statement, to make myself clear. At this moment a door slid back at the other end of the saloon and a cheer went up like a drowning wave. I was sucked in with relief. A wiry fellow with gingery forearms and a chef's hat stood sweating under the weight of his *plat du jour*, presented on a huge silver tray.

'Sucking pig! Hurrah!' The dish transcended language.

I glanced over at Liam. He was glittering like old times, straight into my eyes. I suddenly felt hugely happy. Captain Vig Moller brandished two bottles of claret. 'Come. Come. We drink a toast, ya?'

I shouted out, 'Absolutely!'

*

We woke up with a bump when the tender docked. I crawled on deck. It was late. The Liver and Cunard Buildings, monuments to Liverpool's glorious commercial past, loomed against a starry sky. A little further down the docks arclights glared eerily as men swarmed over a ship. They carried on regardless of the hour. Somewhere farther up the Mersey a foghorn sounded.

I couldn't remember much about our departure from the *Anastassia*, except that it was certainly a milestone in Anglo-Dutch relations. Not to mention the Irish. Back once more in the hold Liam had waxed lyrical on the subject of vibes, body language and international peace and understanding. 'Hands across the sea. Hands across the fuckin' sea, that's what it is! Get the fuckin' frontiers down and set the people free!'

We hadn't been going long when John made the discovery that gave him his good idea.

'Look!' he said. He held up a roll of silver foil as though it were a Dead Sea Scroll.

'Aha!' said Liam. I didn't get it and said so.

'Perfect for a pipe.'

'A peace pipe?' Something about the word association, I suppose, had got into my head.

'Something like that. A hash pipe.'

Hash smoked this way, pure, without tobacco, gives a clean, clear high.

'No paranoia this way, baby. Even you.'

We smoked. We laughed ourselves into exhausted sleep. We slumbered. I dreamed of feather-bonneted Dutchmen with huge red hands chasing pigs across a silver-foil sea.

We assembled with the captain by the Dock Board office building. The few parked cars looked abandoned. There seemed no hope of cabs – it was after midnight. I couldn't help feeling we were more likely to be set upon than rescued. We walked down the Strand. The grand name seemed hopeful, but that was all. The Liver Building clock boomed the quarter.

'Come on.' John sounded edgy. We set off towards the docks, where the lights were. Victorian warehouses loomed and blocked us in. Narrow streets led away from the water.

'We want to go that way.' Liam sounded definite. He led us into a dark alley. Our footsteps rang emptily on the cobbles. We emerged in Duke Street.

'Aha! Duke Street,' said Liam.

'So?' said John, rather uncharitably. The captain grunted something in Dutch, looking this way and that.

'Sounds familiar.' Liam was unperturbed.

'It only sounds familiar because . . .' I began.

Liam held up his hand urgently. 'Listen!'

We all froze. Something like a heartbeat, faint but insistent, nudged at the silence.

Liam said, 'This way!' and was off again. We were reluctant, but we followed. No doubt about it, the beat was building to a definite throb as we went along, enhanced by other, vaguely familiar sounds. We came puffing up on a considerable throng of merrymakers crowded round a hole in a wall. Over their heads neon letters spelt 'G OT O.' On closer inspection 'R' and 'T' had fizzled out. Someone had whitewashed 'GROTTY' on a wall nearby.

Liam dived in among them, soon to re-emerge. 'These cats're havin' an All Niter!'

John said, 'Oh.'

I glanced from one to the other of them. I felt pretty tired.

The captain said, 'Will there be somewhere to sit down, please?'

John said, 'Look, man, we're fucked. Let's go.'

I said, 'I'm knackered.'

Liam said, 'Don't worry about it.'

'What d'you mean, don't worry about it?' John sounded moody.

'I got the answer to that one.' Liam held something out to John in the palm of his hand. John shifted and scratched the back of his head. 'That could make a difference, I guess.' He grinned at me stupidly. Liam's teeth were bared in his most dangerous smile.

I said, 'What? What could make a difference?'

John said, 'Purples.'

'Confiscated from the kids at the Happenin'!' Liam's triumphant smile threatened to cut his head in half.

I said, 'Aha,' and peered at them warily. They looked exactly like their name. 'Not poppers?'

'Not poppers. Don't worry.' I'd popped some amyl nitrate with Liam not long before. The idea of a blackout followed by a heart attack was more than I could handle.

'What is this, please?' Vig Moller lumbered into the debate.

'Somethin' to perk you up a bit, Captain. Yer not lookin' a hundred per cent well.'

'Ah, no thank you. No thank you. I haf my own medicine on board.' The captain pulled a bottle of aquavit from a pocket deep in the vastness of his coat. 'And there's more where that is coming from.'

Once inside the Grotto the need for an artificial boost became acute. The Happening, my comparison, was an oasis of luxury. First came a confrontation with a phalanx of bouncers. The Happening's biggest heavy was a nine stone weakling beside the smallest of these. Their white starched shirt fronts were like snowy mountain faces – insurmountable. We passed through an inner door and were engulfed in a superheated armpit of noise. Conversation was conducted in hoarse shouts from mouth to ear. Our bodies were squashed between those in front and those packing in behind. The whole mass moved rhythmically a few feet below the arched brick roof. At the other end of the tunnel the stage wasn't high enough to be seen from the back. Surrounding pressures occasionally forced me upwards enough for the odd glimpse of four mop-haired lads called the Merseymen. What they lacked in skill they made up for in loudness. The song was just recognisable as 'Dizzy Miss Lizzy'.

Vig Moller was speechless and I could tell he wasn't digging the scene that much. Any hope of a seat seemed remote. I managed by body language to indicate that I wouldn't say no to a swig of his aquavit. I had more faith in it than in the purples, though I had swallowed four. I hadn't felt much in common with the captain but in that moment we were soulmates.

The Merseymen walked to the front of the stage and bowed in unison. This final piece of slickness differed sharply from their playing. They bounced off and were immediately replaced by four more identical Merseymen called the Swinging Merseybeats. They raced through 'Roll Over Beethoven', 'Mister Postman' and 'Sweet Little Sixteen' before unleashing their *pièce de résistance*. One of them knelt on the stage, spread his arms and belted out 'My Prayer'. The drummer staggered squarely along, well behind the beat, but it didn't bother this bloke. With 'My Prayer' he'd found his little corner of local immortality, and once into it only that final high note could get him out. When he hit it the crowd went bananas.

The song was over but singing persisted in my head. Also roaring, and vision fading to black, and uncontrollably grinding molars. The purples and the aquavit were working. When the crowd parted I thought it was my personal vision of the apocalypse. Liam stood before me like St Peter.

'C'mon, baby, follow me.' In a clear moment I saw that behind him was not one of my black spots but the massive back of the biggest bouncer in the world.

We filed through the multitude to an arched recess near the front, beside a door marked 'Green Room'.

'Yis'll be all right here, gents.'

We sat down on rickety chairs at a wobbly table. The bouncer, I detected, was Irish. I looked quizzically at Liam. His grin was bigger than ever, and his eyes glittered.

'How're you feelin'?' I knew he knew I'd been shrinking from the abyss. I took a stab at sounding nonchalant – 'Don't say that fellow's a friend of yours?' – but the voice that emerged was shrill and accusatory.

'Frank's brother.' Frank was chief bouncer at the Happening.

John grinned a lopsided grin and ruffled my hair. 'Stay cool. Just keep taking the tablets, ha ha!'

'I am fucking cool!' I shrieked. 'God!' My eyes stuck out and my teeth ground. 'Is there any way of getting a drink around here?' Liam smiled deep into my eyes and slowly shook his head. 'No fuckin' way. Strictly no booze in this sorta joint.'

I turned a haunted eye on the captain. The bond held. With a devil-may-care flourish he plonked the bottle down.

'Hey, hey!' said Liam.

'Everybody stay cool!' called John, in great agitation and removed the bottle. It was my turn to say 'Hey!'

'Look, man, do you want us all to get fucking killed?' John was getting heavy. 'This place is full of maniacs who already hate us for sitting at this table.'

'I don't care. I want a drink.'

'OK. OK. But there's a cool way and there's a fucking uncool way, OK?'

'OK.'

And so, with John shielding me from the curious, I was able to get a shifty swig under the table. This way we drew the most possible attention. Peering warily up through the chair legs I made contact with two pairs of eyes.

'Hey, John!'

'Huh?'

'Those two birds!'

'Which two? What about them?'

'Behind me. Don't look now.'

'How can I see them if I don't look?'

'You know what I mean. Keep it cool.'

'Oh, yeah. Sure!'

'One's blonde and sexy and the other one's quite large. I think they're interested.'

'What do you want me to do about it?'

'Nothing. I just mentioned it, that's all.'

Liam said, 'Those two birds keep lookin' over here. I think they want some action.'

John stared over at them hard. 'I think the big one fancies Paul.'

'Fuck off! It was the blonde who gave me the eye.'

'She's just lining you up for her friend.'

A succession of groups were shuttled on and off with unceremonious speed. Now came an expectant lull. The crowd buzzed. From backstage muffled oaths floated out over the hubbub. A number of mop-haired lads were dragging something heavy on to the stage.

'Look, John. A Hammond!' Liam was sitting up and taking notice. Even John uncrossed and recrossed his legs with a certain alertness. The Hammond organ was set up near a drum-kit on which was stencilled boldy: THE FORMBY FIVE. There were some war-whoops from the crowd. A small man in a crumpled suit and an obvious toupee bounded on to the stage and held up his hands.

'And now,' he announced in high cabaret camp, 'ladies and gentlemen, for your further entertainment, the moment you've all been waiting for. The Formby One . . . Two . . . Three . . . Four . . . Five!!!!'

And seconds later we all got our minds blown.

In Haslemere the bad part of town was a street called Wey Hill. It wasn't exactly Needle Park, but had there been tracks in Haslemere it would've been on the wrong side of them. At the bottom of the

Hill was a café called The Last Chance. Greasers in black leather jackets and ageing Teddy Boys hung out there. They leaned against the door chewing matchsticks, or tuned and revved up their massive Beezas and Triumph Tiger Twins.

I used to pile the bright young colonels' daughters into my Messerschmitt bubble car and buzz by tauntingly, but they could hardly be bothered. One night two of them did treat me to a chicken run. Their headlights coming straight at me in the dark, I thought it was a car and that my hour had come. They only split at the very last moment, hurtling by on either side. I thought I caught the sound of mocking laughter mingled with the thunder of their exhausts. After that I tended to navigate Wey Hill by a series of discreet detours.

The guy kneeling frontstage pointing his Fender Stratocaster like a lethal weapon was a greaser. He hacked out 'Long Tall Sally', shaking the notes all over the floor and driving the punters wild. The rest of the band were rock solid. The bass player was a man-mountain in a pink suit who never moved a muscle as he played. The drummer was frenzied but spot on. A concave scarecrow with hair much longer than any I'd ever seen played rhythm guitar. A shrimp with glasses and a green nylon shirt sat behind the Hammond. After the first number he went straight into some heavy chords. The lead singer stood up straight at the mike, his guitar hanging free, both hands holding the stand. While he sang 'I'll Put a Spell on You' the audience was hushed. When it was over there was pandemonium.

I looked cautiously at Liam and John. It seemed to me that this group was something else. The need for coolness uppermost in my mind as always, I didn't come straight out and say so, all the same. Warily, I caught Liam's eye and held it. I cleared my throat.

'What d'you think, Liam?'

Liam shook his head slowly. 'Fuckin' fantastic!'

'I must say I think they're pretty amazing. What do you think, John?'

'Not bad. Not bad at all.'

There was a stand-up, honky-tonk piano at the back of the stage. This the leather-jacketed leader now attacked. He went into a boogie-woogie duet with the Hammond, standing up, singing 'Goodbye Joe', into a nearby mike. After this he grabbed his guitar and worked his way through 'Hey, Bo Diddley', 'Around and

Around', 'La Bamba', 'Poison Ivy', and 'Bye bye, Johnny, bye bye'.

'This is the fuckin' greatest R&B act in the world,' Liam declared.

No one wanted the band to go. They finished with 'The Night Time is the Right Time' and disappeared. Someone started playing Beatles records to drown the cries of 'Encore'. Liam got up straight away, without a word, and slipped unobtrusively through the green room door.

The anticlimax seemed to me something that only aquavit could dispel. I turned to the captain but he wasn't there. John was cautiously applying his gold Dunhill to a Rothmans King Size.

'Have you seen the captain?' I asked.

'Mmmm?'

'The captain. He's disappeared.'

John inclined his head. 'Over there. Dancing with one of your girlfriends.'

'What!?'

He was dancing with both of them. The girls had their handbags on the floor between them and were trying hard to look as if they were dancing with each other. He wasn't much of a dancer but he was obviously proving hard to shake. He shuffled around them, bear-like, flapping his arms with no particular reference to rhythm. By the way the girls kept shooting moody glances at him I could tell he wasn't just relying on body language, either. El Capitano was chatting them up.

'Go on over. Kill two birds with one stone. Ha ha.'

'Ha ha.' I supposed I could.

'Excuse me, Captain. Hello, girls. Er, I hate to butt in, but . . .' This jolly banter was completely lost on the birds, whose moodiness deepened. Not so the captain.

'Aha. My good friend.' He embraced me. 'You would like a little something, ya?'

'Ya.'

He brandished the bottle. It was a new one. I knocked some back. The captain gallantly offered it to the girls but they declined. I eased into my Mick Jagger style of sexy dancing, which I hoped would turn them on. The aquavit added a certain looseness to my limbs. Next to the captain, I felt, almost anyone would look good. When I thought I'd exhibited enough to arouse their interest, I gasped, 'That was a good group, don't you think?'

'Yer what?' They both turned indifferently.

'That last group. Terrific!'

They looked back at each other and shrugged.

I danced on, driven by a compelling mixture of beat, hope, booze, speed and extreme horniness. No doubt like all girls they found the ritual of playing hard to get necessary. My chances with the blonde might be a bit uncertain but the big friend was beginning to look more and more desirable.

The blonde suddenly switched her attention to me, twisting up close, forking her naked knees between my furiously jiving legs. She put one hand lightly on my shoulder. Her eyes smiled up from dark patches of mascara.

'What's your name, then?'

'Paul. My name is Paul.'

'That's nice. Like Paul McCartney.'

'Yes.'

'Mine's Maureen.'

'Aha. How do you do.'

'Charmed I'm sure.'

Conversation languished while I struggled to think of something else to say. Whenever I caught Maureen's eye I smiled my most knowing smile, but that was about it. Again she broke the ice.

'Yer wanner siddown?'

'Er . . .'

'Your table looks nice.'

I looked over and saw that Liam had returned with a guest. Slumped at ease between himself and John, smoking and nodding occasionally at Liam, was the star performer of the Formby Five. As far as I could gather Liam was administering Treatment A.

We frolicked over to them, Maureen in the lead.

'Er, this is Maureen, er . . .'

Liam looked up quickly. 'Howareya?'

John said, 'Hi,' and gave her a long, cool look.

Maureen said, 'Hi, Val . . . 'owsitgoin'?'

The rocker looked up with hard-boiled eyes as if she weren't there. I stuck out my hand to bridge the gap and said, rather heartily, 'Hello! I'm Paul Shaw!'

For a moment I thought he was going to give me the freeze as well. My hand wavered but he took it at last, ''Owsitgoin' pal? My name's Val Dainty.'

Val was like a switched off high-voltage wire: drained, hoarse, relaxed by the expulsion of all excess energy. He was big and bony, with a beaky face. His hair was blue-black like Elvis's and looked like Elvis's had in the fifties, with heavy sideburns. He wore a white scarf loosely round his neck. His hard mouth twitched at the corners.

'So yer like scrubbers, do yer?'

His voice had a metallic twang, hard to miss. I glanced at Maureen and giggled feebly. 'Er . . . ha ha!'

'Fook off, Val.' Maureen spoke matter-of-factly, as she rummaged in her bag for cigarettes.

'Ha!' John barked and blew a stream of smoke.

'She's a loovly gerl really. She'll take good care o' yer, won't yer, Maureen?'

'Fook off, Val.' She seemed quite content now, puffing away.

The captain hove to with the big friend in tow. Her name was Janine. She too had become more friendly. The captain had his arm around her ample shoulders and she seemed to be bearing it well. Their arrival swelled the press of flesh within the alcove to beyond busting point. The captain, a beaming mass of ebullience, proposed a solution.

'Let us return to the hotel for zum refreshments!'

Liam lit up. 'Nice one, Captain. Val, how about it? We can rap a while.'

The girls watched Val guardedly. John said, 'God knows what refreshments there'll be at the Adelphi at four in the morning.'

Who cares, I thought. If we can just get these two back there . . .

Maureen said, 'You lot stayin' at the Adelphi? Coom on then. Warrer we waitin' for?'

'I promised me mam . . .' Janine looked doubtful.

Maureen snapped, 'Get knotted, Jan. Let's gerrouta this shithole.'

I said, 'Absolutely!'

'Paul! Wake up, Paul! Come on now . . .' Liam's urgent voice came from far away. The closer I allowed it to get, the greater became the pain.

'No. No, I can't . . .' I rolled over and banged my face on

something hard. 'Oh, God.' My arms thrashed for the protective bedclothes that weren't there.

'Get it together now. There's somethin' important I need you to do.'

'No, no,' I moaned. The hard thing, I noticed, was burning hot. I recoiled, achieving a sort of crouch. I opened my eyes. The light stabbed in like knives. I looked around. I was hard up against an old-fashioned radiator, fully dressed in stiff and smelly clothes. I recognised the sitting-room of our suite. Liam shimmered above me.

'Did you sleep well?' I couldn't answer. I shook my head and regretted it.

John was stretched out on a *chaise longue*, smoking a cigarette. They both looked fresh as daisies.

'What time is it?' I croaked.

'Time you got goin'. I want you to go see that Val cat, and clinch things.'

'Clinch things?'

'Yeah. It's all down to you, baby. The guy liked you.'

Did he? I tried hard to dredge some memories up from the pit. I remembered walking from the Grotto to the hotel. Things went well until we reached the lobby. Then the captain and Maureen kept going round and round in the revolving doors. As they spun they laughed and sang. They went faster and faster until Maureen came exploding out all over the carpet. The captain got stuck. The night porter was anxiously polite: 'Sir, I must ask you to . . .'

'Get me out of here, dammit!'

'People are trying to sleep, sir.'

The captain sang louder still, in Dutch. More senior staff arrived.

'I am the night manager,' said a sombre-looking character in a dark suit. The captain catapulted unexpectedly into his arms. The dark man struggled free and continued, 'I must ask if you are all residents?'

'We are residents. These ladies and this gentleman are our guests.' The captain strode towards the stairs which led up to the magnificent lounge. Waldorf-Astoria chandeliers glittered down on him as he turned imperiously.

'We shall require a light supper, with plenty of champagne.'

'Plenty of champagne,' echoed Maureen.

'Absolutely!' I agreed wholeheartedly.

'The hotel kitchens are closed.'

'Then we shall make do with champagne only.'

'The bar is closed also.'

'Look . . .' Liam placed a bony hand on the upper arm of the night manager and steered him with subdued urgency into a shadowy corner. 'Listen . . .'

Up in the splendid privacy of our suite, it was the night manager himself who delivered the champagne. He brought small stale sandwiches too – 'with the compliments of the Hotel'.

'Won't you have a glass yourself, now?'

'Thank you, sir, no.'

'Better bring another couple of bottles.'

'Certainly, sir.'

'Now then, Val' – Liam applied the same hand-on-the-arm treatment that had worked so well with the manager – 'tell me some more about the group.'

'I do remember singing a couple of numbers with him. Is that what you mean?' I screwed my eyes up at Liam's shimmering form.

'That's it, baby. You were fuckin' beautiful. That's what he liked about you!'

'Oh. What happened to the two birds?'

'You don't remember?' Liam and John exchanged veiled smiles.

'No.'

I shook my head and regretted it again.

Formby was a seaside village which by the nineteen-sixties had become a small, suburban town. Halfway between Liverpool and Southport, it can be reached in half-an-hour by rail from Central Station. Alone with my thoughts in the grimy compartment, I stared moodily out as Bootle docks gave way to flat, watery farmland.

Liam and John had some 'heavy-duty business moody' to settle with the captain.

'Just boring stuff,' Liam urged. 'This scene you're on is where it's at. You just have to handle it. Remember – that group's gonna be fuckin' major!'

'Yes, but . . .' I didn't think I'd ever felt quite this ill, 'what if I can't handle it?'

'Then don't come back!' John was really enjoying himself today. 'Don't worry about it. Think positive.'

'What exactly shall I say?'

'Say anything that sounds good. Tell 'im about the station. Tell 'im we'll bring the group to London and make him into a star!'

These words were ringing in my ears as I arrived at Formby. By now it was early afternoon. I stared after the train until it disappeared.

The ticket-collector told me the way to Sefton Road. It was just round the corner. Number 46 turned out to be a neat semi with red bricks picked out around the pebbledash. I stood in the tiled porch and stared at the stained glass in the front-door. The doormat said 'Welcome'. I didn't feel it. I couldn't help remembering the Brian Jones fiasco, and how freely he'd expressed himself on the subject of managers.

Chimes pealed within. Heels clicked, then the latch. The door was opened by a fortyish looking woman in a rose-flowered apron. Her face was rosy too. She had bright eyes and teeth, and Val's hair, the jet streaked with grey.

'Yes?' She was smilingly inquisitive.

'Hello. Good afternoon, er, sorry to bother you, but . . . are you Val's mother?'

'Yes.'

'Is Val at home?'

'He's asleep.'

'Oh. Er, my name is Paul Shaw, by the way.'

'How do you do.' We shook hands. I was beginning to feel more and more like a brush-salesman. 'Is Val expecting you?'

'Well, er, yes and no.'

'It's just 'e never gets up till tea-time, as a rule.' I tried to imagine my own mother standing guard over my slumbers like this. Early rising and the work ethic was always the underlying theme in my home life. As if she could read my thoughts Val's mother said proudly, ''E works nights, you see. In one o' these beat groups.'

'Yes, well as a matter of fact I know that. I saw him last night. That's why I'm here, really.'

'Oh yes?' Val's mum became guarded. 'Not an autograph hunter?'

'Ha, ha, hardly, no.' I fairly writhed with deprecation. 'Ha, ha!'

'That's all right, then.' She was only just convinced. 'I get a lot o' them. Mostly girls though.'

'M'yes, I expect you do. Absolutely!'

''E's very popular with the girls is our Val.'

I didn't much like the turn the conversation was taking. Blurred thoughts of Maureen still nagged at me, apart from anything else.

'He's going to be a big star, I should think, don't you?'

'He is a big star!' said Mrs Dainty indignantly.

'No, but I mean, in London. Stage, screen and radio and all that.'

'If you want to go on talking you'd better come back later. I got things to do.'

'Oh, OK, fine. Absolutely. What time would be good, do you think?'

''E 'as 'is tea at five.'

'Will you let him know? Paul Shaw.' But the door had closed.

Formby in mid-afternoon is not a hotbed of action. I wandered off back in the direction of the station, at a total loss. The weather had brightened, at least. I remembered that Formby was meant to be a seaside place, although I could see no sign of a beach. A passing inhabitant was helpful.

'Yer go down 'ere about a mile to St Luke's Church. Turn right, over the sand dunes. Yer can't miss it.'

Once past the church the dunes can be seen through the pines, a mountain range of sand. The star-grass rustled stiffly in the breeze as I braced myself for the ascent. My natty suedes weren't ideal, and the walk from the station had been a longish mile, but something about the lonely sea and the sky was calling me. What I needed for a bruised spirit and a sore head, I felt, was to occupy my business in great waters for a while.

I wasn't disappointed. It was the biggest beach I'd ever seen. The sun shimmered on trackless miles of sand on the distant mirage of absent tide.

Bracing visions of buckets and spades and starfish and crabs and nanny engulfed me. Blue suede shoes with pointed toes no longer seemed important. I ground happily along on them, into the timeless vacuum, occasionally collecting a shell. I went all the way out to where the tiny waves washed in over the ribbled floor. I breathed deeply and stared out, a man of destiny once more . . . I put my hands on my hips and turned to view the dunes. They were gone.

A wall of mist swirled like an enemy between me and where I'd wandered from. The sun became a pale disc, then disappeared. All the glory was suddenly horribly grey.

The next time I saw St Luke's Church was three hours later. A short prayer seemed in order. Life had become cold and frightening, and only the power of panic had driven me back over all that uncharted darkness.

The road past the church was clear. The dense mist, which gave up the ghost at the brink of Christendom, closed off the hellish past like an iron curtain. I hurried on into the uncertain future, glad to have one at all. There was still a mile to go and it was an hour past Val's tea-time.

''E's gone out. You missed 'im.'

'Oh dear.' Mrs Dainty and I both allowed our eyes to wander over my beach-stained clothing.

'Got a bit, er, got in a bit of a mess on the beach. Got a bit lost.'

'Oh aye.' The evening sun shone serenely on Val Dainty's mum.

'No idea where he's gone I suppose?'

'Couldn't say.'

'Oh well.' I turned to shuffle off, a broken man. At the last moment the mother in her broke through.

'You could try the pub . . .'

'Oh, I say! Which one?'

'The Railway Hotel.'

The Railway Hotel, Formby, is as near the tracks to the east as Val Dainty's house was to the west. It was his local. The forecourt was cobbled and its jolly sign featured a loco not unlike Thomas the Tank Engine. Normally the idea of lubricating a tricky negotiation like this would have seemed attractive, even essential. But only that morning I had foresworn strong drink, this time for good.

'What's it gonna be then?'

Val was in the bar-parlour with the weedy keyboard player and someone new to me, built on similar lines to the mountainous bass-player. They had turned at my 'Hulloa!' without much surprise or interest.

'This bloke's called John. 'E's from London.' Val was mildly apologetic.

'Paul, actually.'

'All we need is George and Ringo then,' quipped the mountain. 'I'm Moose.'

'How d'you do?' I looked around vaguely, wondering whether I could possibly ask for a lemonade shandy. Val seemed to read my mind.

'Give 'im a velvet mist.'

'Velvet mist?' I hadn't forgotten the beach.

'Guinness with an Irish Mist chaser,' said the weedy chap, looking up from his glass, white foam around the lips. 'I'm Quint.'

I shook hands with Quint. He had a soft Yorkshire voice, without the metallic scouse hardness of Val and Moose.

I said, 'Perhaps just a half of Guinness.'

''E's a fookin' pansy!' Moose spoke as one whose suspicions are confirmed.

''E's all right. 'E'd get it together with berds if 'e could.' Val gave me a knowing look. 'That's what they drink in the 'Ome Counties, 'alves.'

'Look . . .' I groped for coolness, 'that's a load of crap.' I pushed the accent as far out into the mid-Atlantic as I could. 'I've just been having a rather heavy time, that's all.'

'Then what you need, pal,' Moose set a tall black and a small golden glass in front of me, 'is a drink.'

By closing time we were all Irish poets. Moose was a Paddy McGinty's Goat man. I gained a solid foothold with Oscar Wilde, despite Moose repeatedly interrupting to remind us that Wilde, too, was a pansy. When I got to the bit in *The Ballad of Reading Gaol* about the wretched man eaten by teeth of flame, Val rose to his feet dramatically. He held his empty glass up to Heaven.

'The Centre will not hold!' cried Val. 'The falcon cannot see the falconer . . .' He looked down at me quizzically.

'Something about the blood-dimmed tide?' I ventured.

'Cry treason, and let slip the dogs of war!' Val's black eyes glittered.

'No, no. That's Shakespeare.'

'And what's wrong with fookin' Shakespeare?' Moose glowered at me belligerently. 'At least 'e weren't a fookin' pansy!'

On the way back to Val's place Moose draped a sentimental arm around my shoulders. 'Yer not a bad bloke.' The glow of many Velvet Mists stole over me. I felt I could get to like this fellow a lot, even when he added, 'fer a fookin' pansy!'

Val wanted to go back and check his Yeats. 'We could 'ave a sing-song an' all.'

Quint said he was sick of singing and split. The rest of us blundered into the vestibule of Val's neat semi. The stairs were carpeted in red with a bright flower pattern. At the top was another locked door.

'Me own private werld.'

Two rooms were knocked together. Books flowed out of the walls over musical instruments. Aubrey Beardsley Wicked Queenes and frightening images by Edvard Munch and Kirschner hung by drawing-pins. Sketch-pads and record sleeves littered the floor. Assorted guitars leaned next to a G-string banjo and a George Formby ukulele. A fiddle hung beside a picture of Harpo Marx. Against one wall stood a honky-tonk piano and a harmonium with carpet-covered pedals.

'Can you play "Abide with Me"?'

'Fook that!' Moose declared. 'Let's get fookin' pallatic 'n' sing "Waltzing Matilda"!'

'Won't your parents mind the noise?' I said.

'Me dad won't, 'e's dead.'

'Oh, I . . .'

'Died of drink like a true Irishman. Me mam stops downstairs and does the cooking.' Val moved a battered copy of Grimm's Fairytales and sat down at the harmonium. I looked around for something I could bang or rattle.

'Don't you play anything, Moose?' I said.

'Not me, mate. Me broother plays bass in the group. I just fetch 'n' fookin' carry. A hewer of fookin' wood, that's me.'

Val said, 'Beer in the fridge, Moose.' His feet tramped the pedals and his fingers rested lightly on the notes. The first chord droned sweetly into my ear . . . 'If you ever go across the sea to Ireland . . .'

Alone in the musty London train the following day I wondered how precisely to word my report. Looked at in one way things had certainly gone well. When at last I'd got my way and we'd slurred through 'The darkness deepens, Lord with me Abide', the sky had lightened over Formby. The fridge had emptied. So had a full bottle of Canadian Club. We'd worked our way through 'Galway Bay', 'Waltzing Matilda' and 'Danny Boy', as well as some inspired verses we'd improvised to the tune of 'Green Onions'. If mere words are anything to go by we three had formed a brotherhood for life. Val's last act before he passed out was to show me to a mattress in one corner.

'You can crash there, mate.'

'Thanks. Er, Val . . .' I'd said.

'Yeah?'

'Do you mind if I ask you something?' Even in this relaxed state I'd felt my balls tighten slightly. 'Whatever did happen with those two birds?'

Above me Val's face was tired and covered in blue stubble. It lit up at this.

'Ha! They both fooked off with the big bloke.'

'What, John?'

'No. The old one with all the gelt. The Captain.'

I told the cabbie to drive through the park while I organised my thoughts. Liam and John could hardly expect me to have things signed and sealed at this stage, could they? The ice had been well and truly broken. While the word 'management' had not actually passed my lips, I felt sure that if I invited my new friend Val to London to be a star he would be delighted. The taxi rattled to a halt in Draycott Gardens. While I agonised over how to moderate the tip without alienating the driver, something outside the Admiral Rodney caught my eye. I strolled over to take a look. It was a bright mauve Lotus Elite. Rather garish, but I envied it all the same. The motorcars of some patrons presented the only real drawback to living opposite the Admiral Rodney. Many of them made my MG look low-powered and boring. My father had turned a deaf ear to this problem, and to the sociosexual disadvantages arising from it. He said I was lucky to have a car at all. When he was nineteen he hadn't. Many more deserving people still didn't. Etcetera. The Lotus Elite was high on my list of desirables, nevertheless.

I opened the flat door. Laughter floated down the stairs from the sitting-room. It was John. I heard Liam say, 'Fuckin' beautiful setup . . . hangon . . . !'

John said, 'Who's there?'

'Just me.'

I had triumphant words worked out for any question, but no question came. I breezed into the room, relaxed and confident. John stared at me like I was the public hangman. He got himself together with a visible effort.

'Hello, lad! Howsitgoing?' He seemed to be dragging the *bonhomie* up from somewhere around his knees.

Liam rose quickly and gripped both my biceps with bony hands.

'Yer lookin' well. Yer lookin' fantastic!' The gestures were as familiar as the words, but his heart wasn't in it. Liam, for some reason, was floundering.

'I gotta split right away!' he seemed to galvanise himself out of trouble with this thought. He looked me in the eye with an almost normal glitter.

'Oh! OK.' I felt as relieved as anyone.

'John . . .' Liam pointed a long finger at John but didn't say anything, '. . . OK?'

'Don't worry about it.'

'Doesn't anyone want to know about the Formby Five?' I complained, as the door closed behind Liam.

'Of course, lad. I want to know all about the Formby Five.' John rose and placed both his hands firmly on my shoulders. He was giving me his most sincere look: 'Nothing would give me greater pleasure.'

'Well . . .' I moved towards the window, rather against the pressure of his hands, I felt. Glancing out, I exclaimed, 'Hey!' Liam was climbing into the mauve Elite. I pushed closer to the glass. Liam seemed to sense me. He looked up. His grin was positively sepulchral. A nonchalant wave and he disappeared into the driving seat. Seconds later the thing screeched off. Only a slight haze of molten rubber marked the spot. I turned to John. 'What the fuck . . .' but he was ready for me now.

'You never heard of such a thing as image?'

'Yes, but . . .'

'Look, sweetheart, listen to me. We need Liam to get things together, right?'

'Right.'

'OK. Liam needs the car to boost his image.' John's tone was final.

'But I don't understand,' I persisted. 'I just don't understand how he paid for it.'

'Money, money, money! That's all you ever think about. You're as bad as your old man.'

'I bet he doesn't know Liam's bought that car.'

'It's none of his business.'

I looked at John without asking the next question. He said, 'And you're not going to make it his business, are you?' He was looking at me intently. I looked away. John fiddled with a Rothmans pack, and eventually lit up. He blew out smoke like steam escaping from a safety valve.

'Come on, lad. Let's go down the King's Road and pull a couple of birds. I'll show you how it's really done.'

– Four –

'Six bloody months!'

'Yes, Daddy, I know.'

'What's going on, for God's sake?'

'Er . . .'

'You should be on the air by now. It's a bloody disgrace!'

I cleared my throat for want of a suitable reply.

'Jeremy Hammond is staying with friends over in Ireland and insists on seeing things for himself. I want you to arrange it.'

'Absolutely!'

The irate parent finally hung up. The summer of 1963 had been a busy one for me and time, I suppose, had flown. The *Anastassia* had steamed off to some mysterious spot on the Irish coast, to be converted to a radio station. There hadn't seemed much more that I could do. Had even the simplest task been required of me I doubt if I could have accomplished it anyway. My mind was paralysed and I had become incapable of coherent action. In the midst of my few remaining months as a carefree teenager I had fallen hopelessly in love.

Her name was Natasha Roxbury. Pictures of her tantalised me almost daily in the society pages of the papers, and in magazines like *Tatler* and *Queen*. Nightly they haunted my dreams. I was obsessed with a girl I didn't know. And yet I did know her, I felt, and she would know me too, if only we could meet. That was the problem. The press had created her Deb of the Year. Sensing change in the air, they had singled her out. Natasha was not a twinset and pearls girl. She was the wild card in the pack of English roses who annually came out for their 'Season', under the watchful eyes of society dowagers, whose goal in life is to steer their charges into the arms of 'suitable' liaisons and keep the rotters at bay. At the Berkeley Dress Show, Natasha, one of the exclusive twenty chosen for the traditional Charity Parade, wore Bermuda shorts and a rakish cap by Mary Quant. The dowagers murmured and frowned but the hacks loved it. Natasha's legs were good enough for space beyond the Court Circular and Jennifer's Diary. Her hair was black, like jet. Her huge eyes beguiled me luminously from their pale, patrician setting.

I was neither suitable nor a rotter. More of a nobody, I should say. Try as I might, and fret as I might, my name still did not feature on the List. The List was compiled by the ruling matrons of society, whose jewelled hands controlled the flow of those white paste invitations so essential to the mantelpiece of the would-be deb's delight. These announced that the Hon. Mrs So-and-so, At Home somewhere in Pont St., on behalf of her daughter Penelope, would cordially welcome your presence there at seven-thirty for eight. During the season mothers of the Right Sort gave dances for their daughters in the country and in town. Even those Not Quite Right, but Rich, could get the gel brought out by grand but impoverished dowagers-for-hire. Men of the Right Sort went to the dances and to dinner parties beforehand, arranged by the hostess among her cronies. Rotters gatecrashed but didn't get the free dinners. A chap could live well on that list. To some it was a profession, even an art.

In Haslemere a few Hons lurked among the laurel shrubs. From the age of sixteen, when we had moved there, I had had the advantage of a swimming-pool and a bubble-car. They went down well with the daughters, but smacked of unwelcome vulgarity once they got me home among the chintz and the bone china. My Elvis Presley image and views struck a jarring note over afternoon tea on the croquet lawn. Even at a meal that simple I could usually manage some appalling gaffe, and the maters baulked. I caught my first whiff of social obstacles ahead. A hand up a skirt in a bubble-car is a far cry from being listed among the nation's most desirable males.

I explained my problems over a pint or two at the Admiral Rodney to Henry Pelham. Being a viscount he was high on the charts of socially conscious mothers, and knee-deep in invitations.

'You surely can't go to all of them, Henry,' I wheedled. 'Couldn't I just borrow some and pretend I was you?'

Henry shook his aristocratic head. 'Not a hope, old lad. They'd spot you a mile off.'

We sipped in silence while I brooded on the unfair machinations of fate.

'Why the sudden interest in being a deb's delight?' said Henry.

'Well . . .' I wished to stay as evasive as possible – Henry was hardly the man for confidences of the heart. 'There's this girl, you see. I can't seem to get to meet her.'

'What's her name?'

'Just some girl. She's a deb. She goes to all those parties.'

'If you won't tell me her name I won't help you.'

'Will you if I do?'

'I might.'

'Oh, OK,' I sighed reluctantly, 'Natasha Roxbury.'

Henry stared at me and his half-expected laugh was unpleasantly crude. 'You must be joking, mate!'

'Well, I'm not.'

'You can forget that one. The whole world wants to get in there. Anyway, Ned Wessex already made it.'

'Oh?' I felt sick.

'He writes all the gossip. She likes him because he gets her in the papers.'

Happy with the distress he had caused, and with a few more pints, Henry was able to supply a straw to help me on my hopeless way. An aunt of his was giving a ball at the Café Royal in a few days time.

'Leave it to me. Your bird's bound to be there.'

'How do you know?'

'Because Ned will. He wouldn't miss a bash like that.'

I was a broken man, but I got an invitation. In addition a letter arrived on impressively embossed notepaper from a Lady Belchester, who resided in Belgrave Square. She requested the pleasure of my company at dinner before the dance.

It was a perfect summer night. I was nervous in a dinner jacket borrowed from my father. I stood in front of the mirror while John made sartorial observations.

'I suppose in the thirties bum-freezers were all the rage.'

'Fuck off, John.'

'Do you think elasticated bow-ties are *de rigueur* in Belgravia?'

'Look, I'm very nervous, OK? This isn't helping. Let's have a drink.'

Once I'd got some Dutch courage on board I felt better. I tied a white evening scarf loosely round my neck.

'How's that?'

'Speak up clearly when you get there or they'll think you're Clark Gable.'

I parked the MG and walked to the number displayed on my letter. A porch, a single brass bell: no one could occupy the whole of one of these, surely? The building towered above me like a cliff. I peered nervously about. When I turned back to the door it had opened noiselessly, although I hadn't yet steeled myself sufficiently to ring.

'Good evening, sir.'

Towering above me now was the butler – I had never seen one before, except on the screen. He looked down on me as one might who finds something distasteful attached to his shoe.

'Mr Shaw, I presume?'

I was wondering how my fame could have spread to this unexpected quarter when he said, 'Will you follow me this way, sir. The other guests are waiting.'

Lateness was not my only distinction, I discovered, when, after several miles of haughty ancestors, my ponderous guide swung open a heavy, mahogany door.

'Mr Shaw,' he announced, apologetically.

A richly furnished room shimmered before me. It was full of people at least twice my age. Every eye, many lorgnetted, was upon me. My first instinct was to turn and run, but the butler barred my way. The men all wore evening clothes as if they had been born in them. Those not in military costume wore white tie. This detail on the invitation had, in my excitement, escaped me. Looking like a waiter and feeling like a leper I greeted them all with a strangled croak.

'Ah, Mr Shaw.' A woman in a long green dress and a tiara rose graciously from her seat near the fireplace. She didn't actually say 'at last'. 'Would you like something to drink, or shall we go straight in to dinner?'

Witless though I was, I knew the right answer to this. Large double doors were swung back by two liveried footmen, revealing the glittering spread. My hostess attached my arm to someone whose name I didn't catch, and we made our way into a blaze of candlelight.

My knowledge of the Aristocrat at Home was still vague and

half-formed. Association with Henry Pelham had led me to believe that faded grandeur was the thing. Any overt display of wealth was the height of vulgarity, I thought. In Lady Belchester's dining-room yet more ancestors gazed down on a table the size of a cricket pitch. The candelabra were gold. Plates, knives, forks and spoons were gold. Golden flowerpots stood in a row down the centre of the feast, from which sprouted twisted stalks of gold. The flowers that bloomed from them were rubies, amethysts, emeralds, pearls. I sat down mechanically next to my partner, intent on everybody's actions, nearly missing my seat. I was saved by a footman, one of whom stood behind every other chair.

I grinned weakly at the female on my right, who had drawn the short straw with my name on it. She smiled back, encouragingly. She looked younger than most – about forty I should say. At nineteen anyone over thirty is ancient, but I prepared to make the best of it. She wore tiny diamond earrings in the shape of horseshoes. Her dress was modest, almost frumpish. Her hair was brown and curly, her eyes soft and friendly. The absence of cut glass in her voice gave me heart. Perhaps she was another outsider like me, and that was why we had been put together. She had a better grip on etiquette than me, and signalled to a footman, who filled up one of my many glasses with wine. Despite the shakes I got the thing to my lips, and after the process was repeated two or three times I felt quite chatty. I stopped worrying about what to do with all those knives and forks. My new friend was called Joan, and I told her all about my carwash and my radio ship. After lots more wine and many courses, I was able to confide my passion for Natasha Roxbury to her, and the real purpose of my evening's quest. She seemed interested, in a maternal sort of way. We let the rest of the table recede in a vague blur of stars and garters and *croix de guerres*.

This cosy state of affairs was terminated abruptly by the departure of the ladies. The men moved as one to surround our host at his end of the table, the opposite end to mine. They made clipped, yipping noises of recognition, and their conversation had become general even before they'd sat down. By joining them I could hardly be more of a trailing arbutus than by not joining them, or so you'd think. I shifted my way from chair to chair in their direction, like a commando dressed as a bush. I maintained an ingratiating smile, slightly fixed, but all the time I was humming a Little Richard number under my breath. 'You said you loved me and you caint come in, come back tomorrow nite and try it again . . .' I just *knew* Natasha would be able to hear me knockin'.

'Port!'

I glanced up from my reverie. The decanter glowed stationary before my new place on the fringe of a heated discussion about prices at somebody-or-other's shoot in Sussex.

'Oh! Yes, please!'

'£200 per half gun per day!'

'Bloody outrageous!'

Lord Belchester was making a vigorous stirring motion at me with his forearm and finger. 'Keep it moving, there's a good chap.'

I was unable to contribute much to the feast of reason raging about me, even when the topic switched to politics. We rejoined the ladies, with all my music still within me. I was relieved to see Joan looking out for me. She suggested we share a cab to the dance.

At the Café Royal cabs crowded the kerb. After depositing our coats, Joan and I joined the line at the head of some stairs behind a man who banged a stick on the ground and shouted out everyone's name.

'The Right Honourable the Lord Saltash!'

'Their Graces the Duke and Duchess of Belper!'

I grinned sheepishly at Joan as our turn approached.

'He won't have much trouble with mine,' I mumbled.

She went first. The stick-man banged hard, three times.

'Her Royal Highness the Begum Aly Khan!'

'Mister Saul Plore!'

The place was crowded and I was propping up the bar on my own. HRH had joined a table full of friends and I had excused myself on some pretext.

'Well, good luck.' She raised a glass at me.

'Mmm?'

'With the marvellous Miss Roxbury!'

I was the lone wolf. I was the ice-cool hunter in the forest dim. I was Napoleon Bonaparte, stepping down to pluck a new mistress from her mesmerised husband's arms. I was the perfect stranger, across a crowded room. I had switched from wine to whiskey.

My eye swept the crowd. A thin girl with hair piled up, wearing a long, tight dress that flattened her body against it, flickered and then disappeared in a dense corner. At last!

The crowd obscuring Natasha was predominantly male. There was a quality of sleekness about the group. They seemed more dangerously élite, more modern, than the thumping crowd. She sat at the back of a large, round table, away from the room, away from me. She talked secretly to the girl next to her. The girl kept nodding, smiling a rapt smile. Suddenly they burst out giggling and were just girls. They both stared like urchins at a loud ginger man in a coloured waistcoat. Ned Wessex sat on Natasha's other side, ignoring her with care. When he saw her watching the ginger man he leaned smoothly across and whispered to her. The girls laughed. Watching them, I felt unreasonably happy. She left her hand where it was, however, under Ned's.

Ned Wessex rose from his seat and started pulling Natasha's bare white arm. Now she noticed him, turning. She had a high bridged nose, and I could make out the delicate bones in her skull as her jaw moved under luminous, almost transparent skin.

'No, Ned, I don't want to.'

He jerked her hard. 'Well, I do.' Under the play I could sense the anger. She pulled to get her hand away, angry too.

'No, Ned. Let me go!'

On feet of dreams I waded in. This, I felt, whiskey-clear, was the tide in the affairs of men. One or two of the party got handled rather roughly in my haste.

'She doesn't want to dance with you, OK?'

In the ensuing débâcle things were said and done which might, on sober reflection, seem regrettable. Moreover, they failed to impress the woman of my dreams. She seemed to resent my intrusion more than anybody.

'Who is this fellow?' demanded the Earl of Wessex. 'Do you know him, Natasha?'

'No, I don't.' They still held hands, I noticed, now more united than before.

He turned to me. 'What the hell d'you mean, butting in like this?'

'I didn't like the way you were treating her, that's all.'

'Oh, didn't you!'

'It's none of your business!' This from the girlfriend, very shrill. It seemed to strike a chord with all of them.

'Isn't it?' I addressed Natasha, giving her my most burning look.

'No, it certainly isn't.'

'My name is Paul Shaw. I've been wanting to meet you. Would you like to dance?'

'Now look, old chap' – Wessex dropped Natasha's hand and gestured towards my shoulder – 'fuck off, why don't you!'

Throughout this exchange the ginger man had been picking himself up from where I'd knocked him, quite accidentally, off his chair. No doubt inspired by Ned's suggestion, which was chorused heartily by the whole party, he seized me by the collar of my father's constrictingly tight DJ.

'Yes!' he cried. 'Fuck off! You bloody little upstart!'

This unexpected assault from the rear startled me. I fell over, taking the ginger man with me.

The London Season does not cater solely to debs. The grander balls attract all age groups and this was one of them. At the table next to Natasha's a particularly stiff selection of exhibits from the *ancien régime* had already been roused to hauteur by the fracas. When the ginger man and I collapsed into their midst, dislodging one dowager on to the lap of a blimpish gent with a monocle, they were not amused. I soon discovered that the Happening was not the only place in the West End to employ bouncers. As discreetly as possible I was dragged away. Confrey Phillips and the boys broke noisily into 'Fly Me to the Moon'. Over the din I screamed, 'NATASHA! I LOVE YOU!' I felt I had nothing to lose.

I hadn't been seeing so much of Liam. Once or twice when I'd thought I might connect with Natasha at Esmeralda's Barn or the Garrison he'd lent me the Elite to improve my chances. It hadn't, but I was grateful all the same. When I called he'd just returned from one of his intermittent trips to Galveston. I broke the news.

'Jeremy and the old man are getting restless.'

'Excellent!'

'Jeremy's over in Ireland and insists on seeing the ship.'

'Excellent!'

'Liam, this is serious.'

'Excellent!'

'Why do you keep saying "Excellent" like that?'

'Excellent!'

'Oh, God, Liam.'

'Things are groovy. I'll catch you later and explain.' He hung up.

In Texas, to get and stay ahead of the game, anyone at all happening flew. Liam delivered this all-important message during a brief visit to Pandora's Box that evening. John and I were munching our way through a steak and a bottle of Mateus Rosé. John had put on a Hollies album, and watched the dancefloor in an ecstasy of boredom. He turned to Liam without interest.

'Is that so?'

I said, 'I can't see what that's got to do with anything. What about what I told you on the phone?'

'Aha! Come with me tomorrow and you'll find out. I'll pick you up at seven in the morning.' And he was gone.

Brighton & Worthing Municipal Airport was (and is) a group of Nissen huts thrown up around a waterlogged meadow in Shoreham-by-sea. Sea mists are uncannily attracted to it. On clear days huge flocks of gulls settle there. Prefabricated hangars of the Whacko Prang school housed flying machines of similar ilk. The one that was to put us ahead of the game was a De Havilland 'Dragon Rapide'. It was operated by South Western Air Taxi Services, but Liam intended to commandeer it on some sort of permanent basis. The details of the deal were vague. Both Liam and Wing Commander Edward 'Teddy' Tenterden were keen to make it 'happen'. On the way down Liam emphasised the importance of air mobility in the modern age, Texan style. In addition to his other 'duds' he wore a pair of mirrored shades.

'That cat's ready to make a trade-off fer airtime.'

'That's funny, isn't it?' I chortled. 'Airtime!'

John gave me a look of contempt. He said, 'It is pretty funny, considering there isn't any.'

Liam said, 'Aha, that's just it. That's the beauty of it.'

John said, 'I don't get it.'

'This guy's a war hero. He's in the why-not business, right? His thinkin' is radical. We get what we need now. When the big turn-on

comes, the cat has enough airtime rolled up to start a fuckin'
airline!'

Wing Commander Tenterden was the proprietor and sole
'operational' employee of South Western Air Taxi Services Ltd.
Tangible assets of the firm appeared to total one hangar (World
War One issue), and one De Havilland 'Dragon Rapide'. A dirt road
took us to the 'Terminal Building', an Art Deco surprise that made
me think, for some reason, of Graham Greene. From here we
proceeded on foot across the field.

One thing about being rejected by the girl you love is that you
cease to care. Death, you feel, where is thy sting? Events at the Café
Royal and since had affected me this way, and it was just as well.
Only the most reckless disregard for life and limb could induce one
to fly in the machine that confronted us that day. In the first place it
was in bits. A ginger type with a Biggles moustache greeted us
heartily. 'Morning, chaps!' he called from the heart of the debris,
rubbing the side of his head with a monkey wrench. 'Good journey
down? Topping day for it!'

'Hello there!' cried Liam, not to be outdone in *joie de vivre*. 'Yer
lookin' well!' John and I were introduced to the wing commander.
He was a spry individual in greasy overalls with RAF Wings sewn
over the breast pocket. He appealed strongly to the *Boy's Own
Annual* side of me, even if what he called his 'trusty steed' did not. I
thought such people only existed in comics. Teddy, as he wished us
to call him, was the real thing.

The trusty steed was the real thing too, according to Teddy. An
absolute corker! By the early sixties metal bodies had become the
norm for aeroplanes as far as I knew. The De Havilland 'Dragon
Rapide', vintage 1934, had a fabric skin stretched over its fuselage,
which laced up underneath, like a corset. Even in its present state of
disarray we could see it was a biplane. A network of taut wires
seemed to hold it all together. There were two engines, which was
encouraging. They were housed over solid rubber wheels in deco
style similar to the terminal building. Whether they worked or not
seemed dependent on the outcome of major surgery currently in
progress.

'I'll just get some seats in the old bus. Then we'll be off!'

Surprisingly soon the three of us were helping Teddy push the
finished article out of the hangar and on to the soggy grass.

'Jolly good show! Where did you say we were going?'

A salty cross-breeze stiffened the stocking on the tower. Visibility was beginning to look a bit misty. We climbed aboard and settled into canvas seats. Teddy fiddled with the controls and muttered into his radio headphone, which crackled back. I was glad we had a radio. Every so often he turned to us and said, 'Dublin! Hah!' He had a way of tipping his head back sharply and going off like a pistol. 'Dublin! Hah!'

Outside the mist almost obscured the carpet of seabirds. Brilliant-rimmed cumulonimbi gathered ominously overhead.

Teddy hauled on a couple of knobs. Dynamos wheezed and whined. Exhausts banged like guns. Both engines clattered into life, then roared to a crescendo. My teeth rattled in my head and everything went blurry. He throttled back and taxied slowly over bumpy hectares of buttercup and clover. Propwind licked flat swirls of grass around the plane. At last we faced down the strip, into the wind and sun. Teddy gave it the gun. Sweat started out of my palms and my balls shrank. I stared rigidly at the back of Teddy's flying helmet, not daring to look at Liam and John. Through the windshield a million startled seabirds seemed to fill the sky. Everyone got airborne but us. Buildings and tall trees hurtled towards us. At the very last moment we went vertical. The engines screamed in protest. My stomach bailed out. I looked down. Things on earth were getting small. I felt sick. The coastline stretched away against the widening sea.

I dragged my terrified eyes back from the abyss. Staring rigidly ahead at Teddy I became aware that all was not well with him. He appeared to be wrestling with some enemy in his lap. I strained against my harness for a better view. Directly in front of Teddy, where the instrument panel should have been, was a gaping hole. A hopeless looking tangle of wires hung out of it.

I don't know what happened next exactly because everything suddenly went dark. Looking out I realised we were inside a cloud, still climbing hard. I hung on by closing my eyes tight and clinging to the image of Natasha that was fixed indelibly on to the backs of my eyelids.

We levelled out at last. I opened my eyes. Outside was a Jack-and-the-Beanstalk land of bright sun on cotton wool.

I leaned as close to Teddy as I could and yelled, 'Is everything all right?'

Teddy turned his pale popeyes on me. I could see the tiny red veins all over his nose and cheeks. His smile stretched the brush above his upper lip over his yellow teeth. 'Couldn't be better old boy!'

'But what about . . . ?' I nodded down at the wreckage on his knees.

'Soon fix that!' said Teddy with relish.

I watched him shove the whole panel back into the hole, stuffing in wires until it fitted snugly. Teddy went to work on the corners with a screwdriver, and I settled back.

I turned around to the others and we all grinned. John was yelling something over the engines. I called, 'Wha . . . ?'

I caught the word 'Fun!'

'Yes! Yes, isn't it!'

Something was poking me insistently. I turned. It was Teddy's screwdriver. He crooked a forefinger at me.

'Yes?' I leaned forward to him once again.

'Spot of bother with the wireless.'

'What sort of bother?'

'On the blink. Kaput!'

'Can you fix it?' None of this was really sinking in.

Teddy shook his head. 'No can do, old boy.' He seemed as chuffed about this as he did about everything. I gaped at him. 'Better ask the others if they want to push on or call it a day,' he said.

'You mean we could carry on without it?'

'Piece of cake.'

I unbuckled and struggled back to Liam and John.

'Teddy says the radio's fucked. Do you want to turn back?'

John said, 'Yes.'

Liam said, 'No way!'

I sat up front with Teddy in the co-pilot's seat. He would need me to assist with a spot of navigation.

'I shouldn't think I'm much at reading charts.'

'No need for charts, old boy. We'll just pop down whenever there's a break in the cloud. Keep a sharp lookout for landmarks.'

'What happens if there aren't any breaks in the cloud?'

Teddy said, 'HAH!' and grinned ferociously.

In order to stick to the flight plan we first had to pick up Southampton. After that we would set course for Cardiff, Swansea and out over the Welsh coast at Fishguard.

'A dead straight line,' Teddy assured me. 'Couldn't be simpler. Then all we have to do is turn right into Red Fourteen.'

'Red Fourteen?'

'Air Route to Dublin. Piece of cake.'

Teddy peered at his compass, glanced at the sun, then at me.

'Should be just about over Southampton now.'

The carpet of cloud stretched unbroken for as far as I could see. Our shadow buzzed merrily along it, just below us.

'Do we actually need to see it?'

'Can't risk starting from the wrong place. Hah!'

I didn't know exactly what Teddy was going to do next, but I got a sort of kicked feeling in the pit of my stomach. He placed his hands carefully over the earpieces of his ancient leather helmet, as if making the final adjustment. He looked across at me. Whatever madness it was that had enabled our young men to shoot down their young men at the rate of four to one stood plainly in his gooseberry eyes.

'Hang on tight.' Teddy pushed the stick forward hard. 'Tally-ho!'

I'd been to Southampton once before, on another unforgettable occasion. It was the day my Nanny left me to become Chief Nursery Stewardess on the Queen Mary. Wiser heads than ours had decided that at the age of twelve I no longer needed a nanny. I remember feeling completely disembowelled that day, too.

The chief impression it left on me, apart from an overwhelming sense of betrayal by the whole female sex, was of big ships with huge funnels.

Ships rushed up at my half-conscious eyes as we screamed out of the cloud-base. We were roughly level with their masts. I turned desperately to Teddy. His eyes and mouth were open wide. Both thumbs pressed down furiously on the stick.

'Ackatackatackatackatacka! Ackatackatackatackatacka!!' He didn't seem to be pulling out.

'Teddy!'

*

Safe again in serene sky Teddy said, 'Bang on target, what! Still, better safe than sorry!'

There didn't seem much to say to this, even when I had regained control of my voice. As nonchalantly as I could, I croaked, 'Do you think we're on course all right, now?'

'Bang on!'

Back in the passenger area John looked pale. Liam stuck up an exuberant thumb. I couldn't hear him but I could read his lips and mind.

'Fuckin' A!'

We settled down to uneventful droning for what seemed many hours. I stared out at the unreal cloudscape and tried not to think about Natasha; what she was doing, who she was with. The more I thought about not thinking about her the more painful the images became.

Teddy messed about with the radio without much real conviction. It broke the monotony once with an unexpected squawk. Teddy said he thought he might've got a bearing on Manchester.

'Is that good?' I asked hopefully.

Teddy shook his head with grim satisfaction. 'Absolutely bloody useless. Hah!'

The endless cloud-tops were like a snowy mountain range. My mesmeric reflections moved on to the subject of winter sports. I brooded, with some bitterness, on the fact that I'd never been skiing; never penetrated the sophisticated mysteries of *après-ski* at Klosters and Gstaad. The ritual of our holidays had always been rigidly observed during precisely the same three weeks of August, year in year out, at the family hotel on Majorca. Natasha, I remembered reading in *Queen* magazine, was a keen and accomplished skier.

One formation rose up ahead of us, high above the others. I watched it for a while. It looked remarkably real.

'I say, Teddy . . .' I didn't want to disturb his incessant tinkering without good reason, but on the other hand . . . 'take a look at that.' I was, after all, supposed to be the navigator.

Teddy looked up absently. 'At what, old boy?'

'Over there.'

'Good Lord!'

'I can't make out if it's a cloud or a real mountain.'

'Well,' said Teddy, wrestling briskly with the controls, 'put it this way: if we don't take evasive action on the double we're going to crash into the bloody thing!'

'What mountain do you think it is?' I asked him when I thought he'd got over the more urgent procedures. 'It looks jolly big!'

'Look at the altimeter!' Teddy tapped hard on a gauge that meant nothing to me. 'Only one it can be!'

'Really? Which?'

'Bloody Snowdon!'

Teddy snapped this out so testily that I felt a surge of nervous guilt for having spotted it. In an attempt at conciliation I said, 'Well, that's good, isn't it? At least we know where we are.'

'Hah!' If anything his bad mood seemed to worsen.

'Well, isn't it?'

'Too far north. Bad drift.' Teddy banged the compass accusingly.

'Something wrong with the instruments?' I was happy for it to be their fault rather than mine.

'Wish there was, old boy. Look at those fuel gauges.'

'Fuel! We're not running out of fuel are we, Teddy? Please say we're not!'

'Should just about make it.'

'Just about make it! Can't we land and get some more?'

'Not a hope!' Teddy was beginning to perk up.

'Why not?'

'Only hope up here's Liverpool. Never find it without a wireless. Get knocked out of the sky by an airliner. Hah!'

'Only hope?'

'Except Dublin. Dead reckoning. Piece of cake.'

'It's dead reckoning that got us where we are now, Teddy.'

'Got no choice, old boy. Don't see how we can miss the whole Irish coast!' Teddy was back on form now. Soon the cloud broke up. Down below flecks of white winked coldly on the bleak Irish Sea. 'Wouldn't like to ditch in that lot. Hah!' We flew low and slow to conserve our last precious drops. Words like 'watery' and 'grave' kept turning in my brain. I turned round once or twice with a ghastly grin, and got two ghastly grins in return. No one had much to say. Down in the depths I could see Natasha dancing with her head on Ned's shoulder. It was better than looking at death, but only just.

'I say, old boy, how well do you know this part of the world?' Teddy had crooked the finger at Liam, who had hurried up front to join us. I could see the freckles standing out on his pale, damp skin. Teddy's question did at least raise the ghost of a chuckle.

'Which part of the fuckin' world are we at?'

'Irish coast somewhere. Can't seem to find Dublin.'

'Teddy's been doing it by dead reckoning,' I explained.

'That's a good fuckin' word for it . . .' Liam peered down. 'Hold on a minute' – he held up his hand – 'I don't fuckin' believe it!'

'What, what!' I squeezed my face next to his at the wet, misty window. 'Where?'

'Down there!' I could just make out a cluster of masts, derricks and gantries.

'I still don't see . . .'

Liam was beside himself. 'It's the ship. It's our fuckin' ship!'

The victory roll marked our official change of mood. Common sense was relegated to its more usual position at the bottom of our list of priorities. Teddy bristled like an old dogfox who has once again foiled the pack.

Towering up at us from the deck of the *Anastassia* was our brand-new, all-American, 150-foot radio mast.

'Up at last' – Liam spoke with rapture – 'Fuckin' beautiful!'

To get a better view Teddy flew down to something like fifty feet and circled the thing. One set of wingtips seemed likely to sweep the startled knot of onlookers below into the dock. We waved like the madmen we must have seemed to them. The mast bristled with spars and wires, all very capable of snagging a wobbly biplane, I thought.

After this a victory roll seemed almost an anticlimax.

'Just couldn't bloody well resist it!' Teddy's yellow teeth were gritted fiercely.

'Fuckin' beautiful!' said Liam.

John and I, who had ended up wedged together in an undignified muddle of limbs, were just glad it was over, though coolness forbade us to say so.

Worse, however, was to come. One engine gave a sickening cough. Hearts and cylinders skipped several beats.

'Good Lord!' exclaimed Teddy. 'I'd almost forgotten about that!'

'Don't worry about it!' Liam was cool. 'I know where we are now.'

'We need to land pretty soon.' Teddy gripped the joystick with both hands.

'I know just where to land!' Liam's face had assumed its most dangerous gleam.

'There's an airfield nearby?'

'Not an airfield, exactly . . .'

We arrived over our destination by way of a series of shallow dives at roadsigns. We kept going roughly southwest. It wasn't, as Liam had promised, all that far. But with stammering engines which every now and then petered out completely, it was far enough. As he had also promised, it was impossible to miss.

'Good God! We're going there!' Teddy, a true son of the Empire, was impressed.

'That's where jolly old Jeremy's stayin'.'

Castle Drogheda, the largest house in all Ireland, was the ancestral home of the Marquis of Meath, Jeremy Hammond's host. To describe it either as a castle or a house or a home would be misleading. It was a palace.

Three stately chunks of eighteenth-century architecture, each about as big as Buckingham Palace, stood around three sides of a central court. A thing like a porch, about fifty feet high and replete with columns and a good deal of Greek statuary, looked out majestically across the courtyard and down a causeway which ended in an ornamental bridge over a huge lake. Both east and west wings were built round ornamental gardens where fountains played. Beyond the house on the other side, Capability Brown parkland rolled away to the south.

'We can land there and drive right up to the front door. Blow their fuckin' West Brit minds!' Liam had Teddy's shoulder in a fiercely persuasive grip.

'Does it actually have a front door?' Teddy was as overawed by the layout as I was.

'That fuckin' great temple thing, with all those Roman lookin'-cats on top.'

'Not much runway between the lake and that. Bloody great tree in the way, too.'

'You can do it, Teddy!'

We flew down low over the lake. Beyond the bridge a large tree spread its branches directly in our path. We got round the tree, but when we hit the gravel we bounced. The angle of descent was all to cock, Teddy later explained. Also the causeway was uphill, which he hadn't noticed.

'Whoops! Hang on chaps!'

In what I later learned was the Tympanum of the Portico, something heroic in Latin was fast becoming hugely and distressingly legible. The word 'VINQVIT' held me spellbound as Teddy wrestled desperately. Above the portico was a dome; above the dome an orb; a crown; a cross. There seemed no end to it, like the biggest wedding cake in the world, until at last we were looking down breathlessly on the rooftops of the palace. It was like a small town in Italy in the year 1 AD.

We breathed again, but only briefly. Teddy put the protesting Rapide into a sharp turn, but halfway round both engines gave up the ghost completely. That last desperate manoeuvre had finally drained the tanks dry. The propellers feathered powerlessly. All we could hear was the rushing mighty breeze.

Liam said, 'Unreal!'

Teddy broke the spell. 'Mayday time, what? Hah!'

We dumped pretty well straight down on to the courtyard, and shot off back along the causeway. Going this way, of course, it was downhill. The lake grew up at us fast. The little bridge was a dream of old Tuscany, ideal for lovers. Even when crinolines came in it had comfortably accommodated the romantic stroller. But in 1704, when it was built, no one had thought of biplanes.

'Not going to make it, are we?'

'Nope.' Teddy spoke with the grim philosophy of the Few.

In the event only one set of wings snapped off. The others were saved when the impact swung us sharply round. For a moment that lasted an eternity we teetered on the edge of the stonework. Then we went over, into the lake.

*

The butler came to fetch us in a Landrover. He had brought towels.

'His Lordship felt you might wish to clean up and change before dinner.'

We left the remains of the Rapide where it was, languishing in the shallow water. Someone from the estate office would deal with it, our rescuer assured us. His name was Ross. He was dapper and deferential – unlike Lady Belchester's tyrant – in black jacket and sharp striped trousers. A gold watchchain traversed his black waistcoat, adding a touch of gentish dash to uniformity. His shoes glowed like the biceps of a Nubian slave. He conducted me to a bedroom about half a mile down a dark green corridor.

'You will find the main staircase at the other end, sir, when you wish to go down. Dinner is at eight.' Ross disappeared, taking the others with him, Teddy still muttering darkly to himself about insurance.

My luggage hadn't suffered in the crash. There wasn't much of it. My trials at Lady Belchester's dinner had hardly prepared me for the stately goings-on I felt eftsoons must engulf me. One thing I did know, though: any social disadvantages I might naturally possess were going to be greatly amplified by my wardrobe.

I picked over it glumly in my red brocade bathroom. On the wall was a huge diagram of the coronation of Queen Mary. Numbered outlines corresponded with names of the participants below. I might just as well have turned up to that in my metallic jeans and yellow T-shirt. Not even a jacket.

The last minute came and went. I gave myself a final parting glance in the full-length mirror. No Cinderella miracle had occurred.

Silence reigned in the endless passage. Doors stretched away to right and left. My repeated soft knocks, which might have brought forth friends, drew blank after blank. I was resigned to a solo descent into the unknown when someone called out 'Yes!' to my last cursory rap.

'Who's there?' said the voice, vaguely familiar.

'Er . . .' I pushed the door open uncertainly. 'Is that, er, oh, sorry.'

'Yes?'

Someone with their back to me also stood before their reflection: brown velvet suit, yellow shirt with matching tie, unmistakable ferret face.

'Hello, Jimmy!'

'Oh, hullo. What are you doing here?'

'Just dropped in, you might say.'

'Oh, was that you?'

'Yes. What about you?'

'Friend of the family. I'd get another pilot if I were you.'

'Not to mention another plane.' Somehow the discovery of Jimmy Rittenhaus here wasn't the least surprising. Playboys have to fill their time somehow, and this place seemed a match for even Jimmy's bottomless ennui. I decided to test our relationship to the limit with a long shot.

'I say, Jimmy, I don't suppose you've got a spare jacket, or a tie, or anything, have you? I feel a bit naked going down to dinner dressed like this.'

Jimmy's expression, which had been frowning with concentration on the knot of his tie, went wary and defensive. Playboys, and the rich as a class, live their lives on the brink of an abyss of borrowers, and are consequently in a permanent state of readiness. He drew in his breath sharply. 'Nothing I can spare, I don't think.'

'How many clothes can you wear at once, Jimmy? I mean, I'm a bit desperate, you know.'

'I might have a sweater . . .' There was reluctance in every fibre of his being.

'Even a sweater . . .' Well, I hadn't been expecting much. Castle Drogheda's many installations didn't seem to include central heating. A sweater might at least modify the chill if not the discomfort.

Jimmy rummaged moodily. Something was at last dragged from a bottom drawer.

'This is the best I can do I'm afraid.' So was I. Joseph, in his coat of many colours, could hardly have appeared more conspicuous.

'Oh, I say . . .' I wasn't sure, honestly.

'Go on, try it. It's very warm.'

'It's quite, er, big.'

Jimmy was smiling now, adding a quality of malice to his normally discontented features. Not wishing to seem ungrateful, I was obliged to swathe myself, and stood before the glass, a blaze of mauve from neck to knee. Had I been able to foresee the advent of the kaftan, rooted there in that winter of 1963, I might have felt avant-garde. As it was, I felt anything but.

'Look, if we hitch it up with a belt it'll look good. You could start a new trend.'

'I don't want to start a new trend.' I wondered anxiously what John would have to say about it.

'Everybody's doing it. There's a chap here made me this suit. I got this belt from another chap in London called Danny Buckley.' Jimmy was brandishing something wide and stiff with two big metal circles for a buckle. The floodgates seemed to have burst in the weasel soul of Jimmy the couturier. He clasped the thing around my waist, pulled and tugged at the sweater, glancing anxiously in the mirror until he was completely satisfied.

'There!'

You had to admit it was striking, I suppose. The metallic jeans had assumed a new and vibrant meaning when mated with the acid sheens above. I was uncomfortably aware of having become Jimmy's protégé. He was getting quite feverish.

'Everybody here's heavily into fashion. Just say it's the latest thing. Who's to know? You can get away with anything these days if you're outrageous enough!'

Moving through the great chambers below I felt it was easy for Jimmy to talk. As we approached the Long Library, where, he said, house guests foregathered before dinner, I didn't feel outrageous. Ridiculous, perhaps. At least Jimmy knew the way.

The Library was certainly long, the ceiling vaulted and painted with heavenly creatures. At intervals down the length of polished floor, clusters of creamy furniture were grouped around tables whose rich cloths reached down to Persian rugs. Flowers and lampshades abounded. At the far end, almost lost in mist, a cathedral organ fluted its way up the wall in pale blue and gold.

There were a number of people, but my eye was drawn to a tableau near one of the bookcases. A pair of wooden steps stood by to help the reader to the upper shelves. A girl was up them, leaning back, looking out, away from the books, down at a man with a camera. He was snapping her and urging her into different and sexier poses. She moved stiffly, and stuck out her limbs in an angular way, moving her head from side to side, throwing it back in a half-hearted expression of abandon. The way she was stretched against the tilting steps was sexy enough for me, though. She wore something in lace over satin that just reached the tops of her thighs as she leaned back. The photographer kept calling 'Yes!' She stuck out one leg, then swung it stiffly sideways. A small chunky shoe in red and black leather hung from the front of one slender foot, halfway to being abandoned. The man with the camera was Ned Wessex. The girl was Natasha Roxbury.

I stared up. Her neck swivelled slowly in my direction, like fate. Two huge pools of darkness, which I had failed to fathom so many times in magazines, fell full on my face. I could see lamplight reflected in them, but no gleam of recognition. Delicate strokes of black emphasised their long lashes and heavy, languid lids. Her lips were pale, brushed with some subtle gloss. They smiled at me.

'Where did you get that great belt?' She had spoken to me.

I couldn't answer. I just stood there, gaping upwards. Jimmy, to whom she was simply a girl on a ladder, said, 'Danny Buckley. It's mine.'

Her momentary interest in me switched to indifferent Jimmy. I had missed my chance.

'I thought so.' Natasha's voice was light and high. 'Danny makes the most marvellous hand-painted silk shirts for me.'

Jimmy gave me a meaning look, as if to say, 'I told you so'.

The next meaning look I got was from John. He was sprawled on a sofa, his long legs stretched towards the fire. I moved guiltily towards him.

A girl was curled up at the other end from him. She was swaddled in something soft and woolly with a matching woolly hat.

'How's it going, lad?' John rattled the ice about in his glass. He seemed thoroughly at home. I longed to ask him if he knew what Natasha and Ned were doing here.

Jimmy was hovering in my immediate rear.

'Er, John, do you know Jimmy Rittenhaus?'

'Sure.'

'Oh. This is his sweater. He very kindly lent it to me.'

'Did he now. This is, er, what did you say your name was, sweetheart?'

'I didn't.'

'Well, if you tell me now I'll be able to introduce you to these two charmers. Paul here, in the glad rags, and my old mate Jimmy. You'd like that, wouldn't you?'

'My name's Chrissie.'

'There you go. I'm John.'

'Pleased to meet you.'

'And what's your story, Chrissie? What brings you to this neck of the woods?'

'I'm here with me boyfriend.'

'Oh, yeah. And who's the lucky fella?'

'Nicky Beresford . . . 'e's 'ere doing a bit of business with that bloke Ned.' Chrissie was working hard on her tough accent.

I burst in. 'But what's he doing here? Ned, I mean. That's what I don't understand.'

Her cornflower eyes impaled me scornfully. ' 'E only lives 'ere, that's all. This is his pad. Or 'is dad's anyway.'

I looked over wistfully at Natasha as I tried to absorb this. She was busy looking bored by Ned's suggestions. She blended well with the majestic scenario. It occurred to me that I could give myself a considerable break by forgetting about this girl. But just then she turned her head, flicked a stray hair from the corner of her mouth, put her shoulders back. Her small breasts creased the fabric of her dress. I looked away but I could still see her. Jimmy was saying something. His voice came from far away.

'Nicky Beresford's the chap I was telling you about, who made me this suit.'

'Oh?' I tried with difficulty to drag some interest into my voice.

'Here he comes now. Hi! Nicky!' I had rarely seen Jimmy so animated. I followed the direction of his eager cries.

Moving languidly in our direction was a vision in blue velvet. Although his creamy satin shirt, or blouse, or whatever it was, ended in ruffles at neck and wrist, it was his slippers that grabbed me most. They were bottle green velvet, monogrammed. The carnation in his buttonhole was green, too.

Nicky Beresford fell back into the sofa between Chrissie and John. One hand pushed back a heavy lick of dark hair. The other clasped an ivory cigarette-holder in a frozen grip.

'You're late,' said Chrissie.

'I do hope so. Punctuality is the thief of time.' He embraced us all in a curved smile. The vowel sounds were rounded and mellow, but unmistakably, surprisingly, Australian. 'So, Chrissie, are all these hungry boys being naughty to you?'

Chrissie stuck out her tongue. 'That one's Paul. That one's John. 'E fancies 'imself strongly.'

– 78 –

John was saved from responding to this by the shuddering summons of the gong. Jimmy perked up like a pointing stoat.

'Ah, dinner! Old Meath's chef is an absolute wizard!'

The dining-room was the sort of place where you could roll back the rug after dinner and throw a party for 500. Unnerving groups of classical characters watched us from vast, painted galleries around the walls. Each scene was astonishingly three-dimensional, standing out against a surreal backdrop of Michelangelo sky.

On the way from the library I walked directly behind Chrissie, torn between gasping at the grandeur and watching the pneumatic movement of her bottom. When she'd risen from the sofa the rumpled angora had clung to it lovingly, stopping just short of her long, model-girl legs. She moved flowingly without Natasha's arresting stiffness. Natasha was skinny. This was one definitely, professionally, slim.

Liam followed some distance behind, still deep in conversation with a character who, I couldn't help thinking, looked even more out of place than me, deafening sweater and all. I had been half-aware of them for some time, huddled together in a distant window-seat, out of touch with the rest of the room. His large face was pale and smooth, shiny blue around a pink mouth and round chin. He wore a sharp suit with slim lapels, beige, with a beige, button-down shirt of heavy linen, and a black knitted tie. He emphasised a lot with his hands, smiling hard, until the smile faded, leaving his face flat and disturbingly neutral. His receding hair was polished flat on his head. Gold-rimmed glasses gave his careful, steady eyes a deceptive twinkle. At dinner he seemed well-known, even celebrated, to everyone but me. His name was Reggie Turner. He had, he revealed, a number of 'West End interests', including casinos.

Ross the butler fussed around the long, glittering table. The musty air was sweet with forgotten banquets. I was placed opposite Natasha. I both hoped and feared to meet her eye. This, I soon realised, was unlikely. There was something impenetrably indirect about her. All her gestures were a calculated distraction. Most of all she was expert in screening her face behind the black curtain of her hair.

After a minute or so the Marquis of Meath arrived, with Jeremy Hammond. Someone this grand was beyond my wildest imaginings, and I was surprised that we didn't all have to prostrate ourselves or something. He was small, with small hands and feet. He had the high cheeks and hung jaw of the aristocrat, fine-boned and ascetic, with parchment skin. His gun-metal hair was rather long. Rakish sideburns filamented over his large ears. Most striking of all was his smoking jacket. It was sky-blue satin with scarlet facings, quilted. The front fastened with silk-embroidered frogs, also scarlet. Nicky Beresford wasn't the least inhibited about admiring it. Whether or not this was good form I wasn't sure. Certainly the Marquis seemed to like it.

'It belonged to Oscar Wilde.'

'Really. It looks like the one in those New York photographs by Sarony.'

'If you're interested in Wilde, I have quite a collection here. He used to visit the place a lot with his mother. My great-grandfather took an interest in their society for the suppression of virtue.'

Nicky explained that Narcississimus, his planned enterprise in the art of clothing, must exemplify the spirit of Wilde. It would, in fact, go far beyond mere garments. It was a matter of style, a philosophy of life. Clients would be transformed into animated epigrams. Even now small groups of the discerning (with sufficient cash) such as Jimmy Rittenhaus, patronised the embryonic temple to aestheticism at Nicky's small but exquisite house in Camden Town.

Nicky had indeed been hopeful that Lord Meath would allow him to sketch some of his renowned collection. Ned Wessex, son and heir, would be creating a series of photographic masterpieces capable of expressing the true meaning of Narcississimus to the readers of *Tatler* and *Harper's Bazaar*.

'And what about you, my dear' — the Marquis focused his attention on Nicky's charming consort — 'will you be helping in the shop? I shall certainly come there if you are.'

'I'm a model,' said Chrissie, fetching but doubtful.

'She only models mainstream stuff' — Nicky was dismissive — 'Mary Quant, Tuffin and Foale.'

Natasha piped up surprisingly, 'I like Mary Quant. I don't know what you mean, mainstream.'

Nicky snapped back with startling sharpness, 'Being a deb, I don't suppose you would.'

I felt the gallantry rising and took a swig of wine. Natasha twined a strand of hair around a finger. 'I don't see what being a deb's got to do with it.'

Ned, to give him his due, said, 'Natasha has been voted Deb of the Year,' but this only added fuel to the fire.

Chrissie leaned across at Natasha with what struck me as a shocking lack of reverence: 'What do debs do, exactly?'

The object of my pent-up adoration was now definitely under pressure. She grabbed a whole handful of hair and hid behind it. Seizing my opportunity I turned on her tormentor. 'Well, I see Natasha's picture in the paper all the time, and I've never seen yours,' my voice boomed. Faces turned towards me, pale and indistinct. All I could see was Natasha, beyond the detailed flame of a candle fluttering between us. I was speaking at her directly now: 'I saw that one of you in *Vogue*. One of England's six most fascinating women' – I took a strengthening gulp from my glass – 'I must say I rather agree.'

What impact the force of this speech had on Natasha, I couldn't say. On me it produced extreme breathlessness bordering on blackout. John's voice came from far away: 'There you go, lad!'

I'd had about all I could take at the centre of attention when Ned Wessex said, 'Haven't I seen you before somewhere?'

There are times when being unmemorable pays, and this, I felt, was one of them. I had no wish for events at the Café Royal to be recalled, particularly in this distinguished company. I was saved by Jeremy Hammond.

'Bloody ridiculous!' he barked.

I was grateful for the interruption but curious to know the cause. With Jeremy almost anything was possible. Life as he saw it was packed with things that were Bloody Ridiculous, or even Absolute Rubbish. Ross the butler, assisted by two pretty Irish maids, was dishing out *Gujonettes de Veau aux Timbales*, and for a moment I thought it might have something to do with these. When pressed on the point, however, Jeremy said, 'That *Vogue* thing. Absolute rubbish!'

Ned, abandoning any last shred of interest in me, said, 'Why?'

'Not representative. Terrible photography.' Jeremy in

conversation favoured sharp explosions of upper-class barks, like ack-ack, interspersing a loud military err-ing sound. Nicky pointed out that at least some of the pictures had been taken by Ned. Jeremy made err-ing noises that were vaguely conciliatory, then barked, 'By and large!'

Nicky tipped his head back and weighed Jeremy up through half-closed eyes. 'You take a special interest in photography, do you?'

'Have to. Errr. My bloody job!'

'What job is that?'

'Advertising agency.'

'And what do you do, exactly, at this advertising agency?' Nicky was all the way back now, like a cobra.

'I own the bloody thing!'

'Yes, but what do you actually do?' This drew an extra long err from Jeremy, who started turning dangerously red. Even Liam and John, who had been happily engrossed with Reggie Turner, caught the vibe. They broke off abruptly, sensing sport. We were all familiar with Jeremy-baiting and were happy to be dispassionate observers for a change. The thing about Jeremy, once the blue touch-paper was lit, was to stand well back. Under his habitual Guards blazer and Old Etonian tie he wore a shirt with a crimson stripe (white collar and cuffs). When the complexion matched the stripe the wise man got his head below the parapet. It was getting that way now. We held our breath. Jeremy thrust his head forward at Nicky. The veins on his neck were swollen: 'What I do . . . Errr . . . Errr . . . Errr . . . What I do is organise! Bloody so-called creative, artistic types . . . Errr . . . no sense of direction!' A pregnant pause followed this. It was filled by the still, small voice of the Marquis. He spoke like silk.

'Ah, a sense of direction, yes, indeed.' He looked up dreamily at the full-length portrait of another Marquis, painted in the military costume of the early seventeen-hundreds. He wore a luxuriant wig, and a rich coat over his gleaming breastplate. His dog looked up at him adoringly. We all looked up the table at our Marquis in much the same way.

'You know, that's something we've been trying to give the Irish all these centuries.'

Liam said, 'Is that so?'

His Lordship treated Liam to a distant, exquisite smile. 'Oh, yes. Oh, yes, indeed. Of course, quite the reverse has occurred, to my family at least. I myself am quite rudderless.' He spoke the word with relish. 'This country can never be industrialised. That's the beauty of it. No nineteenth century. Nothing ever really happens here. No progress.' The Marquis of Meath spoke the word 'progress' with the utmost distaste.

Liam said, 'Something happened in nineteen-sixteen.'

'Oh, I've nothing against revolutions.' His Lordship smiled sweetly. One white hand fluttered around his glass. 'A bit of bloodletting is always healthy. But you mustn't confuse revolution with progress. Progress is a strictly middle-class affair.'

Nicky clapped his hands with delight. 'Brilliant, quite brilliant! Worthy of the master. I wish I'd said it!'

The Marquis looked pleased. 'You will, dear boy, you will.'

Jeremy, whose angry braying and abrasive laughter were almost indistinguishable, bellowed, 'There's nothing I like better than a good Irish joke!' and proceeded to tell one, with a good deal of err-ing through the gears and gratuitous guffaws, about an Irish space launch.

I watched Liam anxiously all the way to the punch line, fearing reprisals. When the titters and polite barks had subsided, he said, 'Paul here knows some excellent Irish jokes!' I could hardly believe my ears. The treachery was compounded by John: 'Go on, lad. Lay one on us!' The chorus became general, like a pack baying for blood. All eyes were once more upon me. I shifted uneasily on the hard silk. 'Er . . .' It's true that under certain ideal circumstances, usually around closing time, amongst relatively uncritical intimates, I had been known to rise to the occasion, but that was different. This audience, for a start, was all wrong. And the venue. And if I had wanted a warm-up act I wouldn't have chosen Jeremy Hammond. In my agony I caught Natasha's eye. She was smiling. 'Go on.'

'Well, you see, there was this IRA chap –'

'IRA?' the Marquis looked up sharply.

'Yes. He was an assassin.'

'Oh.'

'Er . . .' There seemed nothing for it but to plunge on. The room had become an icy tomb, full of frozen grins. 'Well, anyway, he was waiting up this dark alley, you see, only the chap was late –'

'Which chap?' Now it was Ned's turn to interrogate. I might as well have tried telling jokes to the Spanish Inquisition.

'The chap he was going to assassinate.'

'Oh.'

'Yes, you see, and anyway, after a while this chap, the IRA chap, he looked at his watch and said, "Jaysus . . ." (here Jeremy gave an appreciative grunt), "Jaysus, I hope nothin's happened to him!"'

There was a deathly hush until the Marquis said, 'And then what happened?'

'I don't know. That's the end of the joke. You see, he looks at his watch and –'

'Oh, I see.' And that was just about that. I looked over at Natasha, without much hope, but she was deeply absorbed in crumbling a piece of breadstick. Her pale face was lost in the shadow of her hair.

In the ghastly silence which followed the Marquis turned to Nicky, and was about to speak, when Liam said, 'You're quite near the border here, aren't you, yer Lordship?'

Back in the Long Library I felt better after the port. Natasha had disappeared. Chrissie had taken over on the stepladder. With professional agility she writhed from one erotic posture to the next. Ned, bent over his Hasselblad, cranked away in an uninhibited fever of encouragement. John and I found a couple of armchairs and prepared to enjoy the show. Ross had left a silver tray of liqueurs within easy reach. We had known worse. John muttered, 'Get yer gear off, you little raver,' and we speculated juicily on this rather remote possibility.

A nearby door swung open just as Ned hit level ten. Natasha stood stock still on the threshold, her head cocked on one side, watching.

An ancient square of embroidery stood framed on an easel in the middle of the floor. It seemed to draw Natasha like a magnet. She strolled across and subjected it to the keenest scrutiny. She bit down delicately on one finger, her expression shrouded. Distracted from her briefly by the floorshow I was startled suddenly to find her heading straight towards me. I'd never seen her looking more relaxed. Her smile was an open invitation. My own face froze. My heart beat so hard I couldn't speak.

As it turned out I didn't need to. Natasha smiled on by and perched on the arm of John's chair. John looked up. He didn't seem the least surprised.

'Hullo, sweetheart.'

'Hi.'

John chatted up Natasha. Natasha chatted up John. She played with her hair. She picked at threads in the arm of his chair. She swung her long silky legs. She smiled and laughed. He smiled and laughed. I was locked out but looking in. It didn't bother them. They were blissfully unaware. I didn't like it. I wasn't the only one.

'Come on Natasha. Let's go!' Suddenly the photo session was over.

John looked up. 'Something I can do for you, my friend?'

Ned said, 'I very much doubt it. Natasha, come on!'

Natasha, looking tense, said, 'I don't want to come on.'

'There you go,' said John, 'there's nothing she can do for you, either.'

Ned went red, then white. 'Look, mate, I don't know who you are, but this is my house and that's my bird!'

'And I'm delighted with both of them.' John smiled up at Natasha warmly.

'You get your greasy hands off her right now, or you'll be chucked out of here!'

John held up his hands and glanced at them. 'Never laid a finger on the little darlin', guv'nor' – he looked at Ned blandly – 'yet.'

Natasha got up abruptly. 'Oh, God. This is stupid. I'm going to bed.'

John laughed richly. 'Hold on, I'll come with you!'

'No, thank you.' Natasha looked even angrier than Ned. 'And I'm not anybody's bird!'

Once she'd gone there wasn't anything to fight about. Chrissie, too, had disappeared. Ned looked sheepish. He said, 'Women! Bloody hell!'

John said, 'The little darlings. Where would we be without them?' and waggled his eyebrows at me.

The dying fire popped. An ember died on the hearth. Ned Wessex yawned and stretched. 'Well, I think I'll turn in too.' He stalked away, closing the door softly behind him. John and I did not speak about where we thought he might be going.

No one was left in the long room now except Liam and Reggie Turner, still talking earnestly, back in their window-seat, forgotten coffee cold on a nearby table. I got up to get another kümmel. 'Come on, John, let's see what those two are up to.'

But he smiled an odd, lopsided smile and said, 'I think I'll have to leave you to it, lad.'

'Why, where are you going?' It was hard to keep the fear out of my voice. He leaned over and ruffled my hair. 'Don't worry about it.'

I sat there with cold hands and a pain in my chest that no amount of kümmel could dispel.

Next morning I woke early. The sun shone. The birds sang. My head ached, I felt sick. I got up, dressed painfully, and made my way downstairs. Somewhere in the distance Hoovers droned. I walked down to the lake. When I got there I found Teddy, staring disconsolately at the wreckage of his plane.

'Where did you get to last night?'

'Aha!' He brightened when he saw me. His moustache bristled. 'Always mess downstairs in this sort of billet.'

'Why is that?'

'Better grub, old boy. Not to mention the service.' Teddy waggled his eyebrows ferociously.

'Really?'

'Couple of absolute corkers called Betty and Sadie.'

'Ah.' I felt a momentary twinge of uncharitable resentment. Looking up at Castle Drogheda's myriad windows, any one of which might have been hers, I said, 'I suppose there's only one way to treat women, isn't there? Love 'em and leave 'em.'

Teddy said, 'Absolutely!'

We crunched back up to the front of the house. Just as we reached it Liam and Jeremy appeared, heading for a large black Packard. A uniformed chauffeur held open a door. Liam's face lit up. I seemed to be having that effect on everyone this morning, though I couldn't think why.

'Paul! Teddy! Yer lookin' well, both of you. What's happenin'?'

I said, 'Nothing much. Where are you off to?' Jeremy had already climbed in without a word.

'We're off to see the ship. Hop in, why don't you.'

Teddy said, 'No, thanks, old boy. Got to deal with the old bus.'

I hadn't had my breakfast. On the other hand I had little appetite for meeting John's eye over the marmalade jar. What I needed was clean air and an all-male cast, even if it did feature Jeremy Hammond.

I settled back into the cloth upholstery. 'Morning, Jeremy!' I said, bluff and military, despite my rumpled shirt and jeans. I had discarded the sweater.

Jeremy grunted. He was hunched and silent for most of the way. We followed the road to Dundalk. The Irish countryside flowed richly by. Liam rattled on about Jack Kennedy. The catastrophe in Dallas had shattered him. Camelot was under siege and the bad guys were massing. Liam was convinced of a conspiracy. All his hopes were now pinned on Bobby. We turned off on to a small road which soon became a track. The Packard winced slowly along. We drew up before a high gate in a wire fence. A death's head sign said 'KEEP OUT!' Liam told the chauffeur to hoot five times. Jeremy reached for the doorhandle. Liam placed a restraining hand on his arm.

'If I was you, Jeremy, I'd take off some of that gear.'

'Eh?'

'People round here aren't too crazy about the British Army.'

Jeremy opened his mouth to protest. Then, to my surprise, he shut it again.

'Errr. Yar. Gotcha.' He peeled off the British Warm, on the double. The stripes today were royal blue, the white shirt collar rakishly unbuttoned. The OE tie had given way to an OE cravat.

He climbed out and stood there, ready for inspection, in his cavalry twills.

'Well? What d'you think?'

I said, 'At least the shoes are brogues. Ha ha!'

Liam looked doubtful. 'Yer gonna give me a bad name, I'm afraid.'

As it turned out everything went smoothly. Two silent men in green jerseys opened the gates. We walked down, past rusting Nissen huts and the occasional crane, leaving the car and the chauffeur for reasons of security.

'The less people know about this place the better,' Liam tersely explained. The ship, up against the quay, was an exciting sight, with her huge mast. The name *Camelot Castle* stood out white on the black prow. We got the guided tour with our expensive radio engineer, a highly paid defector from the BBC. He was worth his weight in gold that day to Liam and me. He somehow made it seem as though we were already familiar with the dazzling array of equipment that confronted us both for the first time. All we had to do was look bright. Jeremy erred and yarred his way about, getting more and more excited.

'Well' – his teeth bared across his broad jaw. His eyes glittered. All he lacked was the Light Brigade – 'when do we go?'

'We're ready, really. Just fine tuning now.' Our engineer was confident.

Liam said, 'Fuckin' beautiful.' We all felt strangely overawed by what we'd done, and inseparable. Like Guy Fawkes and his crew, we were getting close to the Big Bang.

As it turned out I didn't see John again until we were both back in London. Jeremy and Liam had forgotten to tell me they were going to the airport straight from the ship. I had no regrets about not going back to Castle Drogheda. What was I leaving behind, after all, but Wooden Hearts, Suspicious Minds, and There Goes My Everything?

I was messing about with a late breakfast in the kitchen of the flat. John was upstairs. I hadn't seen him but I knew he was back. The doorbell rang urgently. It was Liam. He seemed excited about something.

'Listen. This is important. What's the scene with that chick, the skinny one with the black hair?'

'You mean Natasha?' I felt my breakfast begin to rise.

'D'you think you could pull her?'

'Well, er . . .' It was a good question.

'What about John. He can pull anything. John!' We had both heard the stairs creak. John lumbered in, bleary-eyed, wearing only a towel. He was busy lighting up a Rothmans.

'John. Listen to me. Someone has to pull that little Natasha chick and fuck her till she don't know what day it is.'

John blew some smoke. His eyes were hooded. 'Why is that?'

'Her dad's a cat called Sir Anthony something or other. He's in the Cabinet. He's exactly the kinda cat we need!'

John considered. 'I see. Well, it just so happens . . .'

'Hey!' I couldn't take it. My voice broke out like the cry of a trapped beast. They both looked at me with great interest. 'I'd like to have a go, that's all,' I finished lamely.

'All right, lad, all right.' John was all deep-voiced consolation. 'Don't get your knickers in a twist. I was just going to say I've got her phone number, that's all, if anybody's interested.'

'Well I am bloody well interested.'

Liam was brusquely unromantic. 'I don't give a fuck who makes it with her, so long as she ends up doing what she's told.'

'Leave it to me,' I said, bravely.

Before Liam left, he put his hands on my shoulders and grinned coldly into my face. 'I'm relyin' on you, baby.'

After the door closed behind him, John said, 'What we need is a Bloody Mary.'

We mixed a jugful together in silence. When we were sitting down with our glasses, John said, 'I never knew you were all hung up.' I looked at him. There wasn't much to say, or anything I really wanted to know.

'The trouble is,' I confessed, after a sense-blocking tumblerful, 'I don't know if she'll even go out with me when I do ring her up.'

'Tell you what,' said John, pouring me another, 'I'll ring her up and make a date, then you show up.'

Two days later I found myself in a taxi heading tensely towards a lunchtime table at Valentina's, booked for two in the name of John Meadows.

– Five –

'*Mid-Morning Musicale*?!'

'That's it, baby. That's the fuckin' spearhead of their programming operation.'

'I don't believe it. That's worse than *Housewife's Choice*!' John was shaking his head with contemptuous disbelief. I couldn't see the problem.

'That's OK surely? No one will want to listen to something like that!'

Liam and John gave me a patient look. Jeremy, less tolerant by nature, barked, 'That's the whole bloody point, you imbecile. Once these ghastly Australians get started no one will want to listen to any radio ships. They must be stopped. We've got to get there first. If we don't they'll completely steal our thunder and ruin the market and that'll be that.'

'Quite right, Jeremy!' John maintained a congratulatory, back-slapping sort of attitude to Jeremy that Jeremy seemed to like. He would respond with coy public-school horseplay, punches to the upper arm, hearty but gentle.

'What I can't understand, Liam, is how you've managed not to know about these bloody people. You've been back and forth to Galveston the whole bloody time – At great expense, I might add – and this ship's come from there, for Christ's sake, ready equipped, ready to go, ready to pip us at the bloody post. If I'd known about another group with exactly the same bright idea as ours, I must say I doubt I'd've got mixed up in this bloody business!'

Mixed up was right. The excitement of the Irish visit to the ship had gone to Jeremy's head like poteen. Any idea of sleeping partnerships melted in the blaze of his hysterical enthusiasm. Jeremy's greatest wish in the world became to assume command.

Jeremy Hammond had been orphaned at an early age and

brought up by a Trust Fund. The huge size of this fund was directly proportionate to that of Jeremy's desire not to be thwarted. The only thing bigger in Jeremy's life was the bellow he would let out if anything ever looked like getting in his way.

Jeremy liked to be in charge. He had been in Pop at School, Head of his House, and he wanted things to stay that way. Lacking in real life a House to be Head of, he had bought a flourishing advertising agency lock stock and barrel with a prestige building in Berkeley Square. He changed its name to match his own, fired everybody, hired everybody (so everyone knew who was in charge) and moved abrasively into the brand new penthouse he'd built, in record time, on the roof. Jeremy had no problems getting planning permission.

Everything was very modern in his building, with rubber plants and glass. There was an Art Department with glass-topped tables uplit by bright lightbulbs, covered in layouts, and sheets of colour negs of leggy model-girls. Creative types in open shirts spoke stand-offishly down white telephones at the Account Execs on the floor below. Account Execs were trendy too, but wore ties. They too spent much time on the white telephones, making expense-account lunch dates with clients. Everyone was young and confident and talked a lot about David Bailey.

Another floor housed the typing pool. Suburban birds made up to look pretty, rattled briskly on electric machines behind glass partitions and thought a lot about David Bailey.

Everything in Jeremy's building was open plan, so Jeremy could catch out slackers at a glance. People could catch each other out as well in the fiercely competitive atmosphere, and report to Jeremy upstairs. When Jeremy got fed up with sitting by himself in his penthouse he loved to sneak down the stone stairwell and make sudden appearances. He would stand silently behind his victims, just like at school, watching over their shoulders while they worked, breathing noisily through his nose.

As soon as we returned from Ireland Jeremy canvassed all interested parties, my father in particular. What we needed badly was to Get Organised. My father nodded. Right. This meant notepaper, telephones, desks . . . You can't run a business without an office. Right again. All this Pirate Radio palaver might seem terribly different and revolutionary, but, in fact, when you boiled it all down, all businesses were basically the same. My father by now was nodding like an electric dog. It sounded like the gloomiest of news to me. Jeremy, of course, knew just the place. He was prepared to make the necessary sacrifice.

It didn't take the two of them long, either, to select the ideal bearer of these frightful tidings to Liam O'Mahoney. They briefed me until I could take no more, then sent me on my way. No missionary ever felt less zeal. I folded back the hood on the MG and buzzed off up the A3, hoping the wind would blow it all away.

Back in Draycott Gardens the mauve Lotus at the kerbside told me Liam was paying a call. Resisting an urgent summons from Henry Pelham in the doorway of the Admiral Rodney to get in a couple of rounds, I hurried up the stairs.

'Relax, baby, just relax.'

'Yes, but . . .'

'It's cool, seriously.'

'Sounds heavy to me.' John stood by the window, carefully stroking the back of his hair.

'No, no, yer wrong, both of you. It's fuckin' beautiful. In fact' – Liam paused and glittered hard at each of us in turn – 'in fact it's exactly what we need.'

'I'm glad you think so.' John looked rattled. 'That Jeremy's the heaviest megalo of all fuckin' time.'

Liam smiled inscrutably. 'You leave that fucker to me.'

I don't know who knew less about Stanislavsky's 'Method', Jeremy Hammond or me, but we were both learning fast under Liam's expert tutelage. Jeremy was a surprisingly keen student, which was lucky: his beloved penthouse was now 'Studio Sixty-Four', a radical 'workshop' inspired by Lee Strasberg's Actors Studio in New York.

Liam, an apparent lamb to the slaughter, had explained the critical importance of the Method to Jeremy during the key meeting at which Jeremy had been fully prepared for a showdown. John and I went along with Liam to the penthouse pow-wow. The Method itself would be employed in the persuasion process, Liam assured us. Jeremy would be turned on.

'This place is totally ideal, Jeremy. Your thinkin' is so fuckin' radical I can't believe it.' They stood together at the panoramic plate glass window, looking down at the reassuring gleam of brand new Rolls Royces in H. R. Owen's showrooms below. It was all Jeremy's idea! The magic of it was obviously tickling him pink. His err-ing sounded more and more like purring.

'It's all down to communication, as you know.'

'Errr.'

DJs schooled in the Stanislavsky approach to the mike at Studio Sixty-Four would be able to turn on the entire nation at will.

'Everybody out there will be peaking on level ten!'

We moved into Jeremy's penthouse and Jeremy moved downstairs, taking with him his desk and most other traces of his reign of terror. Anything he left behind was either commandeered or disposed of. We found some canvas folding chairs. Liam had the back of one of them stencilled boldly 'JEREMY HAMMOND, DIRECTOR'. Jeremy was delighted. Whenever he visited Studio Sixty-Four he sat in it, err-ing with the air of a slightly self-conscious visiting dignitary, and fielding mild sarcasms from John with boyish good humour.

Two floors below in the sales department, Jeremy's occasional trips upstairs were greeted with profoundest relief. Life had been less than carefree there since he'd unexpectedly erupted into their midst. He gazed out remorsely across the naked vista into the very souls of the account execs. Woe betide the one who glanced up from his labours and caught that cobalt eye. He had stuck little stickers on all their white telephones which read 'STD = LSD, BE BRIEF!'

The man most affected by Jeremy's move was poor old Gilly. Major Clarence Gillingham was the Sales Director of J. W. Hammond. He had never much cared for the name Clarence. Everyone called him Gilly except the girls in the typing pool, who were supposed to call him Major, or Major Gillingham, to his face at least. Gilly called most people 'old boy' or 'dear boy', depending on who they were. If they were women he would clear his throat and avert his gaze and finger his small moustache.

Gilly had occupied the space so abruptly commandeered by his Chairman and Managing Director. Although it was only a glass enclosure, it had been home sweet home to Gilly. He had furnished it with familiar things, many of them heirlooms, he said. These included a fabulously elaborate gothic desk and an Art Deco cocktail cabinet. Gilly enjoyed sliding open the well-oiled doors of this cabinet and exhibiting its mirrored pink interior. He was a great believer in a spot of lubrication when the occasion demanded. Sales, after all, could stand or fall by just the right dash of angostura in a couple of fingers of gin, even at ten in the morning. His philosophy of life was popular among the account execs and they were sad to see him go.

Gilly went down to the typing pool on the floor below. It was the only place where any room could be created for him. A few heavy lads from dispatch were detailed off to help him, but it wasn't long before most of the building got involved. So great was the upheaval that it filtered up to Studio Sixty-Four, and we all hurried down to see if we could help.

The problem was the desk. Gilly wanted things to be just as before, but in only half the space. Although enough partitions to enclose three typists had been removed, still Gilly's desk couldn't be fitted in comfortably. By the time we got down there it was technically in, but only at a diagonal that cut the confined cubicle completely in half. In the tight glass corner behind it, looking rattled, sat Gilly. In the foreground were the cocktail cabinet and the door. There was no room either side to squeeze around, nor was it the kind of desk you could crawl under. It was solid to the floor with tiny secret drawers.

'There's nothing for it, guv. You'll just have to climb over,' observed one of the heavy lads from dispatch. Gilly's eyes shifted anxiously to the glass wall of his cell. You could see what he was thinking. Two dozen mascara-ed lashes batted innocently.

'How about a drink eh, Gilly?' John clapped his hands and rubbed them together. Gilly cast a haunted eye at the cabinet. Next to it, taking up most of the rest of the space, stood a Victorian hat-stand. Lonely on one of its antlers hung Gilly's tightly furled brolly. In that moment it spoke to Gilly of wide open spaces.

'Perhaps we should adjourn to the pub?' said Gilly.

Back in the penthouse we had plenty of room. Action Stations had been our password since Ireland. We urgently needed to prepare something worthy of transmission. Soundproof booths, each one as large as Gilly's new lair, were thrown up regardless of cost. Inside these we could get creative, smoke joints and make tapes of each other laughing uncontrollably.

At least some of this mirth was wiped from our lips by the news about Radio Dingo. Liam's Texan chums had tipped him off. A transmission-ready ship full of Australians was steaming flat out across the Atlantic straight towards our audience. They were opening an office in London. An announcement to the press was due any day. If this happened before ours, we were sunk. Our ship was almost ready. What we had to have to win the punters over and blow the nation away was a hootin' tootin' team of Yankee-Doodle-style DJs on the slick pickin' lines of Dandy Dan Daniels and Wolfman Jack. On this point Liam and programme controller John were 100 per cent sure. Without it, spake John, we would be pissing in the wind.

To this end Studio Sixty-Four had been created. Liam asserted with complete confidence that the teachings of Stanislavsky, once fully absorbed by the subject, would transform him (or her) from his (or her) native clay into whatever role was desired. Look at Brando. Think about Jimmy Dean.

We were all right for native clay. One was an estate agent, one an actor. One had once done a voice-over for a commercial, a real pro. All were more than ready for the limelight. I even made a tape myself, but was rejected.

The common problem with our intake of potentially swinging DJs was they just didn't want to be transformed. They had their own ideas. They were critical of Wolfman Jack, negative about the teachings of Stanislavsky. They knew their audience, they said. Our problem was we found them all so boring. Liam gave up on day one, claiming more pressing business on other fronts, and left me and John to sort it out. We didn't know much about Stanislavsky so we had to improvise and lean heavily on John's superior knowledge of music. We lost a few and found a few, but it made no difference. They were all the same. They were earnest. They argued with us. They got heavy. They took things seriously. In a word they were, to a man, uncool.

Keith Boardman was enthusiastic about being a DJ. In his twenty-two years he'd tried quite a few things but this was it, he knew. He didn't really like the name Keith Boardman. He didn't think it had mass appeal. What did John think?

'Well, you know, I mean, what can I tell you?' For John, Keith Boardman had little appeal of any kind. He wore pale clothes with plenty of topstitching, and patterned shirts which did up like a choker without a proper collar. His light hair was brushed forward in slavish imitation of Paul McCartney. His fringe bounced winningly above his keen, open face. Liam liked him. He thought he was a positive thinking cat.

'He's heavily negative about Stanislavsky.' I spoke up boldly in defence of fastidious John. When we'd told Keith that with the Method he could be anyone he wanted to be, he said he already was.

'He's into it, don't worry about it,' said Liam enigmatically.

First he changed his name to Keith Barry. I said, 'Isn't that a bit like John Barry, you know, the John Barry Seven?'

'But that's a good thing, I thought.' Keith was irrepressible as usual.

'Did you?' said John.

A few days later Keith Barry bounced into our office at Studio Sixty-Four. He sat on the edge of John's desk, said, 'Hi man', and dropped a card in front of him with a finger-snapping flourish. John picked it up by one corner with extreme care. I padded over on my brand new desert boots and gave it the eye over John's shoulder. It said, 'STEVE "THE SENDER" SEMPRINI', and underneath, 'YOU'LL GET SENT BY THE SENDER'. Otherwise the card was decorated with crotchets and minims.

'Well?' the Sender himself was taut with expectation.

John looked up. 'I'm sorry, I don't get it. What does it mean?'

'The *Sender*, man, don't you see? When we go on the air that's what I'm going to hit them with!'

'God,' said John, not without awe.

'I knew you'd like it! What do you think, Paul?'

'Well, er . . .' but he was gone. The door shivered shut. One second later it was open again. The relentless eye of the Sender pierced the blank expressions of his two employers, one thumb raised in remorseless optimism. 'Cheers, ciao, and . . . bye for now!'

The pressing business which had torn Liam away from the uphill struggle with our crew of professional hipsters turned out to be the Formby Five. They were coming to town at last! Liam called me to meet him at my flat: 'No need to rap with all those hustlers around.'

The group had been touring the northern club circuit for the months since we'd met, held back from a gilded and guaranteed future in the metropolis by a management contract which was now null and void.

'That cat's off the scene now.'

'Which cat?'

'The old queen at the Grotto with the dodgy rug, remember? He had some deal with them but it's over.' Liam looked around my sitting-room with an appraising air. 'How much room do you have here, exactly?

'It's all right. They can have my room and the spare room. I'll sleep down here. You'll never see them.'

'Or hear them, I suppose?' John was being negative.

'It won't be for long anyway.'

'Dead right it won't. Have you thought about what Mrs Flowers is going to say?'

'She'll be OK.'

In the event she wasn't.

'These chaps will be staying with me for just a few days, Mrs Flowers,' I informed her on the day, very much the *grand seigneur*.

'Oh, will they now? Over my dead body.'

We were standing all together in a conspicuous knot on the pavement outside the house in Draycott Gardens. Another knot, curious and potentially satirical, was forming outside the Admiral Rodney opposite.

The Formby Five plus Moose had disembarked from the back of a friend's removal lorry. Their own van had died somewhere outside Blackburn. Rucksacks, guitars, mike-stands and the Hammond organ, in particular, were hard to pass off as casual guests. I greeted a pale Val with enough heartiness to drown Mrs Flowers's protests, I hoped. Moose and his brother together looked large enough to fill the Albert Hall. Moose hugged me with untired enthusiasm.

''Owareyer, yer poxy little fooker!'

'Let's get this fookin' show off the road then.' Val looked tired and sour and headed for the front door with a guitar and a large box tied with string. Mrs Flowers barred his way with folded arms. ''Old your 'orses, my lad. Not another step.'

Val turned to me with that hard-boiled look in his eyes. 'Tell yer gran ter gerrout the fookin' road fore I clobberer.'

Just then there was a whizzing noise and a screeching noise and Liam leapt out of his mauve Lotus. In his rumpled suit with his arms spread in a universal embrace he looked more than ever like a demented scarecrow. His eyes were narrow and his mouth was wide.

'Beautiful, beautiful, yer all lookin' beautiful. Val howareya? Yer lookin' beautiful!' Before Val had time to dispute this Liam had waltzed straight over to Mrs Flowers. He executed some jiving steps straight from the hip and made a circle around her with his arms. She was trapped in his eyes like a rabbit.

'You said before we met
That your life was awful tame.
I took you to a nightclub
And the whole band knew your name!
Oh, baby baby baby . . .'

and Liam lifted Mrs Flowers off her feet and swung her round shamelessly.

'Mr O'Mahoney please! Whatever next!'

We trooped upstairs so the banisters shook and the carpeted steps shuddered under our tramping feet. Other tenants peeped out from their doors and hurriedly withdrew. The Hammond was allowed to rest for the moment in the hall. Mrs Flowers made a great exception for Mr O'Mahoney and disappeared into her lair to brew up tea for the poor tired boys from the north.

'I 'ad a friend once from Liverpool. Yes. Very nice 'e was. Couldn't understand a word 'e said.'

Moose wanted to know about closing time in the south. He would far prefer a bevvy to a brew-up, he said. I cast a doomed look out of the window. The moment I had been secretly dreading had arrived. A cold bright winter afternoon had just begun. However pathetic Moose considered the south, I thought him unlikely to believe that the pubs shut at 1.30 p.m. The idly curious group still lounged in the pale sunlight that bathed the Admiral Rodney, pint pots at the ready. I spotted Henry Pelham among them. He seemed to me to epitomise the sharply differing social forces between which I was surely about to be sandwiched. There seemed nothing for it. 'Come on then,' I said, 'anyone else?'

'What you chaps need is some exposure to the people that really matter.' Henry eyed Moose speculatively over the rim of his pint. He had a surprising amount to say about promoting groups. He even bought Moose a drink.

Moose said, 'Oh, yeah?' – still quite guarded. He was ill at ease but hadn't actually hit anyone yet. He'd muttered a bit about nancy boys and pansies, but I had high hopes for the mellowing effect of his third pint of Guinness. The nancy boys and pansies in question were keeping their lips mercifully buttoned in view of the unforeseen interest shown in Moose by their revered leader.

'No good tellin' me, mate. I'm joost the fookin' 'od carrier.'

'Yes but Paul here, I thought he was your manager.'

'Well, er . . .' I got my face hurriedly into my pint.

'That's what he told me.'

'What sort of exposure do you mean, Henry, exactly?' I screamed, hurrying the discussion forward.

'Well, I should say some of the really big deb dances. I might be able to help you out a bit there.'

'Deb dances?' Moose's big face was beginning to redden and sweat. 'What the fook's a deb dance?'

I said, 'I'm not sure if . . .'

Henry went on smoothly. 'Look at the Band of Angels. They're doing really well.'

'Yes, but the Band of Angels all went to Harrow.'

'What the fook's a deb dance?'

'Matter of fact' – Henry tilted back and gave me a look with one finger laid along the side of his nose – 'matter of fact, that bird of yours is having a big bash soon.'

I shook my head. 'Of mine?'

'You know.' Henry took the finger from his nose and poked me in the ribs with it. 'Natasha Roxbury.'

Back in the flat most had crashed where they had fallen amid the kit and the instruments. For me the excitement of being involved in so much action (and several quarts of best bitter) quite cancelled out any domestic inconvenience. Quint sat staring out at the London sky, picking absently at an acoustic guitar. I glanced proudly at Henry. Liam was still there, sitting in one corner with Val, laying down some heavy moody.

'This bloke's a lord,' announced Moose.

Liam looked up. 'Henry! Howsitgoin'?' But his heart wasn't in it.

'Yer wanner gerran earfuller this bloke, Val. Fookin' brilliant!'

Liam looked wary. Val said, 'Yeah?' Perhaps he was ready for a change of tune

I said, 'Henry's got some pretty good ideas about promotion, I must say!'

Liam's lips pulled back from his sharp array of teeth. Val said, 'Warrer you a lord of, exactly?'

Henry smiled. 'This and that. It comes in handy sometimes. Like now.'

'How's that?'

'Henry thinks we should form an action committee.'

'An action committee!' Liam slapped his knee.

'A rather special one.' Henry sat on the edge of a chair and leaned forward. 'People with lots of pull with the press.'

'Like who?' Liam was reluctantly drawn.

Henry shrugged. 'Like me. Natasha Roxbury. Maybe Ned Wessex.'

'Natasha's having a big party soon, where they could play. Remember what we said about Natasha?' I gave Liam an owlish waggle.

'How're you gettin' on with that one?'

'Oh, fine.'

'It's a good gimmick. It's never been done before.' Henry lit a cigarette with hurried fingers. 'The Stones are very into aristocratic decadence.'

'Are they now?' said Liam.

'Paul says you met Nicky Beresford in Ireland.' Henry breathed some smoke deep into his lungs. 'He'd be good. He could dress 'em up a treat. Make a big fashion thing out of it.'

Now it was Val's turn to look wary. Moose said, 'You'd look fookin' great in a dress, Val. The Formby Five Fairies!'

'Fook off, Moose, yer great fookin' pillock.'

'And that's another thing' – there was no stopping Henry now. We all looked up at him – 'that name's going to have to go.'

'Yer what?' Val looked dangerous, ready to kill. 'Yer fookin' what?'

'Val, listen to me' – Liam turned surprisingly into Val's line of fire – 'I want you to hang into this one, baby, just for one fuckin' positive moment of your life.'

Both Liam's hands were spread horizontally at Val, as if something were about to start rising beneath them. Henry, in this moment of destiny, had enough nous to leave it to the master. The room stood still.

'I'm gonna run something by you now, all of you. I want you all to think about it very fuckin' carefully.' Everyone was stirred up, looking at Liam. He rose slowly and moved over to the mantelpiece. 'I'm gonna hit you with one word. It's gonna grab you at a lotta different levels. I want you to think about everything that's happenin' at the moment, musically, politically, the whole fuckin' scene, right? Then tell me if this one word doesn't sum up the whole fuckin' thing. OK? Are you ready for it?' Liam's eyes were so wide they might well have held all the secrets of the universe. We held our breath. He brought one hand down in a single cut.

'The Tribe.'

Eel Pie Island lies in the middle of the River Thames near Richmond. It can only be approached by a narrow iron footbridge. In the early sixties the venue there was a stronghold of support for the Rolling Stones. On a freezing night early in 1964 I drove there. In the passenger seat, really going out with me for the first time, was Natasha Roxbury. That is if you don't count the lunch. It hadn't gone that well.

Valentina's is a wonderful place to eat, whoever you are with. Ornate Italian baroque, marvellous food. Natasha had arrived very late. While I waited I wondered if she would come at all, and drank champagne cocktails, quite a few too many. They blocked rather than loosened my mind. When she got there she was cool in every way. She didn't look like she'd been hurrying. She wore a tie-dyed silk dress with a keyhole at the neck. It stopped about four inches above her knees. The waiters made a big fuss of Natasha. I could only grope and gape and grunt.

Natasha's cold asparagus was excellent. She ate it all in silence, every spear. She licked the butter from her fingers, one to ten. She ordered *cannelloni alla Luigi*. So did I. That turned out to be excellent, too. Natasha was methodical and concentrated in the way she cleared her plate of all trace of *cannelloni alla Luigi*. When she was through she raised her head and looked around, over her shoulder. The effect on the hot-blooded waiters was galvanic, like the click of imperious fingers. Would the *signorina* care for anything else? They fell over themselves to tempt her. Yes, she would like a cappuccino. *Si si si*. And profiteroles? Did they have any of those? *Si, signorina*, yes they did. Cumminga right up.

'And some champagne!' I cried, desperate to get into the flow. But Natasha looked at me in cold surprise.

'No thanks. I don't like champagne.' At least the waiters looked disappointed too.

Natasha hadn't mentioned the fact that I wasn't John. Perhaps she didn't want to seem to have noticed me that much. When the ordeal was almost over I said, perversely, 'When will I see you again?' I still wanted to, more than ever, like the addicted gambler who knows that next time he will win. Just one more turn of the wheel.

'I don't know.'

'We could go out somewhere one night, if you like. To Pandora's Box or something.'

'I don't know. I'm pretty busy at the moment.'

The idea of taking her out to judge a great new group, to see if she would like them to play at her birthday party, where they would perform free, had given me the leverage I needed to ease myself back into the running with Natasha. Even then it wasn't easy. I had dialled a number with a KEN exchange.

'Hellayo.'

'May I speak to Natasha Roxbury please?'

'This is her mother.'

'Oh. Hello.'

'Who is this speaking?'

'Er, Paul Shaw.'

'Who?'

'My name is Paul Shaw.'

'I don't know you. Who are you?'

'I've just said, Paul Shaw.'

'Yes but who, man, who? I don't think you quite understand me.'

'I don't think I do.'

'It's all right, Mummy.'

'Some boy for you.'

'Hello? Natasha?'

'I've got it, Mummy. It's OK.'

'Oh. Oh, well . . .' The aching megaphone voice trailed off into a discontented groan of doubt and was immediately replaced by the Ronettes singing 'Be My Baby' at maximum volume.

'Be my be my be my little baby . . .'

'Hello? Natasha?'

'Be my little da-a-ar-lin' . . .'

'Natasha!'

'Be my baby na-a-ow!'

'Yes, Paul, I can hear you OK.'

'What's going on?'

'Nothing. I just like listening to music, don't you?'

This was a cue too good to miss and I didn't. I wasn't sure but Natasha seemed slightly easier to persuade than I'd expected.

'What do you think of the name?'

'Good.'

'Really?' My eyes left the road to look at Natasha sharply. She was looking straight ahead. 'Really?'

She turned to me with a small smile. 'Really. I think it's good.'

I gripped the wheel with renewed zest and gave a sexy thrust to the throttle.

'Great! I think it's good too. Bloody good. The Tribe! The thing is, Natasha . . .' we tore round an unexpected bend. I hung on masterfully. Natasha didn't turn a hair. 'You see, there's a bit more to it as far as you're concerned.'

'How d'you mean?'

'Well, could be, anyway.' My mouth became a firm line, but she didn't ask again. We drove in silence for about half a minute.

'Don't you want to know what?'

'Not if you don't want to tell me.'

'Of course I want to tell you, dammit.'

'Well go on then.'

I told her all about Henry's masterplan, now official, and the key role we would be playing in it together. Natasha stared through the windscreen at the black, rushing night. 'I only said I liked the name. I haven't seen the group yet.'

Outside the club it was well below zero. There was ice on the rail of the footbridge. Natasha wore a big sweater, longer than her skirt. She hugged herself against the sharp, sleety wind. A small knot of fans stood around the door chanting, 'We want the Stones.'

'I'd like to see the manager, please.' I pushed importantly to the window.

A burly chap bustled out. 'Yes?'

'We're with the group.' I touched Natasha's shoulder with my hand.

'Oh yes? What group's that?'

'The Tribe!' It sounded good.

'You're not, you know.'

'Sorry?'

'If you was' – the chap, I now noticed, was boiling up a bit – 'you wouldn't be 'ere!'

I looked at Natasha. She shrugged.

'The Tribe are playing here tonight, aren't they?'

'How can they play if they're not here?'

I looked at my watch and then back at the manager. 'Golly.'

'Golly is right.' He prodded me with a hard finger. 'You get them here. Fast. Or else!'

'Can I use your phone?'

'No.'

Back over the footbridge was a pub where we'd parked the car. 'Come on' – I grabbed Natasha's arm and started running – 'there'll be one over there.'

There was a public telephone in the pub but we didn't need to use it. Val was standing at the bar, but only just.

'Val!'

He turned and waved vaguely. 'Paul, me old mate, me old pal!' I pushed urgently through to him.

'What's going on, Val? Why are you here?'

''N' a dooble Doowers for me owld mate Paul.'

'Val . . .'

'Know why I drink Dooble Doowers? D'*you* know?' Val poked his bony face at Natasha. 'Gerl?' Natasha shook her head. Val put his arm round my shoulders and spoke into my face at close range. I couldn't find the ideal place for my eyes. 'No marrer 'ow pallatic you are' – Val paused and frowned deeply – 'yer c'n always say Dooble Doowers!'

Moose and Henry had failed to show up with the equipment, that was the problem.

'Well what have we got?' I'd managed to get them all around a table. Natasha sat beside me. I was at my most Napoleonic.

'We've got one bird between six of us,' said Moose's brother Ken. Everybody laughed. I looked at Natasha. She sipped her Coca-Cola, holding the glass with the tips of her fingers. Her heavy lids hid the expression in her eyes.

'Right. Exactly. We've got the whole group.' I was thinking positive. 'What else?'

'We've got the Hammond.' Quint was prepared to try and turn the tide. He'd brought his beloved Hammond in a cab, not trusting it to Henry's borrowed van. The others had their guitars.

'No amps, though.' Val shook his head, but he was getting more into the mood.

'No drums.' Neil, the manic drummer, looked lost without them.

'All the same,' said I, draining my glass, 'let's have a go. What've we got to lose!'

Val went on ahead with the others to 'sort out' the stroppy manager and get set up. They left the Hammond with Quint, Natasha and me. The temperature had fallen sharply. The iron footbridge to the island was glassy with ice.

'You go on' – I could just see her pale, frozen face – 'you'll die out here.'

'It's OK.'

'We need all the help we can get,' said Quint.

Natasha went ahead and pulled while we men pushed from the

rear. At the top of the arch of the bridge she crawled back and hung on with us while we fought to control the slow slide down the opposite slope.

'Are you OK?' I put my arm round her and squeezed. I think she was too exhausted to resist.

'I'm fine, honestly.'

Backstage things were not so fine. We could use the house PA. It wasn't perfect but it would do. There was a set of drums but they belonged to Charlie Watts. Negotiations were still raging. Beyond the stage a mob of mods chanted, 'We want the Stones, we want the Stones.' All but drowning a tinny reproduction of 'Little by Little'.

Any Tribe person who went out front to get things ready got pelted. Quint and I ran the gauntlet with the Hammond. An empty can of Longlife caught me on the temple. 'We want the Stones!'

'Fuck you!'

Finally the Tribe shambled on unannounced and started playing. No one seemed to notice. After a few bars someone switched off a recording of 'Can I Get A Witness?'. The effect on the fans was electric. Missiles filled the air. They chanted even louder. They stamped their feet. 'We want the Stones!'

Natasha and I stayed at the side of the stage. Val and the boys were putting on a brave show with 'Boom Boom'. It had all the loud thumping qualities a number needs to quell a hostile crowd, but tonight it wasn't happening. On top of everything else, drink and the borrowed equipment were taking their toll. The adulation they were used to in the north seemed far away. The south was more pathetic than they'd feared.

Ken Kenyon came forward to emphasise, 'Boom boom boom boom gonna shoot ya right down . . .'

A half-full bottle caught him on the fret hand of his bass.

'Right that's it you fookin' moothers . . .' Ken lumbered to the very edge of the stage. In a daze I watched his hands go to the zipper of his jeans.

'Pissin's too good for yer!' Ken relieved himself on the Stones fans in the front few rows and as far into the crowd as he could sprinkle.

'Well, what did you think?'

'Good. Great.'

'Really!' We had left fast after the lights went out, a frantic retreat past the management, over the bridge, into the car and away. This was the first moment we'd been able to breathe.

'Yes, really!' She turned in her seat. I looked at her and smiled. She said, 'I suppose you thought I wouldn't?' I shook my head.

'You don't know much about me.'

'No, I don't. What do you want to do now?'

'Go home, I think.'

'Go home? Natasha!' I felt I had the world in my hands.

'We've done a lot.'

'Yes! We have, haven't we? I mean, it was great, wasn't it?'

'Oooh! It was. Great!' Laughing at me was a good sign, I felt.

'What about the Tribe? Don't you think they're amazing?'

'They're very, sort of, hard, especially that one . . . Val, is it?'

'Val, yes.'

'I didn't like him much.'

'Val? You didn't like Val? He's great, honestly.'

We drove in silence for a time while I considered my next move.

'I must say I feel pretty hungry, don't you?'

'No, honestly.'

'Hmmm.'

'You're pretty determined sometimes, aren't you?'

'With you, you mean.'

'I mean, generally, in the pub, when they wouldn't go on.'

'Oh, well, you know.'

'Only tonight I want to go home.'

I waited until my voice was properly under control. 'And what about some other night?'

'I don't know.'

'I mean, will there be one?'

'I don't know. Perhaps.'

'Yes or no, Natasha?'

'God!'

'Well?'

'Oh I suppose so.'

'Yes?'

'Yes, yes.'

'OK. Great. Home.'

'Thank God.'

Five minutes later we pulled up in Draycott Gardens. It was quiet, dark outside the unlit house. I switched off the engine. In the silence I couldn't speak. I turned and took a cautious look at her. She was staring straight ahead. I could just make out the shine of her eyes and her breathing.

Casually I laid my arm along the back of her seat.

'Natasha . . .'

'This isn't what we said.'

'Home, we said.'

'My home.'

'OK, in a minute.'

I put my head close to hers, smelling her hair, turned her face towards mine. Our noses rubbed together. I breathed in the musk of her skin, like fever. Her lips were soft. They pushed against mine, kissing and resisting at the same time. She made a tiny sound as she shifted imperceptibly in her seat. Our teeth clicked, our breath mixed in our open mouths. My hand moved down to her waist and pushed hard. Natasha's knees remained firmly closed. Under the sweater, above the waistband of her skirt, a man's shirt with buttons to undo. Her bra was tight under her breasts but loose at the top. Inside, my fingers moved over the incredible softness, curled around the underside, little hard button against my palm.

'Come on, Paul.'

'Natasha . . . oh, God! Come up to the flat for a minute.'

'What for?'

'You've never seen my flat.'

'I've never done a lot of things.'

'Well, then . . .'

'Oh, God.'

I was out of the car with victory in my nostrils, hurrying round behind it before she could change her mind, driven by some hangover of chivalry to open Natasha's door, perhaps to seal our bargain with a flourish. I'd reached the kerb when the MG sprang startlingly to life. It shot away with a squeak and a snarl as Natasha engaged the unfamiliar clutch. Dully I watched the brakelights wink farewell at the bottom of the street. The horn tooted twice.

I didn't see Natasha or my car for nearly a week.

*

'Completely blown away!' Liam was at level ten.

'You're not serious!'

'Swear to God.'

'Talk about the hand of fate!'

'Your man called me up. Middle of the fuckin' night. Found my number at home. Fuckin' desperate state of 'im!'

'What did he say?'

'He said their mast was gone and could we help. Every port in Europe will seize them.'

'Except . . .'

'Exactly!'

Two days later the good ship Radio Camelot set sail from Ireland, bound for a secret destination somewhere off the Essex coast. Testing under live conditions was about to commence. The roster of this historic voyage included Johnny Meadows and Steve 'the Sender' Semprini, as well as some excellent new equipment, unexpectedly acquired.

'Come on, baby! Ray Charles!' Liam's head jerked up and down. His shoulders twitched. The face he raised to mine was a mask of ecstasy, tongue protruding. His bony fingers worked feverishly at the dial of a portable radio. The thing squealed and screeched. Liam was subjecting our signal to the 'Tranny Test'. Also being tested to the limit were our fellow travellers. We sat in opposite window-seats of a first-class compartment on the 5.19 from Liverpool Street to Harwich. The train was packed with tired commuters. I couldn't escape the uncomfortable feeling that these were the coveted niches of outraged regulars. Resentment had increased when Liam insisted on opening the ventilation window as far as it would go. A stiff breeze ruffled the pages of the evening papers worn before their frozen faces.

'For God's sake, man!'

Every paper came down. It only needed one to cast the first stone for the others to find their tongues.

'Disgusting!'

'. . . bloody thing off!'

'. . . drugs!'

'Probably!'

Liam's face shining with innocent delight. 'Rock'n'roll!'

I had been raised on the side of outrage. Packed in here with the hare and the hounds I could only say, 'Absolutely!' as Liam's thumb connected with the volume control.

'The communication cord . . . !'

'Come on!'

'They leave us no choice . . .'

Liam hit the signal. The voice of the Genius filled the stale railway air, marvellously fortified by the Raylettes.

> I know the night-time
> Night an' day!
> Whoah is the right time
> Night an' day!
> To be with the one you love, whoaoh yeah . . .

'This is it, you guys, don't you see? This *is* the communication cord!'

'. . . and then this one chap, sitting next to me, went absolutely fucking bananas!'

'Berserk, he was.'

'Wanted Liam to step outside.'

'Beautiful.' John lounged in the control room of MV *Camelot Castle*. He had made himself at home. Every surface not piled with records was covered with coffee cups overflowing with soggy cigarette butts.

'Liam kept staring at him, like this.'

'Like this.' Liam widened his eyes until they were white all the way round, his face dead pan and accusing.

'Jesus!'

'You gotta get the message through somehow!'

'Here, try this.'

'Is that it?'

'Yup. You just go clonk, like this, and you're on the air!'

'It's that fuckin' simple?'

'I don't know if anybody's listening, but basically, yeah . . .'

'Beautiful!'

We all had a go except the Sender. He had changed his name to simply Steve Sender, but the moment of truth found him wanting. He was locked in his cabin refusing to come out and go on, certain that a lengthy jail sentence stretched before him. The rest of us had a party. Much aquavit was consumed. We played all our favourites into the invisible wasteland of soulmates. I played Marty Wilde, 'Sea of Love'. We told them jokes. I told them Jeremy's one about the Irish space launch. Everything took on a momentous significance. Liam quoted Jack Kennedy quoting Teddy Roosevelt: 'And never be counted among those pale white spirits who know neither Victory nor Defeat!' The Captain sang '*Aus der Jugendzeit*', with a great deal of emotion.

Jeremy was in charge of the press conference that would officially launch Radio Camelot. He 'understood the media'. It was to be held in the Art Department of J. W. Hammond. The creative types were instructed to leave their sexiest layouts lying around: 'The average hack is basically only interested in birds and booze. Errr. Won't do 'em any harm to know what J.W. is up to, into the bargain.'

Into the bargain too were gallons of Bulgarian chablis. Gilly had a 'little man' for this, somewhere in the City. On the morning of the great day I found him laying it out lovingly. 'Remarkably good plonk . . .' Gilly was putting it to the test, just in case. We didn't want to let Fleet Street down. He held out a glass to me. 'Bottoms up!'

'Absolutely!'

The City types, my father included, were giving the press conference a miss, fearing scandal. Jeremy, himself fearing scandal with relish, would appear 'incognito'. This involved turning up the collar of his British Warm, pulling down the brim of his trilby, and wrapping the lower half of his face in an Old Etonian scarf. No one was fooled by this, but at least he was extremely noticeable.

A huge radio had been installed on a makeshift platform. Liam and I gave it the expert eye. We had returned on the Captain's tug, more than confident in John's programme plan of non-stop rock'n'roll with no chat. Without the Sender's input this would be easier to achieve. He had been rehearsing his 'jokes' on me since the days when he was plain Keith Boardman and I thought the fact that he was still locked in his cabin was a definite plus.

John had a stack of call-sign jingles that we had made upstairs in Studio Sixty-Four. We waited until the Bulgarian chablis was flowing freely. Liam and Jeremy took the stand together. Jeremy was in the background, by the set, incognito.

'Ladies and Gentlemen . . .' The room was crowded. Cigarette haze hung shoulder-height over the journalists as they scrabbled for the canapés and wine. The creative brigade had laid on a few leggy model-girls. These struck angular stances and made bored eyes at the feverish photographers. All had their own reasons for finding it hard to shift their attention to the platform. Liam tried again, louder. 'Ladies and Gentlemen!'

'Yew thievin' bastard!'

'What's the . . . Oh, Jaysus . . . Paul, quickly now.'

'What's happening?' I climbed up.

'Get that fucker outa here, whatever it takes!'

From the platform I could get a better view. In the doorway a bright red man, built like a bulldog and wearing an electric blue suit, was attempting to force an entry. Ranged against him was the gentlemanly figure of Gilly. One of the lads from dispatch had him by the arm. The other arm stuck a fist up in the air. 'Bloody hijack on the high seas! Put that in yer papers, yer pommy bastards!'

Gilly and I returned, dusting ourselves off, just as Liam's speech was reaching its climax. With reinforcements from dispatch we had made short work of the Aussie. I had his Radio Dingo button in my pocket for a souvenir, although he said we hadn't seen the last of him.

'. . . and so, you see now, this is it. The biggest turn-on of the twentieth century bar none! Independent commercial radio direct from the high seas!' Liam turned to Jeremy with a gesture. The moment had at last arrived. Jeremy's gloved hand turned the knob on our ultra-powerful receiver.

Apart from a loud hiss nothing but an awful silence filled the room.

– Six –

'Your bird's bash was a bloody good hooley.' Henry Pelham eyed me over the rim of his pint. 'You missed out badly. Don't think there was a single soul there didn't get laid.'

'And Natasha, er, was she having a good time?'

'I should coco!' There seemed no bottom to Henry's knowingness. His smile curved with malice. 'You want to watch old Val though in that department. Still, Ned soon saw him off.'

'Natasha doesn't even like Val!'

'No? Well, she ended up with Ned, anyway.'

I didn't go to Natasha's birthday party. The morning she returned my car she said I must come and then she rushed off. A million last-minute things, Richard Henry hair appointment, caterers, etcetera . . .

The dungeons of the family castle at Battle had been converted into a nightclub. Even in the chaos of my obsession a small voice told me that there among the peacocks and the thousand intimate friends I could only lose.

Those like me who couldn't make it could read all about it in the papers: DEBS DELIGHT IN DUNGEON DEBAUCH. Lurid photos in the *Daily Sketch* filled me with breathless despair, but I couldn't quite make her out in the murky crush of bodies. A new group called the Tribe was reported to have driven the swinging socialites wild. Henry's plan was bearing fruit. Everyone was pleased.

'Still got a problem with transport, though.' Henry wore his businesslike look. I was just as happy not to hear any more about Natasha's party. Henry's fly-on-the-wall reportage of other people's sexual progress knew few equals. Details of a kind I couldn't handle could be just a sip away. I got in another large vodka and bitter lemon. A 100 per cent proof against pain.

'Absolutely! That Eel Pie thing was a bit of a fuck up!'

'Not my bloody fault. Really reliable wheels are what we need,' Henry sipped his new pint in silence for a while, his eye unfocused on a photo of the Australian cricket team (1913) over the bar. 'The Beatles have got a bloody great Rolls.'

Debonair Carriageworks occupied premises in Pavilion Road, just off Sloane Square; a garage below a mews cottage. The proprietor of this prestige establishment happened to be a friend of Henry's. His name was Nigel. Nigel had dark wavy hair and a dark blue pinstripe suit. He wore a dark red silk handkerchief in his breast pocket. He rose from behind a small wooden desk when we walked in. Almost every other inch of space was taken up by a car.

'All our motors are one-offs, oh, God yes.'

'Pretty fucking smooth this one.' Henry pressed an appreciative forefinger against the bust of the silver lady.

'Oh, God yes.'

'What is it, exactly?' I spoke up.

'Basically a P6. Special body, of course. One-off.'

'I see.' I looked intelligently at the sheer expanse of the thing. My father had Rolls Royces, but they were like Dinky Cars compared to this. Henry nudged me furtively. 'Be bloody perfect, don't you think?' Hot breath on my ear.

'Care to step into the bar?' said Nigel.

'Why not?' We rubbed our hands.

'Saloon or Public?'

'It's got a public bar?'

'One inside, one in the boot for pissing off the proles. Look.' Nigel raised the boot-lid without effort. The upward swish propelled smooth pneumatic reactions. Leather stools and a walnut table folded out. Behind them crouched a walnut cabinet, like a shrine. Nigel stretched in a snowy cuff and came out with a magnum of Krug Brut Imperial.

'Picnic time!'

*

'It's got a fishing-rod holder under the running board.'

'God.' Natasha looked a bit lost in the cavernous interior, her feet invisible in deep pile. I had called her the following day at Henry's suggestion. Nigel had strongly recommended as much trial running as we liked.

'Get her in the back of that, well' – Henry's finger along the side of his nose – 'you can't fucking fail.'

'Hello? Oh, hello Paul' – Natasha had been slightly peevish on the phone – 'why didn't you come to my party?'

'Oh, I don't know, you know. Hell of a lot happening at the moment.'

'It was good.'

'I heard. Listen, Natasha, the thing is, I wondered if you'd like to come out, you know, to see a film, or something?'

'I don't know. When?'

'Tonight. It has to be tonight.'

'God!'

'I've got something rather special to show you, that's all.'

'Well, OK, I suppose.'

Now she sat well away from me, huddled in the corner. Far from Henry's lascivious implications, moves across this wasteland of sheepskin were doomed to run out of steam before even the halfway mark.

Not helping things along much was the eagle eye of Moose, miles away in the driving mirror, yet far too close for comfort. Henry had roped him in to drive for the evening. Any decision about transport for the Tribe needed his support. He entered into the role like an honours graduate of the Method. Outside Natasha's house he ate her up with his eyes as he held open the door.

'Don't do anything I wouldn't do!' Now he was going to make sure.

'What do you think?' I broke a longish silence.

'What about?'

'You know, the car.'

'God, I think it's awful.'

'Awful?'

'I think it's silly. Why do you need it? Just trying to be a big deal all the time, aren't you?'

'Not at all! Just typical of you to say that.' I stared moodily at the evening traffic, most of which stared back. 'You just don't understand about image.'

'Well I don't like it anyway. I want to get out.'

She stuck it to the Odeon, Charing Cross Road. It wasn't far, but it seemed like an age in the monumental silence. Moose was crestfallen to learn that his services were no longer required, but he managed a parting shot.

'Next stop back row, eh? Oooooer!'

In *Cleopatra* Richard Burton and Elizabeth Taylor succeeded in altering our mood. Extravagance and passion, however silly, found their way into our blood. Natasha had a lot of Cleopatra in her, I thought, with her black hair and huge dark eyes and her Egyptian rings. She had even appeared as her among the Bewitching Women of History at the Earls Court Book Fair.

We huddled out together into the cold real street. 'Come on, let's get something to eat.'

'OK, good.'

We got a taxi to Alexander's in the King's Road. Camillo was vairy pleased to see Natasha. It was full of all her friends. They were pleased to see her, too. I was relaxed and friendly in the warm blush of candles and wine with all Natasha's friends. I did not get jealous and uptight. They laughed and looked over and came over and joked, full of good food and drink and private whispered words. I looked at Natasha and smiled. 'I suppose you might be right about the car.'

'Of course I am. How ever much is it costing?'

'Erm . . . quite a bit, I think.'

'God. What about your radio thing? That's what you should be thinking about, not your stupid image.'

I told her about the press conference. 'Not a bloody column inch. I think they thought it was some kind of hoax.'

'God, what a drag. And is it really working, the signal?'

'Of course. The one place you can't pick it up is Jeremy's stupid building. Something about freak pockets or surrounding steel or something.'

Natasha looked thoughtful. 'I think I might have an idea that could help you. Get everyone talking about it. I'd have to be sure though.'

'Sure?'

'That there really is a signal.'

I had ordered a large kümmel. Natasha sipped her coffee. In the warm shadows, at the small table, in our private pool of guttering light, our hands casually close on the cloth, anything, I felt, might be possible. I drank my kümmel at a gulp. The heat of it helped me breathe and speak. My voice sounded far away.

'It comes through awfully well at my flat.'

At five a.m. it was still dark. A light drizzle fell. Natasha and I huddled in the MG, pinched and cold and silent. I had to get her home before her house woke up. The wipers droned, tyres swished, headlights tunnelled along the deserted streets.

'Stop here.'

'Natasha . . .'

'Shhh. See you.'

I leaned across but she was out of the car. I watched her go, light and quick, head down, a moment of rummaging on her doorstep, then the door opened and closed.

Later on I called her. How long to leave it had bothered me almost as much as what to say.

'I didn't wake you?'

'No.'

'How do you feel?'

'Fine.'

'I must say I feel rather, you know, amazing. Look, Natasha . . .'

'I spoke to Daddy. He says he'll do it.'

'Great! Look, Natasha, what are you doing for lunch?'

'God, masses of things.'

'Well put them off, can't you? I can't wait to see you!'

'Look, Paul, let's not get all, you know . . .'

'How do you mean?'

'Anyway, I don't want to do that, you know, again, for a while, anyway.'

'God, why not?'

'I don't know. I can't explain now. There's a reason.'

'Look, let's have lunch, can't we, and talk about it?'

'No, honestly, I can't.'

*

Shortly before midday the telephone jangled. Three rings for coolness then I grabbed it up. 'Natasha?!'

'Is that you, Paul?'

'Oh, hello, Daddy.'

'What the hell's going on?'

'In what way?'

'What do you know about an outfit called Debonair Some-bloodynonsense?'

'Erm . . .'

'Because they say you bought a car from them.'

'Well that's absolute rubbish!'

'The signature looks like yours.'

'Signature?' This was not a good morning for phone calls. My voice had that old faraway ring.

'On the order form.'

'I don't remember . . .' I could remember the ice-cold Krug.

'The car is in the drive. You gave them this address.'

'Gosh. I didn't really, did I?'

'The chap's looking for twelve thousand quid. Considering the size of the thing I don't blame him.'

'God . . .'

He did blame me, though. By the time he hung up I knew definitely that it wasn't my day. It was all I could do to totter over to the Admiral Rodney. Having a few stern words with Henry Pelham wasn't my only reason for going there, either.

Sir Anthony Roxbury's question in the House of Commons a few days later provoked the kind of howl in the press that any amount of pandering to them by us had signally failed to do. One might have thought we had been keeping the whole thing a closely guarded secret. According to the headlines an outrage rivalled only by the Spanish Armada had been fearlessly exposed off the English coast. A band of 'Pop Pirates', possibly foreign, were threatening the nation's eardrums with unrestricted music, much of it subversive. Teenage morals were in jeopardy, not to mention shipping lanes. Radio frequencies sacred to the emergency services were belatedly found to be jammed. Chaos loomed. Something must be done.

The gentlemanly government of Sir Alec Douglas-Home, the last of its kind ever to rule the twilit Empire, already rocked to its roots by the scandals of Profumo, Jellicoe and Lambton, scratched its head. The thing was shocking, of course, but not, on reflection, half as much of a bore as the apparently endless testimonies of prostitutes. After all, at least this was something one could shoot at. Their Lordships of the Admiralty were consulted. After careful consideration a gunboat was despatched.

Liam and I were up in Studio Sixty-Four trying to make a demo tape with the Tribe, when Jeremy burst in, very red faced. It was Friday afternoon.

'What the bloody hell's going on, Liam?'

'Hold it down, boys.' The group thumped and twanged to a gradual standstill. 'What's the problem, Jeremy?' Liam was cool.

Jeremy stared round wildly at what had once been his sanctum. Beer cans littered the tops of speakers. Wires snaked across the ravaged parquet into soundproof booths. The bluish air was tangy. Liam had pointed out that step one in a creative endeavour such as this must be to get stoned. We all stared back at Jeremy with expanded minds and grins.

'We're all going to end up in the bloody Tower, that's what! Listen to this.' Jeremy strode over to one of the huge radio sets he had installed along with a towering antenna on the roof. The thing was pre-set to Camelot. He flicked it on. Out came the Rolling Stones singing 'Fortune Teller'.

'Sounds good to me!' said Liam.

'Sounds fookin' lousy to me,' muttered Val, sourly.

'Can't you buggers take anything seriously? Just now that absolute bloody moron John was talking on the air about a gunboat!'

'So?'

'So the game's up, I'm telling you! They'll seize the ship, if they don't blow the bloody thing out of the water. I should've known. The British Navy aren't going to worry about all your international law mumbo-jumbo, I realise that now.'

'Bollocks!'

The Stones were cut abruptly by the mocking voice of John.

'Hear this, folks. At this time I'm proud to report a glorious victory by our very own, yes, folks, yours and mine, the gallant Captain Vig Moller . . .' Here were heard many background whoops and yeahs. 'That's right, folks, let's hear it for the captain. He's sent the imperialists packing and saved your favourite station for the nation! That's right, folks, we're all you got! Camelot! Take it away, John . . .'

BOOM BOOM BOOM BOOM,
GONNA SHOOT YA RIGHT DOWN . . .

We all cheered madly and waved our fists in the air. Jeremy's brick-red features deepened way beyond the safety mark. The flesh-rending molars snarled, 'Get out!'

He seized a speaker bodily. With a howl like a wounded mastadon he hurled it through the plate-glass window. We folded into helpless heaps.

'I want you bastards out of here by five o'clock tonight!'

Liam and I lay in chairs back at my flat later. We still felt weak. The Tribe had wandered off to their pad in Olympia, which, thank God, had been found for them. The demo tape hadn't happened, but otherwise they were happy. Keeping a group happy was the most important thing in management, Liam had taught me. 'Ya gotta keep 'em up there, baby,' he would say, stretching his hand up to heaven, fingers spread, 'whatever it takes!' Unhappiness and moaning is the natural state of pop groups when not actually performing, and the Tribe were no exception. If unchecked this can lead easily to them signing with some rival management. We would cut another demo soon, maybe even go 'straight into the studio'. The time to flex our muscles at the record market had arrived. A snap national poll had confirmed listeners beyond even Liam's wildest dreams. More than half the population, it seemed, were tuning themselves in and turning themselves on to Camelot at least once every twenty-four hours. It was all happening, in the words of the Genius, Night an' Day.

I was sipping Southern Comfort on the rocks when the telephone rang. Whenever this happened my balls went tight at the thought it might be Natasha. It never was. In order to be cool I never called her either. It was Gilly.

'Hello?'

'Hello?'

'Is that Flaxman 2763?'

'Yes.'

'This is Gillingham speaking.'

'Hello, Gilly. This is Paul.'

'Bit of a problem here at the office. About fifteen of us were working late and we seem to be locked in.'

'Golly.'

'Some bright spark's changed all the locks. Very fancy patent jobs, too. Need a key on the inside. Don't suppose you've got one, by any chance, have you, dear boy?'

I put my hand over the receiver. 'Jeremy's changed all the locks like he said.'

Liam smiled. 'Yeah?'

I fought down a spasm. 'Trouble is' – I took a deep breath – 'he's gone and locked in half his own people.'

Liam took the receiver. His face was a mask of joy. 'Gilly, what's happenin', baby? . . . I see . . . the whole art department . . . I see, yeah . . . No. No way, baby. We're the fuckin' reason he did it. He didn't tell you anything, no. Sure it's fuckin' typical. Off to Hampshire for the weekend, sure. That figures. Well' – he put his hand over the mouthpiece, 'This is fuckin' beautiful! – Gilly, listen to me now, there's only one thing for it. You'll have to call the Fire Brigade . . . Yeah, yeah, I know it is. Oh, and Gilly, when you do get out, come on over here and have a chat, why don't you?' Liam kept looking me in the eyes as he gave Gilly my address. 'No, I'll be here all evening. I'll wait for you. You won't be sorry. I promise you.' Liam replaced the receiver on its cradle with exquisite gentleness. 'Beautiful.'

The Marlborough Club was situated somewhere in the maze between Lower Regent Street and Piccadilly. The place was plush, with doormen in long coats and top hats on the door, plenty of pink quilted silk on the walls. It had a costly hatcheck, an intimate bar, and a stage. Tables with rosy lamps were looked after by girls in fishnet hose who sold cigarettes by the thousand at quite fantastic prices.

After the cigarette course what these girls wanted most from the customers was an order for champagne. They were very persuasive.

'You boys look lonely.' Our girl looked us over professionally.

Liam grinned. 'Sure,' leaning back. I shifted uneasily, glanced over at Gilly. Yes, he was lonely too.

'Would you like my friend Barbara to join you?'

'Sure.'

'You can call her Babs.' Babs came over on powerful fishnet legs and sat down. She wore a green satin bodice and a green satin bow in her hair. Babs was a redhead, with big pale hands and terrifying nails. Our girl, whose name was Denise, was a brunette. Her outfit was similar to Babs, only pink and black. She said, 'Would you care for something to drink, Babs?'

'I'd love a glass of bubbly,' said Babs vivaciously. She smiled round the table at her gallant little group. A look of serious concern passed across Denise's face.

'We only sell magnums of champagne . . .' A very large man in a dinner jacket had already appeared behind her holding an ice bucket on a stand.

'Er . . .' I leaned a little into the pink light. 'How much would a magnum be?' Denise bent down to me; crimson lips, panstick caked in the intimate glare, a whiff of BO. Her eyes slid from mine to Babs and back. Liam leaned in on the awful secret. 'A magnum of Moët is a hundred pounds. It's all in the cover if you stay and watch the floorshow.' I felt a pressure on my thigh. Looking down, the meaty claw of Babs seemed almost more outrageous than the price. 'You wouldn't want to miss anything, would you, love?' she whispered.

Liam lifted pale fingers in the direction of the bouncer. 'Make that two, baby!'

Denise joined us as well. As Babs said, it made it more of a party. So did a girl called Mandy. Mandy seemed much younger than the other two, cuddly like a teddy-bear, with a fringe of honey hair and an outsize bosom. I liked the look of Mandy. I stopped worrying about the bill so much and worried instead about how I might detach her from Gilly. She kept calling him Clarence. Gilly didn't seem to mind a bit, except when someone wanted to take our photograph for twenty-five pounds. Then he drew the line. 'It's not the price so much as the publicity.'

'Not ashamed to be seen with me, are you, Clarence?' Mandy

nibbled his ear, but he wouldn't be persuaded. Liam ordered another magnum instead to keep everybody happy.

I managed to get tensely across to his ear, ignoring Babs, and hissed, 'Honestly, Liam, what about the bill? It's going to be thousands!'

'Don't worry about it.'

When Reggie Turner appeared the atmosphere of the place underwent a subtle change. Everyone suddenly seemed more conscious. He moved through the room, greeting people and smiling his bland smile. His glasses twinkled in the cosy light. He wore a white tuxedo. His sleek hair shone. He came over to our table.

'Mind if I join the party?'

'Reggie! What's happenin'? Yer lookin' well!'

'I'm feelin' well, my friend. Evening girls.'

'Good evening, Mr Turner.' They were good as gold.

'Me and these gentlemen have some business to discuss.'

'Do you want us to disappear, Mr Turner?' said Babs.

'Not if they don't want you to, an' I'm sure they don't.' Reggie Turner turned affably to Gilly. 'There's precious few secrets between me an' my girls, are there, girls?'

'No, Mr Turner.'

'Besides, there could hardly be a more kosher transaction than this one' – a huge bouncer put a glass of milk in front of Reggie – 'simple case of supply and demand.' He raised the glass.

'What transaction?' I asked, bewildered.

'Reggie here has something we want,' said Liam.

'Need,' said Reggie.

'Need by Monday, to be precise.' Liam glittered at me in the light reflected off the shallow fizzy glasses.

'Badly,' said Gilly, looking owlish. I shook my head.

Liam said, 'Think about it.'

I thought about it. 'Unless, I mean, I suppose we need an office?'

'Aha. An office building!'

'A beautiful office building!' Reggie moved his cigar from one side of his mouth to the other.

'Oh. Where is it?'

'Heart o' Mayfair,' said Reggie proudly.

'It's a fuckin' beauty all right.' Liam shook his head.

'A jewel in anybody's crown,' Reggie leaning forward, 'just a question of agreeing on a fair and reasonable rent.'

Liam and Reggie and Gilly went into a huddle. They talked about tenure and percentages and square footage. I listened for a while and tried to join in, but the floorshow started and anyway it seemed rude to ignore the girls completely. I gallantly poured some more champagne all round. 'Bottoms up!' said Babs. The girls and I toasted and laughed. Some other girls moved energetically about the stage, expertly discarding their clothes.

'Well, that's settled!' Everyone looked pleased. The girls said 'Hooray!' I raised my glass.

'Tell you what,' said Reggie, 'let us adjourn to the Private Side and celebrate. Join all the old faces.' Reggie winked broadly at Liam and rose.

Behind the stage, through a door, down a passage to another door. We waited in a bunch while Reggie buzzed and muttered.

Once through the door we passed into another world, an art deco realm of aspidistras and smiling croupiers. '*Faites vos jeux, mesdames, messieurs, faites vos jeux.*' The dice rattled, wheels clicked as they spun. Beautiful girls with bootlace ties dealt *chemin de fer*. More beautiful girls carried drinks around on trays. In one corner a ravaged youth with blue-tinted glasses and lank air tinkled the ivories; variations on 'Smoke Gets in Your Eyes'. As Reggie had promised, the place was full of faces. I saw both the Kray twins, standing impassively, surrounded by men with faces like masks. Women with beehives and bracelets clustered round the tables. On a low sofa I saw the Marquis of Meath talking earnestly to a black girl dressed in a leopard-skin. Standing by the fireplace, holding balloon glasses, Lord Boothby and another, older man laughed gaily with two much younger men.

The girls were still with us. Reggie waved, greeted, issued instructions. All deferred to Reggie Turner. Even the Krays gave him a nod. I had managed to switch partners with Gilly. Mandy said, 'Do you feel lucky?'

'Absolutely!'

'The wheel over that side of the room is always lucky for me.'

We pushed through the press, apologising, giggling. Mandy and I were getting on well. Just before we reached the table she stopped me and gave me a long, lingering kiss. Her mouth was soft and sweet with champagne, her tongue ferocious. I felt sure there must be more to it than just business. Light-headedly I looked around the green baize for the first time. Sitting directly opposite us was a young man, perhaps a little older than me, with a chalky, pockmarked face. He wore shades, and a black suit, like an undertaker. The only dash of colour was his mouth, thin and bright, like a cut. The air of menace I felt from him was charged by the presence of the girl standing at his side. She rested her hand lightly on his shoulder as he played. She was black and white, too: battered black leather jacket and skirt, black hair, black eyes which looked up for a moment and met mine. Her expression hardly flickered as she took me in. After a few seconds in which my whole life seemed to flash before me she returned her attention to the table.

'Natasha!' I could've played it cool, but I didn't. I barged through the throng, around to where she stood, leaving Mandy without an explanation. 'Natasha, listen . . .'

Reluctantly she turned to cope with me. 'What is it, Paul?'

'What the hell's going on, Natasha?'

'God, not so loud. Can't you be cool?'

'Yes, but . . .' I tried to lower my voice, 'what are you doing?'

'Same as you, having a nice time.'

'Look, I'm not, I mean, I can explain . . .'

'I don't want to have to explain things.'

'Natasha, look . . .'

'Oh, God, Paul, please, go away!'

Back with Mandy I gave Natasha one last look, but she didn't seem to notice. A little paler, more tense, perhaps, but concentrating hard on her partner's chips.

'Is that your girlfriend?'

I looked at Mandy. She was so jolly and friendly. There was nothing really cuddly about Natasha. Everything seemed so much simpler with Mandy.

'Look, I'm getting a bit fed up with this place. What d'you say to the idea of coming back to my flat?'

'Do you want me to stay all night?'

'Well, yes, I suppose I do.'

She leaned close to whisper. She smelled of face powder and wine. 'It's a hundred pounds for an all-nighter, I'm afraid.'

I thought for a moment. 'God, will you take a cheque?'

'You seem like a nice boy. It's twenty-five pounds extra, though.'

A few days later, at the violet hour, John came home, fed up with life on the ocean wave. I cheered him up with all the latest news – Camelot House, our huge audience. 'It's all down to you, lad, after all, I mean, without all that ultra-cool programming . . .' I reassured him.

More reassuring still were the confident predictions of Gilly. Those inevitable yet still elusive millions would surely engulf us now we had a professional advertising man like Gilly on board. 'Contacts, my dear boy, contacts. That's what counts.'

We met Liam at the Picasso. Mulling things over with omelettes, chips and a carafe of wine we concluded that our next logical step must be to have a huge party at Camelot House. Such an event would also provide the ideal launch for the Tribe's first disc. All we needed to do was record one. We would go 'straight into the studio'. John assumed command of the production. I was put in charge of decorating the many thousands of square feet at Camelot House in time for the great event.

Decorators work in daylight. Records can only be made at night, so I was able not to be completely left out. We decided on a Buddy Holly number. Getting everyone to agree on which one wasn't easy. The one to which the least number of people had violent objections was 'Heartbeat', though Val still thought 'Rave On' more rocking while John considered 'I'm Gonna Love You Too' more chartworthy. 'We'll cut a few tracks and see how we go,' said John, decisively.

We booked plenty of studio time at Highnumber Sound in Putney. I had never been inside a recording studio. I admitted it to John on the way there in the car.

'Neither've I, lad, between you and me.'

'How d'you know how to make the record, then?'

'Don't worry about it' – John held up a lump of hash between forefinger and thumb – 'just get loose and let the music flow.'

A number of rather stale-looking people who obviously spent

most of their lives inside a recording studio were hanging about the place when we arrived. They managed to be bored and impatient at the same time.

'Are you the producer, man?'

'Yeah.'

Val and the lads were set up in a hangar-like area beyond our glassed-off lounge. They looked professional in their headphones. A bit lost, perhaps, like strangers on a set of the moon.

'When d'you want to start?'

'Right away, man.'

'OK. You'll have to handle the board yourself, though. The engineer hasn't showed up yet.'

John and I gave the board the once over. It was about five feet wide. A large number of knobs and levers were on display.

'Maybe we'll just run through a few numbers until he does.'

'Bleedin' 'ell! John!'

'Oh, God!'

A flash of unforgettable fluorescent orange, and the King of the Mods was in our midst.

'Don't you ever take that horrible garment off?' John was the first to get over the shock.

'Watchoo two wenkers doin' 'ere?'

'One might easily ask you the same question.'

'I fuckin' work 'ere, dunneye!'

'Bleedin' Buddy 'Olly, man.' Manny sat masterfully behind his board and shook his head. We had all gathered round. 'I dunno.'

'Warrer bout 'im?' Val gave Manny a dangerous look.

'Buddy 'Olly's a bit of a wenker, if you ast me.'

'Nobody did.' John was having to work hard to maintain his authority. We had run through our three numbers before Manny arrived. Then they were run through some more while Manny worked on the levels. Then it was the high hat. Getting the sound of that right so that Manny and Neal and Val felt happy reduced me and the Official Producer to a state of numb dismay. The clock on the wall crawled through the endless hours. The group lounged listlessly around the control room. The air was stiff and unbreathable with assorted layers of smoke. Ken played the pinball machine in the corner. We passed a bottle of warm whiskey around. It tasted sour and made no difference. I had never in my life felt quite so bored. I'd only perked up once, when the thought of ringing Natasha occurred to me. I asked John what he thought.

'She might get turned on by a recording session.'

'Forget it.' John needed every ounce of energy to figure out what Manny was up to at the controls. Manny was unnervingly slick and full of bright ideas.

'Nunner my business, o' course. I mean you blokes is the experts.'

'If yer don't like Buddy 'Olly what the fook do yer like?' Val was aggressive and inquisitive at the same time.

Manny's features twisted in thought. 'Sumfink a bit more soulful, I'd say, wiv a group like yours. Sumfink you can work up that 'ammond an' get a real tasty sound. More heavy blues than R&B, or rock'n'roll.'

Val looked thoughtful. He snapped his fingers. 'Quint, c'mon!'

The group stood around the Hammond while Quint and Val worked intently. Val's voice came into the control room over the mike. 'Wanner try a new arrangement of something I think could be good.'

'Whenever you're ready.' Manny was cool and relaxed. An hour went by.

'We'll just go live for a while, OK?'

'OK.' Manny flicked a few switches.

'Two, three, four . . .' The sound came over the monitors.

> . . . I'll put a spell on you
> Because you're mine . . .

'All right!' Manny turned to me and John with illuminated eyes. 'Vis is fuckin' beautiful!'

'Listen, Manny, how much longer is this going to take?' John, after an hour or two, looked at his watch.

'I dunno, man. We can start mixin' soon, I reckon.'

'*Start* mixing?'

'As soon as we get the organ track right.' Manny was as elated by progress as we were depressed.

'Not feelin' knackered . . . ?' Manny reached into a pocket of the orange jacket, which hung on the back of his chair. He came up with a handful of purple hearts. 'Muvver's little 'elpers.'

'Maybe we should take a break, Manny. Come back to it fresh tomorrow.'

'You must be fuckin' jokin', man! We can be all done by morning if we keep going.'

We hung about a bit longer, playing pinball.

'I think Manny's got things pretty well covered, don't you?'

'Absolutely!'

'It's the finished mix that interests me. Manny, we're gonna split now.'

'Whatever turns you on, man.'

'Bring me the tape in the morning and I'll give it the old ear.'

'Yes, sir, boss!' Manny twisted his stunted body around to bestow a hideous leer of farewell. We waved to the lads, but they were absorbed.

I went down to Haslemere and the family home. My important work at Camelot House was reacting badly with the constant demands of the night, and I was becoming a spent force. I needed a break.

Not nearly enough water had passed under the bridge since the episode of the Rolls Royce. I arrived late for lunch. My father peered out at my MG in the driveway.

'Same old car?'

'That's right, Daddy.'

'I just wondered.'

There followed a subdued passing of peas and polite enquiries from my mother before the old man got himself sufficiently worked up to launch his main attack.

'Had an Aussie down here to see me last week. Nice chap, wasn't he, dear?'

'Very nice.' My mother swallowed hard, pursing her lips and looking wildly from the peas to the potatoes to the mince.

'Oh, yes?' A bit stretched out, perhaps, I had failed to scent lurking danger, the puff of smoke on the horizon which would turn out to be the whole Sioux nation.

'He says you boys are playing silly buggers with his ship.'

'Not that Australian!?'

'Randy Windrush. You've treated him disgustingly. I don't like it!'

'But, Daddy, that had to be done, didn't it?'

'Maybe then, but not now. Give it back. I don't want to be mixed up with a lot of crooks!'

'Jeremy thought it was a good idea to grab it. Is he a crook?'

'Not any longer, he doesn't. He's been talking to Randy, too. We've both got a lot of time for Randy. Sound ideas. We think we should negotiate a merger with these Aussies.'

'What!?'

'They've got years of experience in Australian Radio. You boys've got no experience, and it shows.'

'How does it show?'

'Randy says we should be running the whole damn shooting-match from one room – and Jeremy tells me you've found the biggest bloody white elephant in London!'

'It does sound rather silly, dear,' said Mummy. I wanted to explain to them about image, but something told me not to bother.

'We had to get what we could in a hurry. Jeremy chucked us out.'

'And with good reason, from what I hear. Bloody long-haired layabouts!'

'Those long-haired layabouts, as you call them, if you mean who I think you mean, have just made a hit record!'

'I don't think any of you know the first thing about the music business. Randy Windrush has years of experience. First class ideas about programming too.'

'Such as?'

'Things he's tried and tested on a real audience. Things like the *Mid-Morning Musicale*.'

'Jaysus! And did you tell 'im it's a radio station and not a fuckin' sheep station?' Liam and John and I were sitting on the newly carpeted floor in our white elephant.

'I didn't have a chance. He banged straight on about what all this is costing.'

'What is it costing?'

'I don't know. That was the trouble.'

My small army of workers wasn't that small. Miles of carpet had to be laid, acres of wall painted, hundreds of telephones installed, furniture humped, sophisticated sound equipment plugged in.

'I mean, it's all very well talking about budgets, but if you have to have certain things, you know, you just have to have them.'

'Jimmy's a cool enough cat, but his generation aren't turned on to the image thing yet.'

'Absolutely!'

Every room was wired for sound. Every nook and cranny of the vast edifice must be able to receive the Camelot message. On party night Liam's revolutionary approach to making a record deal was to be unleashed. Important executives from the record companies (there were only two, three if you included Pye) were invited. Manny's final mix of the Tribe's first single would be played throughout the building at the right psychological moment (we had all three given it, John a little grudgingly, the high sign). Acetate copies would later be presented. The highest bidder would be awarded a limited contract with the Tribe. The record would be plugged massively on Radio Camelot. The executives were keen to come to the party. Camelot House at that moment in history was the place to be.

'Natasha?' All I could hear down the phone was Dionne Warwick singing 'Anyone Who Had a Heart'. 'Natasha?' The volume was very slightly lowered. 'It's Paul.'

'Oh, hello.'

'Have you heard about the terrific party we're giving?'

'No.'

'At our new building. You must've.'

'I haven't.'

'We're having a Grand Opening – to launch the Tribe's first record. It's really incredible. John and I . . .'

'. . . trains and boats and planes go passing by . . .' Dionne had changed tracks.

'Natasha?'

'Yes. I'm here.'

'Don't you want to come? You're on the Tribe promotion committee, don't forget.'

'I don't think I can.'

'Why not?'

'I'm already doing something.'

'I haven't told you when it is yet.'

'I'm doing things every night at the moment.'

'Who with?'

'Different people.'

'Ned?'

'Sometimes. Why not?'

'Why not with me then?'

'No reason.'

'Look, just try and come to the party, OK, Natasha? Please.'

'I might come for a while if I'm around there.'

'Don't you want the address?'

'I'll find it.'

The Tribe didn't really have an 'image', and any attempt to impose one on them made them very unhappy indeed. The Stones, by contrast, all looked Neanderthal. The Beatles were a fab foursome made in heaven for a strip cartoon. Our lads were 'different' all right, but only from each other.

Val was a leatherbound greaser. Ken Kenyon was stuck in a fantasy created by Nudie of the San Fernando Valley: hot pink suits and thick crepe soles with soul. I thought we might expand this to embrace the whole group. At least I helped by discovering something nobody could dig. 'There's a lot of things happening at the moment, lad' – John took me aside – 'but the fifties isn't one of them.' Quint was into green nylon shirts. Manny, the King of the Mods, to whom nattiness was the only thing that mattered more than speed, said the group's visuals gave him the horrors.

'You blokes wanner tell vese wenkers we're not in bleedin' Manchester now. Nobody makes it vese days wivout the right gear.'

The right gear, it was decided, was to be sought at Nicky Beresford's temple of decadence, Narcississimus.

'Fiddling while Rome burns! The perfect analogy for the pop group of today! Of the hour!'

'I guess so.' John stood with his hands in his pockets and looked down dubiously at something Nicky Beresford was proffering on a velvet cushion.

The group of the hour hung moodily about among the terracotta busts and the onyx leopards and the jade figurines, like stray cattle in a cottage garden.

I stood beside John, avoiding eyes, gazing at the items on the cushion. I was as bemused as the next man. Two massive facsimiles of Ancient Roman coins rested on their velvet bed. They had been fashioned into cufflinks.

'Decadence, don't you see? That's the theme we're groping for here, I feel.' Nicky cast an appraising eye over the members of the Tribe. He pushed back his heavy slick of hair with a pale creative hand. 'Nero was the most decadent of all.'

'He was, absolutely.' I was on *terra firma* with Nero, as it happened. I gave John and Nicky a profoundly knowledgeable look. 'Still, I don't quite see how these –'

'Well of course you don't' – Nicky stretched wicked witch fingers at me as if I was a hex – 'how could you?' We all started back. Nicky's hands fluttered madly. 'They are only a starting point, don't you see? For me! Like the very first brushstroke on a blank canvas . . . My God!' Nicky hurried from the room, clutching his brow.

'What's oop with 'im?' Moose was enjoying himself more than the others, happy for once not to be a member of the group.

'Gone fer a Tampax,' Val said sourly.

Nicky reappeared with a flourish. He held a bolt of material and a sketch-pad. Deftly he cast a rich black stream of velvet across the floor. 'Voilà,' he cried, 'the muse has struck.'

But on the night only Quint came even close to co-operation. He even said he liked it – the velvet trousers with matching sleeveless jerkin, anyway. Of the full-sleeved satin shirt, with its Imperial climax at the cuff, there was no sign. The faithful green nylon, complete with static cling, hung as usual from his weedy frame.

'Whaddyer think?' In the dense throng it hardly seemed to matter. There were six floors at Camelot House, not counting the dome, and each of them was packed to capacity. I squeezed and shoved my way about, hunting in vain for anyone I knew, preferably Natasha. Everyone else seemed to know everybody, anyway, and were obviously all having a good time. I saw Teddy Tenterden. He was talking to a tall woman in a flowered dress. His eyes popped. He raised his glass. 'Bloody good show, this. A bloody good show!'

'How are you, Teddy?'

'Absolutely ripping, old boy. I say' – Teddy bristled at my ear, his breath sweet. His eyes swivelled in a yellow leer – 'piece of cake, this one.'

I made it to the third floor, where I had managed to create an 'office' for myself. It had an old armchair as well as the green metal filing cabinet I had installed in all the offices. I opened the door. The room was in darkness but I could hear heavy breathing and grunts. Indignant at this invasion I switched on the light. My armchair overflowed with half-dressed limbs, most of them writhing. A bare bottom, male judging by its hairiness and the pinstripe trousers from which it protruded, shone up in the naked glare. The boiling face that belonged to it twisted to confront me. 'Oi! Oh, it's you, Paul.'

I could not deny it. 'Hello, Gilly.'

Somewhere in the mix-up was a girl. Gilly said it was Beverley from the typing pool at J. W. Hammond. I had to take his word for it as she seemed unwilling to expose herself further.

'You remember Beverley. She'll be coming to work for us here.'

'Jolly good.'

Back on the crowded stairs I got goosed by hard invading fingers. Viscount Pelham, from a long line of conquerors, gloated.

'Can't fucking fail tonight, eh?'

'Absolutely.'

'Where's your bird?'

'I don't fucking know, do I?'

'Forget her is my advice. Plenty of fish in the sea.'

Over the hubbub the twenty-four-hour broadcast of Radio Camelot was coming in nicely through the sound system. At that certain psychological moment it was interrupted by the voice of Liam O'Mahoney.

'Ladies and gentlemen. Welcome to the mad place. You think

what you're hearing right now is groovy, and you're right. But wait, we have something for you, something heavy. A group you haven't heard before which is going to blow your minds. Before that, though, something even more incredible is goin' to happen to your heads that you're not gonna fuckin' believe. Live, on the telephone, direct from the US of A, I'm gonna bring you someone with a message which is, believe me, the message of what this whole fuckin' scene is all about. Just hold on, now . . .' The air filled with static, a loud hum, then through the hum the unmistakable sound of a telephone brr-ing, the way they brr in the States.

'Hello?'

'Hello there. May I speak to Senator Robert Kennedy, please?'

'Who is this calling?'

'The Youth of Britain.'

'Hold the line.'

A hush fell over the huge crowd while the speakers buzzed and hummed expectantly. Liam's breathing could be heard.

'Er, hello?' The familiar twang.

'Is that you, Bobby?'

'Mr O'Mahoney?'

'That's right. Do you have anything to say to the Youth of Britain tonight, Senator. Any message?'

'I, er, at this time . . .' a heavy hum descended on the Kennedy message, but we all caught the word 'peace'. Then, 'I want you to tell your government from me that nothing should be allowed to stand in the way of the cause, I should say the message, of Freedom.'

'Does that mean you're with us, Senator?'

'With you all the way.'

A loud cheer went up that shook our white elephant to its foundations. We went about with shining eyes and the hair standing up on the back of our necks. I sought out Liam and hugged him.

'Unbelievable, unbelievable. I just couldn't believe it.'

'Too much. Just too fuckin' much, baby.'

I bumped right into Natasha. 'My God, what did you think of that? Wasn't it fantastic?'

'God, it's awfully crowded here. Wasn't what?'

'You mean you didn't hear it?'

'I've only just arrived.'

'Liam spoke to Bobby Kennedy on the phone' – I waved my arms – 'all over the building.'

'God.'

I looked at her properly. She wore the same black leather jacket and skirt she'd worn that night at the Marlborough Club.

'Who did you come with?'

'I'm on my own.'

'Oh. That's good. Do you want a drink?'

'No thanks.'

'You found it then, anyway.'

'Yes. It's pretty big.'

'Yes. Hard to miss, really, I suppose.'

'Why do you need such a huge place?'

'Oh, I don't know, you know. We've got a lot of things happening. D'you want me to show you around?'

'OK.'

It wasn't the ideal evening for a guided tour. Apart from the crush, Natasha seemed to know many more of our guests than I did and we had to keep stopping for her to enjoy animated bursts of recognition. Not that we were really going anywhere, but I always wanted to hurry her on, away from people. Henry Pelham spotted us and made a revolting gesture with his fingers. I couldn't help thinking of my occupied office with a pang. We struggled gamely through the floors.

Eventually we made it to the fourth. I was running out of things to say. It was then that I remembered the dome.

'There's something interesting up here, Natasha, in fact.'

'What?'

'I'll show you.' Behind a pile of junk was a small door. I had discovered it and kept the secret to myself. 'Through here.' She went ahead of me. I closed the door behind us. It was dark and smelly and strangely silent after the noisy party.

I could sense Natasha's presence in the darkness. I was close behind her. I said, 'Go on.'

'I can't see.'

'Just follow the steps.'

'God, this is awful.'

'Go on, Natasha.'

'Why? I don't like it. Where are we going?'

'You'll see.'

'Don't push like that.'

'Well, go on, then.'

'God.'

The steps spiralled up and soon got lighter. A short flight brought us on to the level stone floor under the dome. A balustraded wall ran all the way round at chest height. Above this the place was open to the sky, a home for pigeons. The dome was supported by stone columns.

'Well, you've got me up here. Now what?' Natasha turned to face me, pale and belligerent in the eerie light.

'How do you mean, now what?'

'What do you want?'

'I just wanted to show it to you, that's all.'

'Oh, sure.'

There was a pile of sacks in one corner. Natasha went over and sat down on them.

'Come on then. What are you waiting for?'

'Honestly, Natasha . . .'

'This is what you want, isn't it? Like with that girl the other night. How was it with her?'

'How was it with Ned, I could say.'

'Come over here and I'll show you.'

'God, Natasha . . .'

'Come on. Let's get on with it.'

When it was over I stood leaning on the parapet, looking over London. It all seemed rather distant. Light streamed out from the windows below. The party was still in full swing.

'The trouble is, Natasha . . .'

'What?' she said, after a long pause.

'The trouble is I think I might be in love with you. I suppose you think that's stupid?' She didn't answer. After a while I said, 'D'you think you might be in love with me at all?'

'God, I don't know. I hope not.'

– Seven –

June 1964

I woke up in my bedroom at the flat. Sunlight bathed the threadbare curtain-backs. They stirred lazily in the breeze. Through the open window I could hear sparrows squabbling over bread on Mrs Flowers's bird-table.

After a bath there seemed nothing for it but to get dressed and go to work. It was getting on for midday. John and I usually had lunch together at a pub in Shepherd's Market, and I didn't want to be late.

I paid the cab and strode into the vestibule of Camelot House. A mountain of mailsacks bulging with requests and competition entry forms blocked the way. Halfway up the staircase to my HQ a face popped out at me from a doorway, a bright, breezy, open face. 'Hi, Paul!' His thumb was up as usual.

'Hello, Sender.' We just called him Sender now.

'Pretty groovy, eh?' Always first with the latest, there was nothing the Sender liked better than laying it on those who, like me, were not.

'What is?' My mood was sunny but becoming clouded.

'The Tribe! Number one again this week!'

'Oh, yeah, great.'

'Putting a spell on the punters an' spinning 'em into spending. That's what I call sending.'

'Absolutely!'

'All down to us though, eh? Twenty plays a day – up and away!' Like all good DJs the Sender's mind worked in patterns of mindless jargon.

'Going back to the ship soon, Sender?'

'Just try and stop me! Ciao!'

Beverley came bustling towards me in a creaking leather mini-skirt. Gilly had made a wise choice in Beverley. Her defection from J. W. Hammond and Partners had maddened Jeremy almost as much as Gilly's own. On the rare occasions when I wrote a letter she would 'take it down' for me, perched on the edge of my desk, her bulging thighs inspiration enough for any writer.

'Good morning, Beverley!' I beamed.

'Oh, hello, Paul.' Beverley glanced at me anxiously, smiling a smile which flickered on and off. 'Are you OK?'

'Fine, yes. Why?'

'Oh, nothing. That's all right then.' She hurried on her way. I watched her bottom for a moment or two, puzzled, and turned into my door.

I'd added a large desk to my armchair and filing cabinet. The desk was bare. I'd seen a picture of Paul Getty in his office at Sutton Place. His desk was bare too: the grim, ascetic look masking undreamed-of power.

The main attraction, the thing that really drew me to the office every day, was my top-of-the-line swivel chair, in black leatherette. Tilted back in it with fingertips pressed judiciously together, the most momentous decisions could be contemplated. In the face of it my comfy armchair had seemed incongruous, but I hadn't the heart to throw it out. It now occupied an unobtrusive corner. When I tired of power it was a good place to sit and read about Bertie and Jeeves.

Seated in it now was John. He was reading the paper. When I walked in he looked up with theatrical surprise. He must have heard me in the passage.

'Hello, lad!' I saw traces of the same look I'd spotted in Beverley's anxious eyes. I slid into position, put my elbows on the desk, fingertips together.

'What's been happening today? Anything?'

John looked uncomfortable. 'Well, lad, as a matter of fact . . .' He got up and sauntered over, slinging the paper casually across. It was the *Daily Sketch*. 'Something you should read.'

I looked down at his pointing finger, then up to his face.

'What is it? Something awful?'

'The front page. You'd better take a look.' He loped back to the armchair. I looked down. I could hear blood shaking my heart. Under the headline RUMOURS OF ROMANCE, half the front page of the paper was taken up by a large photograph. Natasha Roxbury, eighteen-year-old daughter of Sir Anthony Roxbury, an unfamiliar look of unconcealed rapture on her luminous face, gazed into the eyes of the nation's number one heart-throb, Val Dainty, twenty-year-old lead singer of the Tribe. The happy pair, I noticed, were holding hands. They had been snapped the night before at a charity event. The Tribe had topped the bill. Last year's celebrated and delightfully unconventional Deb-of-the-Year, coupled with this year's Top-of-the-Pops, was a union both newsworthy and made in heaven, according to 'Staff Reporter' on the *Daily Sketch*. 'He just put a spell on me, I suppose,' the vivacious Natasha was reported to have quipped.

I looked up dully at John, no blood left in my face. Something loud was buzzing in my ears. He shook his head. 'Fuckin' little whore. Are you all right, lad?'

'I'm OK.'

'You won't commit suicide?'

'Not yet.'

'Let's go and get some lunch.'

'I'm not that hungry.'

'Just have a drink, then. It'll make you feel better.'

'No, honestly . . .'

'What are you going to do?'

'I don't know.'

'You're not going to call her, are you?'

'Well, I . . .'

'Don't do it, Paul, believe me.'

'I think I've got to.'

'Then you're a fool. Have you no conception of coolness?'

'If I don't call her I'll never know, you know . . .'

'Never know what?'

'Oh, I don't know.'

'Everything you need to know is right there in the paper, if you ask me. The chick is no good for you, never was. Just forget about her. Do yourself a favour.'

'Look, John, just leave me alone, OK? I'll be all right, honestly, OK?'

'Whatever you say, lad. You're the boss.'

Listening to the ringing tone I felt sick. It rang for a long time. I was about to hang up when a breathless voice said, 'Hello?'

'Natasha?'

'Who's that?'

'Paul.'

'Oh, hello.'

'Who did you think it was going to be?'

'I don't know.'

'I do.' There was a long silence. 'I saw your picture in the paper.'

'Oh.' Another silence.

'Natasha?'

'Yes?'

'It's just . . . I don't understand what's going on, that's all . . .'

'Nothing's going on.'

'In the paper it says you said Val's put a spell on you. What about that? You don't even like Val, I thought.'

'That wasn't what I said anyway. They just make those things up, you know that.'

'So you mean there's nothing going on between you and Val?'

'I don't know.'

'Have you . . . you know, with him?'

'God, Paul . . .'

'Well, have you?'

'No, as a matter of fact I haven't.'

'Are you going to?'

'God, I don't know.'

'You mean you might?'

'I have kissed him.'

'God.'

'Anyway I've got to go now.'

'No, please, Natasha, hang on . . .'

'Honestly, I've got to go. I'm really late for something . . .'

'Couldn't I see you later?'

'I might be doing something.'

'You mean you might be seeing Val?'

'Maybe.'

'Look, have dinner with me tonight, Natasha, please!'

'Oh, God . . .'

'We could go to Valentina's.'

'Honestly, Paul . . .'

'Please!'

'Oh, OK. We'll have to eat early though.'

'OK, fine. I'll pick you up at seven, OK?'

'OK.'

'Definitely?'

'Oh, yes . . .'

'See you later then. It'll be fun . . .'

'Bye.'

When I got to the pub Liam and John were sitting outside watching the whores go by. They looked up when I arrived and asked me how I was. I said OK, really, OK. I went inside and ordered a Pimms No. 1 with a quadruple shot of Pimms. While I waited I knocked back a schooner or two of ice-cold Tio Pepe.

'I don't know how I'm ever going to face Val, though . . .'

'I got news for you, baby. Yer not gonna have to.'

'Of course I'll have to, sometime.'

'Maybe not.'

'I don't get you.' I looked from one to the other of them. Their features seemed strangely distinct. My head was full of a fierce clarity. I felt wildly high.

'Your little girlfriend isn't the only one who's abandoned ship.' John stroked the back of his head and looked at Liam. Liam shifted in his seat and looked at me. His eyes, I noticed, were flecked with tiny dots of green. 'Seems like Val and the boys have signed an exclusive contract with someone else to handle their careers.'

'God! Who?'

'This you are not going to believe.' John shook his head from side to side and grinned a sick grin.

'Go on.'

Liam said, 'Emmanuel Garfinkle!'

I looked blank.

John explained, 'Manny, get it? The King of the fuckin' Mods!'

'No way!' My head sang louder.

Liam said, 'The King of the ferkin' managers!'

'I don't believe it!' I took a deep pull at my Pimms. 'But what about us? I thought we were their managers. Don't we have a contract?'

Liam shook his head vigorously. 'No way, baby!'

'Contracts were made to be broken.' John spoke with extreme worldliness.

'Yes, but . . .'

'You see' – Liam fanned his fingers at me – 'you see, baby, people either got soul or they don't. There's no fuckin' soul in a piece of paper. These guys,' he shook his head eloquently, 'what can I tell ya? the amount of soul they turned out to have, they're not gonna make it anyway.'

'They're number one in the charts.'

'You can't see it, can you?' John tore the wrapper off a new pack of Rothmans. 'Raised on a diet of balance-sheets, that's your trouble.'

'You gotta think Ray Charles, see, Paul, that's the thinkin'. That cat's got heavy heavy soul and that's what makes him the fuckin' number one cat, never mind any fuckin' charts.'

'We don't have a deal with Ray Charles,' I pointed out.

'Ha!' John drained his glass. 'Among other people. We don't have a deal with anyone.'

'Don't be so sure about that one' – Liam was looking at me with peculiar intensity – 'I gotta mind boggler . . .' He tapped his head, 'Somethin' so beautiful you won't fuckin' believe it. No one will!'

I began my pop singing career that night with uncharacteristic reluctance. There's no doubt I wanted to be a pop star. What nineteen-year-old does not? Furthermore, my bruised ego and shattered heart demanded it. I didn't need Liam and John to point out the obvious benefits to a man in my position. And, as they said, a chart-topper sung by me could settle various scores. We would show them. I would show her. The only drawback was my last-ditch dinner date with Natasha.

'For fuck's sake, man, if you could do just one cool thing in your whole life . . .' John buried his head in his hands.

'Paul,' Liam fixed me with maximum intensity, 'listen to me now. Forget the chick, OK? Being pussy-whipped is not the way to go for you at this time. Face it, she's just a fuckin' groupie. When you're up there she'll be back dying to fuck you along with all the other groupies. You won't want to know then and you shouldn't want to know now.'

'Face it, lad. Liam's right. What's the scene with a chick like her and a guy like Val? Think about it.'

It was the last thing I wanted to do, but Liam could see I was. 'If you just stood the bitch up fer once, 'stead of lettin' her walk all over you, you'd feel better, never mind when you're a fuckin' star!'

Sitting in the Terrazza in Dean Street that evening (step one in the star-making process) I had to admit that Liam had a point. I imagined Natasha, anxious on her doorstep, looking at her watch for the twentieth time, glancing up and down the street, dreadful realisation slowly dawning. There seemed little doubt that I had snatched victory from the very jaws of defeat. I twirled my glass of Frascati. I was through with her once and for all. She had had her last dinner at Valentina's with me, laughed for the last time at one of my jokes. I was never going to see her or speak to her again. The relief was almost too exquisite to bear. Never again would I lie awake at three a.m., wondering what she was up to and with whom. In the words of Martin Luther King, I was free at last.

'If you've got the blues,' declared Liam, 'you may as well sing them.' To this end a unique opportunity had been seized. We were dining with Sonny Boy Williamson.

Sonny Boy, the reigning King of the Blues, was staying with Georgio Gomalsky. The following day he was to begin a nation-wide tour with an impressive line-up of bluesy old Tennesseean cronies like Shakey Jake and Willie Dixon. Tonight, and tonight only, he was free for dinner.

John and I went along to the restaurant. Liam took the Lotus to pick up Sonny Boy. The great man should travel in style. In its confined interior he might also find difficulty escaping the softening up Liam had in store for him on the subject of my musical début. Sonny Boy Williamson, if he only knew it, was candidate 'A' for the position of my guru, mentor and possible accompanist. This was a formula that could not fail. 'You may not realise it,' Liam explained, 'he may not realise it, but chartwise he can't make it on his own. The kids aren't ready yet for one old spade-cat in baggy trousers.'

His idea was that teamed up with white, youthful me, plus a bit of judicious twiddling in the studio, a duo both deeply symbolic and unstoppably commercial would emerge. Peter and Gordon with a big, big difference.

The element of sacrilege in all this was not lost on me and John. To us just meeting Sonny Boy Williamson was charged with the profoundest momentousness. Our eager anticipation was shot through with the gravest doubts. These we doused with rum drinks after the Frascati. Rum drinks, we thought, had a Dixie sort of ring to them.

An hour-and-a-half past the appointed hour, when the waiters were beginning to suggest a smaller table, Liam and Sonny Boy appeared in the tiled atrium. As duos go they were not without interest. Ours were not the only heads to be raised in their direction. Both wore suits, as the restaurant strongly recommended in the evenings, and ties, but only in the very broadest sense. Liam's jacket of pinto hide was matched by trousers. Around the neck of the rhinestone shirt he wore a bootlace held in place by a star-spangled eagle. His height was amplified by cowboy boots and a ten-gallon hat. Sonny Boy, too, wore a hat, and neither of them seemed keen to take them off. They moved smiling through the diners to where we had risen to greet them. The King of the Blues occasionally adjusted the tilt of his bowler at any females who caught his rheumy eye. The thing had a rusty sheen to it, enough to upset the *maître d*'s of lesser joints than this, and was worn rakishly towards the front of his grizzly skull. The trousers of his suit were, as Liam had observed, baggy. They were also brown and, I noticed as he drew nearer, duo-tone. The front panels were lighter than the back. Violin-case shoes completed the picture.

Whether or not he'd been successfully softened up by Liam in the car it was hard to say. Sonny Boy was a man of many gestures and few words. Don't start me talking, was his message, or I'll tell you everything I know. We got on with the business of eating and drinking. Sonny Boy ordered a steak. When they didn't have sourmash whiskey he settled for bourbon. Whenever he felt a response was needed he blew gently on a harmonica which he kept secreted in his cheek. The grille of the instrument would occasionally appear between his teeth for special emphasis. It didn't seem to interfere with the eating process. He moved it around his mouth with his tongue along with his food. Yellow limpid eyes rolled to the music beneath their heavy reptilian lids, signifying the blues.

In the liquor glow of the meal's end, when all was finished save my profiteroles, the chewing and chat languished in favour of Sonny Boy's harp. He could blow and sing as well as he could blow and eat. The blues were infectious. Lubricated by kümmel, I found myself wailing along. Lyrics sprang to my lips: 'Ooooh, baby baby baby.' Liam was right, I saw it now. It was only a question of kicking out the jams and going with the flow. Reproduced on stage or in the studio Sonny Boy and I could not fail.

You have a strong constitution, an' I'm not going to let you down
You have a strong constitution, an' I'm not going to let you down
An' if you never lie to me, darlin', I'll always be around and I won't
  let you down
Yeah man . . .

Liam kept flicking his fingers at me and shooting me inspired glances. 'That's it, baby, that's the scene!' The management came over and requested us to leave.

'The song I'd really like to do is "Crying".' John and I were in the kitchen at the flat next morning. John was smoking. I was making tea.

'"Crying"?'

'You know, "I was all right for a while, I could smile for a while, But then I saw you last night, you held his hand so tight". That one.'

'OK, OK.' John clutched his brow. After a heavy pull on the Rothmans he said, 'I doubt if old Sonny Boy's going to dig it. Him and Roy Orbison aren't in quite the same bag, are they?'

'That's just it. I'm not absolutely sure if Sonny Boy and me are really in the same bag.'

'I know what you mean. What brought on that particular song?'

'I don't know. Just instinct, I suppose.'

'Nothing to do with Natasha?'

'God, no. No way.' I had forgotten to remember to forget her for a moment when I first woke up, but it was all over now.

'That's all right then.'

'I mean I dig Sonny Boy and all that, a lot, he's the absolute greatest, it's just this . . .'

'Black and White Minstrel Show?'

'Well, absolutely. People might not know quite what to make of it.'

'Whether to laugh or cry, you mean?'

'I might feel a bit ridiculous.'

'We can't have that.'

'If it was anybody but me, Mick Jagger or someone . . .'

'I don't know how we're going to tell Liam. It'll break his black weasel heart.'

The telephone rang. John picked it up. 'Yeah? . . . Yeah? . . . I guess so, yeah . . . That's too bad . . . No, I'll tell him, don't worry about it. We'll think of something. Bye.' He gawked at me. 'That was Liam. The deal's off with Sonny Boy.'

'Billy Fury has screaming girls.'

'Screaming girls?' Liam was trying hard to adjust to the new situation.

'You know,' I said, 'like at a Beatles concert. I've got a record of his where most of it is screaming girls. He goes, "Last night a million stars shone down on me", then there's this terrific screaming noise. It's great.'

'Jesus!' John agitated his hair tensely. 'Still, it might cover up the fact that you can't sing.'

'What the hell d'you mean, can't sing?' I had been in the choir at my prep school. Rehearsals of 'Crying' in my bath had been going well.

'Not quite as well as Roy, let's just say.'

'Some of the high notes are pretty high, especially at the end,' I was forced to admit.

'By that time all these birds'll be creamin' themselves uncontrollably.' Liam was coming round fast. 'I like the thinkin' here. Get somethin' primal happenin'. Could be a major turn-on over the air!'

'The only problem would seem to be how to get thousands of birds to cream themselves over Paul.' John lit a cigarette with exaggerated nonchalance. 'I've been listening to him in the bath. It does make you feel like screaming, I suppose.'

'Don't worry about it' – Liam was glittering on all cylinders now – 'leave all that moody to me.'

One thing about the Happening, it was small and pokey. Inside it a small crowd looked big. The core of Liam's thinking was that it could be made to sound big, too. Phil Spector did it all the time. 'You get the screamin' track down, see.' Liam stood enthusiastically in the midst of a mass of borrowed recording equipment. 'Next thing you know' – he executed obscure technical gestures with his hands – 'ya gotta cast o' fuckin' thousands.'

I was nervous. I found it hard to take an interest in what he or anyone else was saying. Questions of recording techniques and hits, of fame and wealth and vengeance, the fact that we had the only portable echo-chamber in the country, all left me cold. The only thing I could think about was that in all too few precious minutes I would be called upon to do something which I now realised I very badly didn't want to do. The idea of that sea of faces, even a small, heavily 'papered' sea, looking expectantly up, was too much. I had watched them on the door coming in. The Ladies Only rule was being enforced with strong and silent relish by the heavies. The ladies themselves looked happy enough at getting in free, blocked enough to have a good time with almost anything, but would that include me? Above and behind where I would shortly be finding this out a large sign had been rigged. When lit it flashed the word 'SCREAM'.

'Just in case they don't anyway, lad.' John was in charge of production. There was a rented crew of pallid electrical types.

Ray Sharkey and the Sharks had been roped in to back me. They were quite well known on the London circuit. Also Brian Augur on Hammond organ and Vibes. John thought the Hammond track on 'Put a Spell on You' was what had made it a hit. My rendition of 'Crying' would have one too. Added to the screaming my singing seemed to matter less and less. I hoped so, anyway.

'Ready, man?' Ray Sharkey poked his head behind the curtain where I was skulking. The Sharks all wore sharkskin suits and black suede Beatle-boots with cuban heels. Ray needed all the height he could get. He was a tiny, wired mod with bright, beady eyes.

'Hang on. Just a sec.' I stared desperately at my image in the mirror. My wrists and knees thumped with adrenalin. Could this really be happening? One Christmas at my prep school I had sung the second verse of 'Once in Royal David's City' in Old Woking parish church. All my childhood fears came flooding back. That night I had appeared before the multitude with a ruff around my neck, a red cassock, and a snowy surplice. Staring back at me now was a pale, acutely uncomfortable stranger all in black. It had been Liam's idea. 'Head to toe, baby. Give 'em somethin' positive to identify with, you dig? Like, spades and white cats, good and evil, positive and negative, that whole trip.' I wore black winkle-pickers, black leather trousers and waistcoat, a black polo. I had drawn the line at one black glove, and at dying my hair black, like Elvis.

'Come on, man,' Ray twitched, 'it's showtime.'

Ready or not, I was on. The solitary mike-stand, which might as well have been a hangman's noose, looked a million miles away. I stepped gingerly towards it across the Sharks' equipment. Seconds later I was out there. The stage lights were bright and hot in my eyes, blurring the room. A few whoops went up. Only the faces in the front rows were really clear. I looked down, smiled, cleared my throat. The live mike slapped the sound back sharply. I looked over my shoulder at Ray.

'Ready, man?'

'Ready.'

'From the top . . . three, four!'

I missed it on the intro first time round. The crash of the group right behind me startled me off the beat. Take two and I was right there.

'I was all right for a while, I could smile –'

'Hold it, hold it . . .' The group lurched to a halt. 'We're in the key of G, man.'

'Aren't I?'

'Doesn't sound like it.'

'I don't think I can sing it any other way.'

'Run through a couple of bars for us, then.'

'What, on my own?'

'Sure.'

I could feel the restless room. Liam and John had said we didn't need rehearsals. It was too much to get together twice. You'll be all right on the night, they'd said. I looked down desperately. I wasn't so sure. A girl in the front row caught my eye. Dark fringes of mascara framed her soupy blue eyes. They gazed up at me adoringly through her blonde fringe. As we made contact her pale pink lips came slowly together in a kiss.

'I was all right for a while,' I bellowed, 'I could smile fo-o-or a while, but then I saw you last night . . .' She wore a tight pink sweater, I noticed. Suddenly the whole room erupted. At first I thought every girl in the place had picked up on my single fan vibes. I stopped singing and looked behind me, ready to make a run for it. That's when I noticed that the sign was lit. In the heat of the moment I had forgotten the sign.

'Whaddya think, man?' Ray was restlessly eager as ever.

'Pretty good,' said John.

'Absolutely fuckin' beautiful!' said Liam.

'You got it down OK?'

'No problem.'

'You was all right, man.' Ray put his arm along my shoulders and squeezed. I had got rather into it. By the final crescendo, screeching 'O-O-O-O-ver you!' into the mike, the Sharks thumping out the last da-da da-da dum, I had no way of telling if I'd hit the high note or not, so overwhelming were the screams of my fans. 'Fancy a bevvy?'

'Absolutely! What are you chaps going to do?'

'Don't worry about it,' said John.

'Where are you headed?' said Liam.

'Goat's Head,' said Ray.

'See you there,' said I, with just the right amount of indifference for a pop star.

She wore a pleated miniskirt, very short, and white plastic boots. I caught a blur of pink in the corner of my eye as Ray Sharkey and I emerged into the cobbled yard outside the club. She was standing under a streetlamp, talking to her girlfriend, apparently absorbed. Ray and I kept walking. We could feel their glances but we ignored them. I spoke to Ray out of the corner of my mouth, 'See those two?'

'Course.'

'What d'you think?'

'I think we're in luck.'

'Shouldn't we say something?'

'Course not.'

'One of them was in the front row, the blonde one. I think she's definitely interested.'

'You don't say.'

'Are you sure we shouldn't say something?' We had crossed the street. The Goat's Head was on the corner a few yards down.

'Look, man, you're a fucking star now, right?'

'Right.'

'So you step inside here, right? Saloon bar, of course, and the only thing you need say, to that nice barman over there, is, "Bring me two loverly large bevvys, my good man," right?'

'I suppose so, right.'

'And let nature take its course.'

'Right.'

'That is what being a star is all about.'

Our negotiations with the bartender satisfactorily concluded, we were leaning back against the counter, when the girls walked in. They had obviously found a mirror in front of which to kill the necessary time. Eyes, lips and backcombing had all been freshly fixed. They scanned the room from the doorway, then walked up boldly to the bar, about a foot away from us. The barman at the Goat's Head, I noticed, didn't bother to ask them their age. While they waited for their drinks (a gin and lime and a port and lemonade) they talked intently to each other in giggling whispers, taking care to keep their faces turned away from where we stood.

'I saw the Kinks last night, in Wimbledon.' The blonde spoke to her friend but looked into the mirror behind the bar. Her voice was raised to the level of a general address.

'Oh yeah?' The friend, dark and chubby, responded even louder.

'They were great.'

'Wish I'd come.'

'That Ray Davies is really cool.' My leather trousers creaked as I turned. She was smirking into the mirror, looking at me sideways through her hair.

'D'you like the Kinks, Ray?' I said.

'Not much.'

'Nor me.' I was looking straight at my bird now, very cool.

'You just like Roy Orbison, I suppose?' She looked up innocently from sipping her drink, the top of her head about level with my chest. Dark roots along the parting.

'Sure, why not?'

Her eyes took in my outfit briefly before coming back to my face, 'No need to try and *be* him, that's all.'

I hadn't worn this gear with any real conviction. It seemed an irritating irony to need to defend it now. 'This was only for the record, you know.'

'People can't actually see you on the record.'

'I know that, but . . .' Why couldn't she stick to being silent and adoring? 'Anyway, looking like him wasn't the reason.' I hesitated at a full description of Liam's plan for my image.

'What's your name, anyway?' She was quickly bored.

It was a relief to get on to solid ground. 'Paul Shaw.'

She thought it over carefully. 'Is that your real name?'

'Of course.'

'It's just, like, my real name's Jeanette, but I'm a model, so I call myself Tiffany. Ringo Starr's real name is Richard Starkey. See what I mean?'

'You mean you think I need to change my name?'

'How long you been going out as Paul Shaw?'

'Not all that long.'

'You haven't built up a huge following or anything yet?'

'I've never heard of him,' said the friend.

'What about Ray here' – I was getting fed up with this – 'd'you think he needs to change his name?'

'Ray Sharkey and the Sharks is a great name,' said Jeanette, fervently.

'We've all heard of Ray,' said the friend, 'he's really groovy!'

A little later I said I thought we should go for something to eat. Since we were in Soho, I said, what about Trattoria Terrazza? I felt a feverish grip on my upper arm as Ray hissed in my ear, 'You fucking crazy, man? Fish'n'chips, these two, man, fuckin' rock salmon, know what I mean?'

The friend's name was Audrey. Once she started talking there was no stopping her. There was nothing and nobody Audrey didn't know. Luckily for me the long list included somebody who'd eaten at the Terrazza once and thought the food was terrible. She knew someone else who had a friend who used to work there and she said, the friend that is, that the chef spat in the food when he was in a bad temper, which was most of the time. We ended up in Chinatown, eating Cantonese. Audrey knew all about Chinese food and so did Ray. They were soon absorbed in disputes over the menu. Ray ordered for me, advising against every suggestion of Audrey's. The indifferent waiter stood inscrutably by. I had trouble with my chopsticks. Jeanette fed me with her fingers.

The rice wine made Jeanette's face melt, her soft mouth squashy as the pink rubbed off, her damp eyes blurred and violet. 'Ooh, Paul,' she said, 'you are super. I've never met anyone like you.'

She said she had a bedsit in Kilburn. 'If you really are serious, Paul, that is. We have only just met.' I said I was, really.

The first thing that struck me, apart from the great distance of Kilburn from anywhere I'd ever been before, and the great price of the after-midnight cab, was the smell. I had noticed it earlier, faintly clinging to Jeanette's hair and clothes. Three creaking flights up in a dark terraced house full of unexpected obstacles, through her flimsy door whose lock was heavier than its wood, and it hit me. This was no mere odour. It overwhelmed all the senses. It qualified as an atmosphere. Had it been visible it would've been yellowish green. I was once in a chip-shop in Hull which came close.

'Sssh!' Jeanette didn't turn on the light. Lumpy outlines loomed faintly in the glimmer of streetlight through the uncurtained window.

'God,' I said.

'Quiet, Paul, please!' – her nails dug into my hand – 'we mustn't wake Benny.'

We did wake Benny, but at least he didn't rise up and smite me. Benny was not an outraged boyfriend or husband, but a child of two. His father was a stockbroker but not, it would seem, a gentleman. He had failed to do the decent thing by Jeanette. Neither she nor Benny were too happy about it. Jeanette's tale of woe unfolded against the background of Benny's wails. Some of the details got drowned. She squatted on the end of the bed with him, rocking to and fro like a grieving African. After an hour or so most of my desire and all my hopes had faded. I took off my jacket and shoes and crawled in under something lime green and slippery.

Warm it wasn't. A slim pillow covered in the same stuff, smelling strongly of stale, greasy head, gave little comfort but made my hair crackle. A thin persistent stream of freezing air trickled in on me under the rotten window frame. By twisting my neck out of its path and my nose into it I could at least breathe. I fell into a fitful doze. I dreamed I had capsized my pram dinghy on the gravel-pit in Burton-on-Trent where my school sailing club used to be. Trapped under the sodden sail I was gasping, drowning . . .

'Paul . . . Paul.' Jeanette beside me in the bed, bare and warm, shook my shoulder. Grey light in the strange room proclaimed another morning. 'Benny's gone to sleep now. Come on, wake up.'

It was when I met Benny properly at breakfast that I started to feel protective. He ate sitting up in the pram which served him both as bed and high-chair. The bib around his neck was encrusted with remains of meals that I suspected dated back for most of his young life. Yet he was a jolly little chap. Every time he looked at me he laughed, allowing the loathsome concoction in his mouth to drool down his chin.

'He likes you,' Jeanette stressed. 'He doesn't like just anybody.'

We sat on the grass in Royal Hospital Gardens. Pensioners pottered about. Benny played happily by himself, chasing birds and falling over.

'I like Chelsea,' said Jeanette wistfully.

'Yes,' I said, 'I was born in Chelsea.'

'Gosh!' The adoring look returned to her rather slack face. 'I don't think I ever met anyone who was actually born in Chelsea.'

'My flat's in Chelsea, too.'

'Do you live there by yourself?' Jeanette pulled thoughtfully at a blade of grass.

'No,' I said, 'I used to, though.'

'You don't live with a girlfriend, do you?'

'No. My friend John. He's my best friend, really.'

'I wouldn't want to be stealing you from someone.'

We'd been to the Food Hall at Harrods and bought a picnic. Jeanette liked Knightsbridge, too. I'd left her there shopping happily while I went for the MG and some cash. It was a relief to get out of the leather gear and have a thorough wash. When I returned I paid up like a man and loaded the stuff into the car. There was enough food for a week. We ate the ice cream first because it was melting, washing it down with wine in plastic cups. There was smoked salmon and chocolate cake. Benny drank Dandelion and Burdock. Jeanette had bought a bottle of Pimms but no lemonade. We mixed it with champagne. I wasn't sure if I really liked her but I thought I did. She was getting melted and blurry again, making me feel strong and protective, something I'd never felt with Natasha. Jeanette dipped a piece of cake in ice-cream and popped it into my mouth.

'Living alone is a drag,' she said. 'Well, you know . . .' We both looked over at Benny.

The mews cottage in Pavilion Road seemed ideal. The street manages to be in both Knightsbridge and Chelsea. We went there to see Nigel at Debonair Carriageworks. I had an idea he might take us all for a spin in a Rolls Royce. Jeanette said she'd like that. He was a bit negative when he saw me but softened when he saw Jeanette.

'The old girl's laid up just at present.' Nigel patted the paintwork of his current model. It was similar to the last one but not exactly the same. They were both one-offs. 'Spot of bother with the distributor. Why not pop back?'

'Oooh, I'd love to!' Jeanette gazed about her in an enraptured way at the cobbles and the bijou window-boxes. 'This is a super place!'

'We like it.' Nigel ran a manicured thumb up and down his Honourable Artillery Company tie.

'Do you live here?'

'Over the shop.'

'Must be lovely!'

'Well . . .' Nigel pushed both hands deep into his trouser pockets, 'as a matter of fact . . .'

It was a charming little place a few doors down, not too pricey when all was said and done, the property of a friend. Nigel thought that something might easily be arranged, if we were really interested, that is. I looked at Jeanette and little Benny. These fragments I had shored against my ruins. It seemed as though we were. Nigel, as it happened, had the key.

John was unimpressed by the plan. 'You're out of your fucking mind.' I said I'd go on paying my share of the rent at Draycott Gardens until he found someone to replace me. 'Until you come crawling back, you mean.'

'Come on, John. You know how it is.'

'Yes, but do you?' He looked at me with a funny kind of hurt anger. 'Oh well. Everyone has to suffer I suppose. Ain't no soul without suffering.'

The place was furnished and we moved in right away. Jeanette was thrilled by the twee fixtures and frilly décor. There was gingham linen, willow-pattern crockery and cutlery with bone handles. Our bedroom had an alcove for the dressing-table papered with Regency ladies fluttering fans in temples. Benny had his own room, next door.

Because of my impending launch I needed to be more image-conscious than ever. With this in mind I opened an account for Jeanette, or Tiffany as she preferred to be known in such places, at Mary Quant's Bazaar. Apart from any question of reflected glamour, the manageress was friendly with Natasha. We had been there together a lot. I didn't want her necessarily not to know that I was doing fine.

Jeanette, in thigh-length leather boots and a variety of outfits, was soon ready to take society by storm. 'Couldn't we give a dinner-party soon, Paul, and invite people? All we ever do is stay in and watch telly. I'm bored.'

'We have to stay in because of Benny.' I was getting quite attached to Benny, and had bought him a cowboy hat and a large teddy.

'I saw Nigel today. He's really super, isn't he? A real gentleman. He thinks we ought to give a dinner-party.'

I invited Henry Pelham, a touch of class for Jeanette. Jeanette shone in the candlelight, eyes brimming with wish-fulfilment, pouting mouth prattling attentive banter to her guests. 'More white wine anybody? Nigel? There's going to be red with the meat course. Paul, bring another bottle through, could you?'

In the kitchen nook, feverishly tilting at *filets mignons* in a spitting pan, familiar fingers gripped me by the bottom. 'Your new bird, eh?'

'What do you think?'

'Better than that skinny bint you had before.' Henry took a swig from the neck of my beaujolais bottle.

'Really?'

'God yes. Sh'think she goes like an absolute snake, doesn't she?'

'Is he really a lord, your friend?' In the debris, Jeanette had reluctantly bidden farewell to the last of them.

'He said so, didn't he?' No peer in the realm could drop his own name like Henry Pelham.

'I thought he said he was a viscount.'

'That too. Come on, let's go to bed.'

'Is a viscount the same as a lord, or what?'

'Better. Come on.'

'Gosh. Is he terribly rich?'

'No.'

'No?' Jeanette looked gooey and puzzled. 'I think he's super anyway.'

Benny was an early riser. Once he'd woken me up every day I had a quick bath and made the breakfast. Jeanette would come down blurry in a silky pink thing which wrapped around her and fell open when she bent over us boys. She enjoyed the domestic ritual of kissing goodbye on the doorstep. I strode off to work each morning primed by the slither of rayon over plump flesh.

Playing house with Jeanette was not my only reason for submitting to this enterprising routine. At journey's end lay Camelot House and the all-important question of my record launch. Great confusion reigned at HQ, and to my chagrin I found nothing happened on my personal front unless I went about daily canvassing people. The people I had to canvass most were Liam and John. Liam had obtained a recording contract from a major label with no advance for me. Far more exciting to me than mere money was the arrival of my promo platters. The three of us tore the package open together. My reaction was acute disappointment.

'Who the hell are Johnny and the Jokers? They've sent us the wrong bloody discs!'

'You don't like the name?' Liam was watching me with glittering expectation.

'How d'you mean?'

John cleared his throat. 'You see, lad, we thought we needed something a bit more happening. The record company guys didn't dig the name Paul Shaw.'

'A bit borin', they thought,' said Liam.

'Well thanks a lot! Thanks a lot for consulting me!'

'We thought we'd surprise you.'

'God!'

'Nothing's definite yet. Don't get excited. These are only the promos, lad.'

'Anyway I thought I was a solo artiste. Johnny and the Jokers sounds like a group.'

'Johnny, sure, is solo, don't worry about it.' Liam pushed the packing paper across his desk dismissively. 'The Jokers don't matter. Just session guys whenever we need 'em.'

'But what about gigs? I thought I was going to gig with the Sharks.'

'No need fer gigs.'

'No gigs?' I was in two minds myself. I craved stardom, of course, but I would've given a lot never to appear in public again in those leather trousers.

'Too much hassle. Just *Ready Steady Go* and *Top of the Pops* when the time comes.'

'Let's give the bloody thing a whirl anyway,' said John.

'Crying' by Johnny and the Jokers was indeed a disc which would be hard to reproduce live without wholehearted audience participation. Great gusts of screaming filled the room, masking the occasional twang. Of the singer's voice there was hardly a whisper.

'Golly,' I said, when it was over, 'what d'you think?' They were both shaking their heads.

'Jesus, that was awful,' said John.

Liam instinctively picked up a telephone and held it halfway to his ear. 'Get that fuckin' thing out to the ship right away!'

'You liked it?' I was hopefully incredulous.

'Fuckin' level ten all the way, baby! Gonna blow their fuckin' minds!'

But the time for *Top of the Pops* never did come. My promo discs were dispatched post-haste to the DJs on the ship with strict instructions for one play per hour at least. And for one hour per hour at least I listened in. I never heard it once.

The truth was the blood-dimmed tide was beginning to engulf us. Tin Pan Alley had rapidly assessed both the strength of our signal and the weakness of our organisation. A small armada of camelhair overcoated cigar-smokers in medium-sized boats kept our gallant vessel under constant siege. They were armed with hot-pressed records wrapped in cash. Even the most high-minded DJ could not resist for ever. A new word crawled into our vocabulary: PAOLA.

But the blow that blew Johnny and the Jokers finally out of the water came from a different and completely unexpected quarter. Ray Sharkey and the Sharks' management served a writ on our record company. A wide range of malfeasances was claimed, not to mention breaches of both faith and promise. The nub of their case revolved around the proposition that whereas the group playing on the aforesaid 'Work of Art' (hereinafter to be known as The Recording) was not *de facto* Johnny and the Jokers at all but the plaintiffs, Ray Sharkey and the Sharks. *Quod erat demonstrandum.* Royalties and substantial damages were to be mulcted forthwith and remitted to the offices of the above named.

Liam issued an uncompromising *nolle prosequi* by way of defence. 'That's a loada fuckin' crap! They were paid for the session. That was the deal.'

'How much?' I asked, worried about my future.

'Eight quid.'

'Eight quid?'

'Listen, most groups down the Happenin' only get a fiver.'

'Yes, but, I mean, on a record . . .'

'Whose fuckin' side are you on anyway?'

'No, no, absolutely! It's just that, you know, I can see their point of view, in a way.'

So could our record company. 'Crying', by Johnny and the Jokers, was withdrawn from sale forthwith.

Liam dealt this final blow in the same breath as telling me he was off to sunnier climes with his girlfriend.

'God!' I said. 'But what about, what about . . . ?'

'Yer absolutely right, baby. The perfect moment fer a holiday. Come along, why don't yer?'

'Er . . .' I didn't see how, really.

Getting away from it all, though, at least from the eyes of those in the know, did appeal to me. I hurried from the building.

Going home, I knew, was no good. Jeanette was unlikely to lend a sympathetic ear to a fallen idol. She had been counting on my stardom even more than I had. Without it our relationship would lose much of its essential glue.

I headed like a homing pigeon for the Admiral Rodney. I sat in a corner, wishing to be alone, nursing my pint.

'Shaw, you old bugger, what'll it be?'

'You're not buying, are you?' I said, startled.

'Seems only fair since you're buying lunch.' Henry Pelham held up two menus.

Smoked salmon, game pie and two bottles of Château Palmer put things in perspective. I was better off, no doubt about it. After all, a decent lunch like this could hardly be enjoyed whilst being mobbed by hordes of screaming fans, could it? Absolutely not. And that's what it would've amounted to, no doubt about it.

'No doubt about it,' Henry concurred, mouth full of pastry, 'no doubt about it at all!'

Strawberries and cream were advertised that day. 'Let's have a bottle of champagne with them!' I said. The idea just came to me.

'Why not?' said Henry.

By the time we were spooning Stilton in port, Henry was telling me how much he'd always liked me.

'Honestly, old lad. I mean it, really.'

I shook my head, looked through the blazing window. My eyes were glazed and shining, 'It's a funny thing, isn't it . . .'

'What is, exactly?'

'What? Oh, I don't know. God this stuff tastes good. Shall we see if they've got any kümmel?'

My vision was ringed with darkness. It was a struggle to make sense of both our voices. Through the mist I heard Henry say, 'There's something I've been meaning to tell you . . .'

'Fire away, old bean!'

'It's about that bird of yours.'

'Oh yes?'

'Yes. Well, the fact is, I think you ought to know this . . .'

'What, Henry, what?'

'I'm afraid that rotter Nigel's been fucking her in the afternoons.'

I was shocked but not surprised. The lunch took some of the brunt. I felt like a peculiarly light lump of lead. Henry went on, nodding owlishly. 'Regular as clockwork, I'm afraid.'

A hollow voice said, 'Are you sure? How do you know?'

'Well, this is the bit I really wanted to say, you know, the hard part . . .' Henry shifted in his chair, crossed his legs the other way. 'The fact is, Paul, I may as well just spit it out. We're old pals, aren't we?'

'Absolutely!'

'Share and share alike, and all that?'

'I suppose so, yes . . .'

'All for one and one for all?'

I nodded my head up and down. The action felt good, I noticed absently.

'The fact is, old lad, I've been dipping my wick in there too.'

With slow fascination I followed the motion of Henry's arm as he peered at his wristwatch. 'Tell you what,' he exclaimed, suddenly brightening, 'if we get round there quick we can probably catch them at it!'

That evening I returned to Draycott Gardens. I still had my key to the flat. I wanted to let John and Mrs Flowers know I was interested in rejoining the ranks of the rent-payers there. Later on Liam came round. We smoked a joint and watched TV with the sound turned off, listening to Mose Allison. He and Carmen were off to Ibiza the following day. I decided to join them.

– Eight –

The first thing that hit me as I walked, still sunflushed and sandyheaded, into Camelot House, was the chandeliers: great byzantine mounds of candlepower that shattered the dim winter afternoon like an electric shock. Behind a massive marble reception desk in the uncompromising glare, an unfamiliar brunette with bouffant hairdo and a dress that looked like a rugger shirt challenged me as I headed for the stairs. She had an ungenerous mouth that shone with some pale and lustrous gloss.

'Can I help you?'

'Er. . .'

'Who do you wish to see?'

I wasn't sure that I wished to see anybody. My intentions in coming here had been vague and exploratory. I just needed to make it to my office unnoticed, and this scrum-half of a girl wasn't helping.

'Do you have an appointment?'

I had now drawn level with her and I noticed that the rugger shirt stopped short high on the upper slopes of thighs not unlike the marble columns that surrounded them. I looked them over appreciatively, and gave her what I hoped would be a winning smile.

'I don't think I need one. I work here, you know.'

The creature's hazel eyes took me in with ill-disguised contempt. The mouth pressed into a thin line as she brandished a list of names and numbers.

Helpfully I played my trump. 'I'm Paul Shaw.'

But the earth failed to move and swallow her. She studied the list and shook her head. It was as she had thought.

'No, sorry.' The eyes came back, luminous now with triumph. 'No one here by that name.' I was cancelled out by the weight of this evidence. 1965 was all over now and the times, it seemed, were a-changin'. I had come back from Ibiza with some reluctance, and ever since I'd stepped on to the rainy runway I'd been wondering why. People had tracked me down. Even those who'd normally run a mile to avoid me in the end became victims of their own curiosity. They'd imagined, no doubt, that if not dead I must have been having too much fun without them. And it should be stopped. 'We haven't heard from you, dear. How are you managing? What are you doing, exactly? Things over here are much the same. We miss you. It's your birthday. . .'

I was fine, as they had all glumly suspected. After the hollow resonance of Liam and Carmen's departure from Santa Eulalia I had settled down to a life of near-ethereal peace. But now that was over.

I hovered and seethed before the rugger girl, unsure whether to indulge a pleasant urge to yell her into submission or grovel. I was saved from this decision by the timely, swinging appearance of the Sender. He was wearing a flowered shirt and a suede tabard.

'That's all right, Jenny. He's OK.'

This was reassuring, if not quite the banner headline I might have chosen for myself. Jenny pulled around in her chair, stretching the stripes across her balloon chest, revealing lots more thigh and a clear, pinkish glimpse of underwear.

'Creeping up on me again, are you, Steve?' She arched, a different girl now.

'I'll catch you bending one day!' The Sender spoke to her but looked at me, transmitting a knowing wink.

'How've you been keeping, you old maniac.' He held up the familiar, inevitable thumb.

'Oh, OK, you know . . .'

'We all thought you'd died. Where was it? The Costa Brava?'

'Somewhere around there.' I smiled like what I hoped was one of the boys, and started to edge past them both towards my old goal, the stairs, and the dark anonymous freedoms above.

'Have you met our Jenny?' Jenny batted her black forests winningly. I paused briefly to leer. 'Paul used to be around at the very beginning.' This use of the past tense twanged a bit in my brain as I headed upwards, two stairs at a time.

Suspicion congealed into dismay as soon as I opened the door to my sanctum. The light was on; not the subdued glow playing on wood and book and bottle, but a bright hellish pulse of disco-strobes. Across the desk, in my chair, behind a rampart of record sleeves and tapes, the loathsome features of Manny, King of the Mods.

'Manny, you hideous gargoyle, what the fuck . . . ?'

'Can I 'elp you, my dear fellow?' He took me in with liquid insolence in his black fathomless eyes.

'This is my office!' I howled, trying not to sound too peevish. 'Bloody Hell!'

'Don't bloody 'ell me, man. I've got work to do. Go away. This is my office now.'

'Oh, is it?'

'Yes, it is.' He moved his hand dismissively.

I didn't have a plan, but my body was ahead of my boggled brain, and in an instant I found myself in a hands-on situation with the desk. It shifted with unexpected ease on the haircord carpet. Once in motion, all I had to do was not get in the way. Manny, on the other hand, did. As the desk responded to my controlling hand he got caught in the backlash when we swung towards the door. With a terrible cry he became one with a wastepaper-basket and an anglepoise lamp. The desk and I cruised unimpeded through the doorway to the stairhead. Here, after the briefest teeter, it was launched and went down broadside.

The aftermath of silence boomed louder than the descent. In the slow motion of time I stood in awe, looking down on my handiwork. The spell broke abruptly as the boardroom doors burst apart, revealing a short, dark, angry man. A halo of greying hair stuck up wirily around his inflamed pate. His shirt collar stood open, and a maroon tie embellished with blue diamonds stuck out at right-angles to a knotty, bucolic neck. His hairy hands clenched and unclenched as he stared at the wreckage. His jaw muscles worked dangerously on the end of a revolving cigar.

'What in the name of Satan is going on around here?' Randy Windrush looked up and his bloodshot eyes met mine.

'This bleedin' wenker threw my bleedin' desk down the bleedin' stairs, Randy.' Manny appeared beside me, adjusting his velvet jacket.

'Did he by jingo!' Windrush was puffing up alarmingly and starting to expand. 'And who might this joker be?'

The time had obviously come to announce myself. 'My name is Paul Shaw. I don't think we've been introduced.'

For the second time that afternoon someone seemed unimpressed.

'That doesn't explain why you should feel it necessary to come into my place of business and throw the furniture around!'

'Manny has taken over my office without my consent.' Randy Windrush raised eloquently enlightened eyebrows at the King of the Mods.

'Paul used to work here in the early days.' Manny was smooth with subtle deprecation, like ironing out a wrinkle in one of his yellow silk cuffs. He had come a long way from the orange suit.

'I'm Liam O'Mahoney's partner!' I howled with outrage.

'Liam doesn't have any partners now except me. That's all you need to know.'

'Let's speak to Liam. He'll sort this out.' I peered and craned in a frustrated bid to see around the Australian into that green, familiar space which surely could only be occupied by himself.

'You won't find him here. He isn't around much any more. Now get out, or you'll go the same way as this desk!'

In the rush-hour taxi home I had time to brood on the subtleties of wit and strategy I might have deployed, if only . . . Manny! That slimy traitor! I should've thrown him down the stairs. Oh well. One day, one day. Revenge is a meal best eaten cold.

Comforted by this reflection I stared out through the rain at wet, shiny London.

Earlier in the day I had left my suitcase in the hall of the Draycott Gardens house, unable, for some reason, to make my latchkey work in the door of the flat. Now, as I stamped in out of the wet, panting like a hart for cocktails and enlightenment with John, I was brought up short at the foot of the stairs by Mrs Flowers.

'Hello, Mrs F. How are you?'

'Not so much of the "Hello, Mrs F.". Where d'you think you're going's more to the point!'

I stared at her slackly. 'How d'you mean? This is my home.'

'Not here. You doesn't live here now.' In the stale atmosphere of damp dust and overcooked cabbage I began to feel the fog of madness closing in. The Mediterranean morning seemed a long way off. I was tired. I had had my fill of shocks.

'Look, Mrs Flowers, please. I'm tired. I've had a long journey. I don't understand what you're talking about.'

'You mean you doesn't know?' Her face softened from hostile to just sour. 'You've moved out. You doesn't live here now. Mister John, he says to me – not so much as a word of notice, mind – he says, "Mrs F.," he says, "we're moving. Moving on to better things," he says to me. The nerve!'

I put up my hand and clutched a handful of rain-soaked hair. 'Oh, God. Mrs F., I don't suppose you've any idea where to?'

The Bunch of Grapes in Brompton Road lacked the friendly warmth of the Admiral Rodney. I fretted at the turgid crawl of time on a bum-bruising mock-chesterfield seat, listening to the drab chat of passing trade. There was no one at my new home to let me in. Every so often I'd lurch along to my impressive new address, heavier-than-ever suitcase in hand. Each time I was a little less steady and a little more cross.

The house peered down at me haughtily as I peered up, tall and brooding with indifferent windows and shiny bricks. It had a basement with railings and steep steps down, and still more steep steps up to a narrow front door. Scaling and descending these as much as my failing puff and patience would allow in the dismal darkness, I could find no access point, no sign of life, and only a single bell whose lonely chimes could be faintly heard within. For the life of me I couldn't figure out which flat was meant to be mine. Some hours after the genteel matron behind the bar had barked, 'Time, gentlemen, please' I found out. Dozing fitfully on my case in the porch, the indignant voice of a girl who had unmistakably bettered herself without elocution lessons broke painfully into my nightmares.

'John! Come quick! There's some weirdo asleep on our steps!'

'Sweets for my sweet!' Martine loaded sugar into John's mug and gooed into his ear, one hand on his balls while the other mussed his hair. 'Oooooh, you old hornswoggler!' She looked up at me with dishy eyes. 'Don't you think he's an old hornswoggler, Paul?'

'Well, er' – I caught a sheepish eye through John's tangled locks – 'I've never really given it much thought.'

'I call him Dangerous Dong.'

We were sitting around a homey wooden table in the big basement kitchen drinking coffee and smoking and getting up to date. Martine made most of the running, while John and I just chimed in occasional responses. She was an overwhelming blonde bombshell of a girl, with the sort of pneumatic eagerness for play that most men can only dream about while leafing through the pages of glossy magazines. While her uninhibited appetite for John left nothing but the pips, she still had enough fizz left to bubble over me, lest I should feel left out.

'Ooooooh, I think you're super!' – this one straight in the shifting eye – 'I think Dangerous is really, really lucky to have a friend like you.' She couldn't wait to be den-mother to both of us.

This she had made abundantly clear from the outset, as soon as the identity crisis on the porch was resolved. 'Hello, lad!' John was only slightly surprised. 'What're you up to?'

A fragrant arm slipped through my damp one and she gave me the guided tour, chatelaine-style. Any question of flats had been removed along with the entire centre of the house from the ground floor up, leaving in its place a vaulted chamber of astonishing cubic volume whose most practical feature was a minstrel's gallery. Organ pipes of fluted blue with gilded mouths flourished up one wall. A harp and a Steinway Grand stood idly on a Persian rug of the sort that takes two thousand bloodstained years to weave. Record sleeves and magazines were slung about on deep sofas adding a lived-in air to the towering grandeur. John went and fiddled about in a distant corner. 'I've managed to rig the stereo up to those pipes.' He grinned across the expanse. 'Oooops!' A crack, a warning hiss, then with the force of a pneumatic hammer Mose Allison slammed into the vacuum: 'Hello, little schoolgirl . . .', the shock of one impact cancelling out the other and nailing my queries to my lips.

In the master bedroom suite, decked out in apricot satin, I kept catching glimpses of myself in tinted mirrors. I hesitated to broach the subject of what the hell was going on – I would wait till some suitable future moment when John and I were alone. At present I couldn't cope.

In my own little den I felt better. Perhaps down here, among the clusters of fat, dusty pipes, I would eke out a life separate from the rest. And from the rent that must inevitably go with it. Martine led me there after our jolly conflab in the kitchen. It was conveniently close. She stopped with arch emphasis at the door.

'This is as fár as I go!'

'Well, good-night.' Without warning she smothered me in a hug that kept sleep at bay for several hours. 'Oooooh, you're so lovely!'

'So, John, what is the story around here? I mean, je ne comprendez vous pas, for fuck's sake.'

'*Non?*' John loafed back into the deep cushions with heavy nonchalance. 'I'll put you in the picture.'

Martine had wafted off early, David Bailey bound, with bulging model-bag, leaving perfume in seductive smudges all around the house. She'd encountered me, grey and twitchy, poking nervously around for much-needed tea after ague in the pipes had startled me awake at dawn. 'What are you creeping around for in the dark, you dirty old devil? You won't catch me that way, you know! You go back to bed, you old hornswoggler. I'll bring you something.' This suggestion accompanied by much play about the eyebrows. I shuffled off.

Minutes later she brightened up my room. 'Here!'

'Thanks a lot!' She plonked down a steaming mug, then knee-hopped on the bed and went, 'Grrrrrr! I'll see you later.'

After a short while I recovered myself enough to pick it up: it was coffee.

We sipped in silence at first, then John said, 'Now, lad, what do you want to know?'

'This house. Why have we moved out of our perfectly good flat and into this . . . this castle in the air?'

'Onwards and upwards! Have you no ambition?'

These words triggered a picture of the previous day's setbacks. 'That's another thing. I went into the building yesterday . . .'

'Oh, yeah?' His eyes narrowed slightly. 'You have been busy.'

'I got chucked out.'

'Ha ha ha! Join the club.'

'By that ghastly Australian.'

'That's the word for him all right.' John grinned but his eyelids drooped.

'He said Liam wasn't around much any more.' My voice narrowed into my theme. 'I can't understand how he's got in there like that. Is it something to do with Jeremy?'

'Something like that . . .' John the insouciant boulevardier now giving way to a shiftier, more familiar John. 'Liam's around OK. We just don't work out of that place really any more . . . basically.'

The darkness deepened. I shook my head. 'We?'

John looked away and flipped a creamy cuff back from his watch. When he looked up at me again it was with the deepest sincerity. 'We. The three musketeers. Remember?' He cleared his throat elaborately. 'I think it's about time you talked to Liam. It just so happens we're having lunch together at Valentina's. You come along and I'll let him fill you in about Interplanetary Promotions.' John pronounced this last with a certain unveiling flourish to the voice. My face, though, was still a question mark. With slightly irritated grace he gathered himself up and leaned over to give my hair a moody flick. 'Come on, lad. Let's go. I happen to know there's something really important he needs you to do for him.'

'What exactly is Interplanetary Promotions, Liam?' I enquired as soon as seemed decently cool to do so, amid the mid-morning clamour of Valentina's and the enthusiastic ministrations of Nino and Orlando, harvesting me home to the fold.

'Meesta Shaw! Issa very very nice to see! You wanna champagne cocktail?'

'On the house?'

'Oh, vairy funny, vairy funny! Meesta Shaw, you sure havna lost youra sensa humour!'

'I'm deadly serious, Orlando, as per usual!'

'Meesta Meadows, he pay. He gotta lottsa money now.'

Which did indeed seem to be the case, although John, looking out of the window, appeared not to hear.

'It must be doing awfully well, whatever it is.'

'Awfully well.' Liam parodied me with his most lupine leer.

'But what's going on at the building?' I could already sense the pedestrian quality of my questioning.

'Listen, Paul, listen to me now.' Liam had me in the direct narrow beam system from which there is no escape. Two fingers rested lightly on my knee.

'You're lettin' your thinkin' get earthbound. You have to let your mind float free to understand what's happenin'.'

John made an inane grimace and said, 'Yeah!'

Smiling, Orlando arrived with the drinks on a tray and set them down. I took a good pull at mine. Surely I would soon see things clearly.

'You see, baby, it's best to let the heavy business cats get on with doing their own thing, while we get the freedom to get on with doing ours.'

I nodded in the overdue if misty dawn of understanding.

'That building's basically just a load of overheads.'

One of the 'things' we were doing, it transpired, at Inter-planetary, apart from helping bands get exposure 'for a small fee', was what Liam called a 'Major Operation' in the north.

'Things are cool in the north. We got two ships now. *Camelot Castle*'s in the fuckin' harbour at the Isle of Man. There's no aggravation with those cats. I'm workin' outa Douglas all the time. We got the plane and Teddy up there. You wait and see!' In Liverpool, where the northern ship's greatest audience lay, we had 'acquired' that hallowed spawning ground of pop, the Grotto.

'Which is where you come in! We're going to re-open the place in a major way. Guess what we're gonna call it?' Liam's eyes were as bright as my mind was dull. He didn't wait for long. 'The Shrine!'

'Aha!' I was hep to this.

'The fuckin' Shrine! Don't you see the beauty of it?'

'Absolutely!'

What Liam wanted me to do was go to Weybridge and persuade Val Dainty, now a fully fledged rock star, and the rest of the Tribe to top the bill at the Grand Opening.

'He won't like it, Liam. People like him don't want to go back.'

'He'll do it for you.'

'Why?'

'You're the one who put in all the heavy graft in the early days. You had the faith. He'll be loyal to that.'

'It didn't stop him running off with my girlfriend.' The old wound twitched.

Liam lit up more brightly than ever. 'Aha! Don't you see? That'll be the clincher!' I shook my head.

'The guilt, baby! The fuckin' heavy guilt trip!'

Weybridge, Surrey, so much beloved of my mother, had, inexplic-
ably to me, exerted the same magnetic pull on certain senior
members of the rock 'n' roll fraternity.

A matter of keenly felt indifference to my father, Weybridge did,
in fact, possess a geographical pecking order. Our house, substantial enough, had been in the comfortable, but modest, semi-rural
vicinity of the railway station, but the apex of the peeking order was
an address on St George's Hill. Houses here, in impressionable
circles, could reasonably be described as 'mansions'. They had
'grounds' rather than mere gardens, whose nether regions flanked
the exclusive golf-course.

As I drove along this wide, quiet thoroughfare, looking for
'Hightowers', I found my thoughts wandering to home, and to
where my father might stand in all this corporate murk. I had
wanted to go to Haslemere to complain about my treatment at the
hands of Randy Windrush, but since seeing Liam, an inevitably
confusing experience, I wasn't sure whose side my father would be
on. Worse, I wasn't sure whose side I was on myself, or even what
sides were available.

John had been distressingly direct on the subject. 'People generally
tend to show up on the side of their bank account. Your Dad's just an
old crook like all business guys. You've got to think of yourself.'

If I was thinking of myself, I brooded, I certainly wouldn't be
here. I stood staring apprehensively through the heavy metal of
something more like a portcullis than a gate, at the turreted façade
of a Hammer Gothic structure. Childe Roland, I felt, to the Dark
Tower came. Numerous statues in the Greek Classical mould stood
incongruously about, casting long evening shadows down generous
slopes of lawn. Their genitalia, it took me a startled second look to
comprehend, had been grotesquely painted in.

'Whaddya want to drink, man?' A pale acolyte with lank hair down
to his weedy shoulders brandished a bottle of White Horse
suggestively. It occurred to me that Scotch was what a real man
would drink, but I decided that if I was going to steel myself I might
as well start now.

'Have you got any white wine?'

He bent his head, scratching peevishly with the whiskey-bottle hand, but didn't answer. Overwhelmed apparently by the unwelcome novelty of my demands, he issued, after a lengthy period of reflection, an expiring sound, and moved disconsolately towards one of the many exits.

I felt lonely when he'd gone, and regretted passing up any sort of stimulant. So far things had gone badly. Both gate and front door had been fraught with humiliation.

'Oo?'

'Paul Shaw.'

Long delay.

'Sorry, man, 'e's not up yet.'

'Oh, come on!'

Long delay.

'No one's evererduvya.'

'Jesus!'

There followed a very long delay, during which it got dark and I began to hope positively for rejection, so I could go home and take comfort in failure.

I was about to suit these negative thoughts with appropriate action when a new voice chimed into play. 'Fookin' 'ell! It's yoo!' And Moose Kenyon, looking offensively affluent in a pinstripe suit, provided an unwelcome reprieve.

'A thorder noo that ploomy voice! 'Ow the fook areya, yer fookin' pansy!'

'OK, I suppose. How are you?'

Moose had risen sharply in the world, in keeping with Val's position in the charts. He was willing to be friendly enough to patronise me though, and I had little choice but to dig it. He was in management now.

'As opposed to transport?' Moose flickered for a moment at this, before deciding to josh along. I didn't represent much of a threat, after all.

'You owld fooker!' The punch in the ribs drove his message home with memorable emphasis. 'Those were the days, eh? No fookin' danger!'

His undoubted influence at least elevated me above the mêlée of liggers that thronged the several large rooms through which we passed before reaching the relatively exclusive one in which I now sat, alone in the midst of suspicious-eyed strangers. Here Moose abruptly abandoned me, overcome with sudden bored preoccupation.

'Seeyer later, mate.'

'What about Val?'

'I'll leddim know. Don't worry boudit.' And he hurried off, eyes newly alert with the fear of contamination.

The predominant décor in the room, as in all the others I had seen, was overwhelming Baronial Baroque, enhanced by British Rail Plush. Forests of antlers jutted from the dark panelled walls, festooned with items of intimate feminine apparel.

I glanced about, avoiding eyes. My seat, hewn from the living oak to a design popular in the Dark Ages, gave unsympathetic support to a series of nonchalant postures. My bum hurt, and I was becoming morosely conscious of my feet.

Despair was unexpectedly pipped at the post by the reappearance of the roadie, this time brandishing, with some distaste, a horse of a very different colour.

'Is this white wine?' he demanded.

'Absolutely!' Even from a beer-mug there was no mistaking a treat in store. He dumped the bottle beside the greasy glass, chill drops sweating down the unmistakable label: Taittinger, Compte de Champagne, 1950. All I had to do was open it.

The next twenty minutes or so saw a marked improvement in my affairs. Another bottle arrived, and in its wake a select group of new and charming companions. My head sang in sympathy with my heart. Moose swam back into the picture, to my great delight, and joined the throng. It was he who thought a third bottle would be a good idea.

When everyone's attention suddenly shifted from whatever-it-was to something else I had to reel in hard to get abreast. I peered around; the corners of my eyes were going dark.

Behind and to my left a short flight of balustraded steps ran up to an arched door. The fact that this had opened was having an electrifying effect on the collective nervous system of the room.

Val stood etched on the moment of his entrance with the dramatic anticlimax of multiple expectations fulfilled, pausing for a beat as if to take the wind out of his own sails. He wore a crushed plum velvet suit and Cuban boots; pale satin shirt ending high under his chin in a choker. He looked taller than when I had seen him last. His black hair was longer, and tousled from recent sleep. He was sucking hard on a joint like it was pure oxygen.

He clumped stiffly down the few stairs and over to the back wall where stereo components stood stacked in an expensive heap. Seconds later Jerry Lee Lewis ripped through the room and everyone began relaxing vigorously.

I took another good pull at my mug and thought hard about not thinking about Natasha and Val together. The music shook my nerves and rattled my brain: too much *lerve* drives a man insane. I ached not to show or see anything in the eyes when we met. I was the only person in the room who hoped he wouldn't join them.

''Ullo, Paul. 'Owsitgoin'?'

My eyes flinched up to find we'd both forgotten to remember to forget. His hand was stuck out and I took it. The rest of the room shimmered like the dim fringe of a cameo. Then it was over. Val sat boisterously down and drained every glass on the table. Moose got busy getting more booze.

''Ere, mate. Try summa this.' Val held the joint across to me like a pipe of peace. Measurement of time and memory and what people last said and when and why soon became surreal. Val at some point got a far out dose of the munchies.

'Man, a could eat a fookin' 'orse!'

Immediately the spinning room became a regular mare's nest of suggestions: what was available in take-away and where, competing violently with the many expert opinions on what Val liked best. We had just heard that in Esher a vendor of jellied eels stayed open all night when Val exploded.

''Ere! A joost wanna fookin' Wimpy King, OK? An' a wannit now!'

The whole place drained away like a sink as the multitude stampeded to obey. Moose flailed his arms – 'Don't let the fookin' grass grow!' – then returned to the table with a mollifying air. ''Ere, Val, this'll take the edge off while you wait,' cracking a small glass phial into his drink. 'Go on!'

'What the fook is that?'

'Liquid meths.'

'Ah!'

Methamphetamine in liquid form works fast. We were a good deal speedier than the foragers when they finally returned. First through the door was the Wimpy King.

'What's that?' Val gazed up stalk-eyed with jaws grinding at the triumphant bearer.

'Your nosh.'

'Ooer, fookin' 'ell. Take it away!'

'Huh?'

'A couldn' eata fookin' thing!'

The consecrated fodder was borne reverently away to an uncertain future and a chorus of conflicting opinions.

'Puddit in the fridge! 'E'll want it later.'

'In the oven. Keep it warm! 'E's bound to want it soon.'

'Fookin' 'ell!'

'What we need's a bitter peace' – Val's big bony body jerked upright like a manic marionette – 'Paul, d'yer wanner coom'n see me new ooble-booble?'

'Sure!' I was just capable of speech, though insufficiently so to fully express the huge affection I was feeling for my great friend Val. I marshalled my disembodied limbs with elaborate care and we set unsteadily off.

The Holy of Holies was fashioned very much around the central theme of the hubble-bubble: thousands of Islamic patterns on walls, floor and even ceiling; huge cushions strewn about; incongruous Tiffany lamps; incense sticks fizzling. Val wore a suede bag tied to a leather thong round his skeletal waist from which he now selected a suitable lump of shit. 'Afghani Black,' he grunted as he hacked away with a delicately engraved silver clasp-knife. 'Pure opium base.'

In the dream familiar faces leaked back in, white and frightening, through the walls. Time at one point turned in a sickening trick of *déjà vu* as Val reared up with a face like death and spoke in a voice that dropped into the acorn centre of my brain like shards of crystal. 'Man, a could eat a fookin' 'orse!'

Another age went by. Someone seemed to be weeping: Moose, fat cheeks wet with tears, breathing like a grampus: 'Ooooh, fookin' 'ell!'

Val said, 'What's so fookin' foony?'

More unmeasurable time, then, 'Someone et it, Val!' Moose wailing like a woman in pain.

'Ate what? Whaddya fookin' talkin' about, ya pratt?'

Moose was screaming now and we all started sobbing and shaking.

'Your fookin' burger!'

Burger Burger Burger Burger Burger. The word was suddenly revealed to us in all its limitless absurdity. Laughing like unlimbered drains we repeated it over and over and over again, like a mantra in a colony of frogs. It had no meaning, and it had all the meaning in the world.

I woke like a ghost in the throes of a nervous breakdown with the dawn light stealing into a tiny room I couldn't recall: I was alone. Empty to the point of levitation yet with feet of lead I stole downstairs through the resonant gloom. Snores on the ground floor shuddered from the slack faces of the fallen; all at peace now, unlike me.

The massive front door was locked and barred and bolted, but most of the windows were open wide. Out on the wet lawn the morning chill felt good. Blood began to make the rounds between my head and feet without me fainting.

Thoughts started to form as I climbed over the wall, sending my nervous system into instant shock. 'Oh, dear,' I thought, 'I don't think I got round to mentioning the opening of the Shrine!'

But as the MG thrummed into optimistic life against the still desolation I saw the silver lining: how would Val remember what we'd said?

'So he was definitely definitely interested?' Liam's face later on was pale and lively, believing with utter faith all the things he wanted to hear.

'Absolutely!'

'That's it, baby! Pack yer bags. Liverpool here we come!'

– Nine –

I went to Liverpool to be manager of the Shrine, determined to make a go of it. I was on my own, as I had been in Ibiza. In Cala Llonga I had survived by selling my labour and building dry walls in exchange for bed and board. I felt sure these foundations of independence would pay off at the Shrine.

In Liverpool I found bed and board just around the corner from Lime Street Station. On the evening I arrived it was raining hard. A porter directed me and my baggage to the conveniently situated Churchill Hotel in Lord Nelson Street. Here I made myself as comfortable as twelve shillings per night allowed. A Full English Breakfast, advertised on a white card in the window, drew me to the place against stiff competition from almost every other house in the street. Though excellent, it was the only meal provided. I discovered this on the first night when I enquired hungrily about dinner. 'Strictly B&B darlin'.' Mavis Fanshaw (prop) leaned seductively against the rickety green banisters which led up to my new home. Mavis was a painted temptress of the old school. The closer you got to her the older you realised she was. She had invested a lifetime of immoral earnings in the Churchill, named after the sexiest man of her generation, she said. 'What a client he would have made! No dear, you'll 'ave ter go to the Cosy fer yer tea.'

The Cosy Dining Rooms was two doors down from the Churchill. It catered to the bed and breakfasters who lodged in Lord Nelson Street and its environs. It was run by an Italian but was not an Italian restaurant. I unwisely ordered steak. 'Cominga right up!' said Carlo, which it did. He disappeared and reappeared with the speed of a conjuror's rabbit. Two old men at a nearby table stared resentfully at the mention of steak. I avoided their eyes by looking down at my plate. It was hardly worth getting hated for. I poured on some Daddy's. It came out in a rush, swamping the greyish meat. I caught Carlo's eye, then looked away again, too dispirited to complain. In the window the stark interior of the cafe reflected dismally against the wet darkness. I felt a profound sense of self pity stealing over me. I paid the bill, carefully adding ten per cent, and crept back to the Churchill.

Through the glass and wrought-iron door of the TV lounge I could see Mavis sitting in a sophisticated pose. She was holding court among a small but spellbound group of commercial travellers. I slipped past and up to the bleak privacy of my room and book.

Under the yellow candlewick the narrow bed sank sharply in the middle when I sat on it, with a loud creak. The icy sheets might or might not have been damp. It was too cold to tell. A bronze flex curled dustily over the floor. It led from a small brown plug in the opposite wall to a straw bedside lamp with a pink shade. I drew the curtains, shutting out the strange city, and switched it on.

Morning came crisp and bright. Merseyside shone under an empty sky. By eight-thirty I was on my way briskly to Button Street. The mighty commercial monuments reflected my mood. Every gene in my body hastened to be in the office by nine. I would start out as I intended to proceed. I would set an example. Business is business. My father was right. The club would stand or fall by the work ethic. I wore a suit and tie.

Outside the club was much as I remembered it. Daylight stripped most of the romance from the black warehouse bricks and mouldering flyers. The name had changed but not to the Shrine. The remaining letters now read G O O. I made a mental note to deal with the matter at the first opportunity. At eleven forty-three precisely this opportunity arose when someone at last showed up with a key.

'Good God! What on earth time do things get started around here anyway?' I had got to know every brick in Button Street by heart.

'Sorry, mate. Place don't open till ternight.' My deliverer was shaggy and unshaven in sheepskin and Spanish boots.

'You don't understand. I'm Paul Shaw.'

'We've all got problems, pal.'

'From Interplanetary Promotions.'

'Oh shite! Why didnyer say so? Coom on in.'

The words 'MANAGER'S OFFICE' were stencilled in black on

the frosted glass of a door to the left of the coatcheck. I headed for it.

'Oi! Not in there, pal. That's private.'

'Look . . . I'm sorry, what was your name?'

'Woody. Still is.'

'Well, look, Woody – hi by the way, I'm Paul. And I'm the new manager, OK? That's my office, obviously.'

'Warrerbout Lionel?'

'Who's Lionel?'

'Lionel's the manager!'

Lionel Prewitt, according to Woody, was a Liverpool living legend. He had been manager at the Grotto from as far back as anyone could remember. Every group on the Mersey who ever got a break owed something to Lionel. His ear was an institution.

Lionel had the only key to the office. He rarely got in before five. Beyond this Holy of Holies every nook and cranny in the club was the province of Woody. He was the lighting man, sound technician, chippy and maintenance engineer. He knew where the groups stashed their dope and proudly revealed the little hole he had drilled for what he called berdwatching. 'You wouldn't believe what those tarts gerrupto in the bog.'

Without Lionel there wasn't much option to Woody's guided tour. My masterplan for the Shrine, with which I was bursting, needed at least a telephone if not a meeting to get off the ground. My only outlet was Woody. I described it to him in pitiless detail. The Shrine would boost its revenues by opening in the daytime. There would be lunchtime sessions and a coffee-bar. Most of all there would be a boutique. I was particularly keen on the boutique.

'People round 'ere don't 'ave money fer a boutique.' Lacking my vision, Woody couldn't see it.

'But the latest fashions, Woody, don't you see? They won't be able to resist them!'

'If they wannem that bad they'll steal 'em.'

'We'll make money hand over fist!'

Woody brooded into his Manstons. We had decided to continue our discussion at the Grapes. 'Sounds like a lorrer work fer yours truly.' He wasn't as turned on by the work ethic as me.

'They said you were coming, sure, but they didn't say why.' Lionel

Prewitt spoke, glancing at me absently, shuffling piles of paper on his desk. I sat opposite him in a hard chair. Signed photos of assorted mop-haired lads festooned the walls. But it was Lionel's own hair that captured the attention. I remembered it right away. On stage it had been merely noticeable. Here in the small drab room it was irresistible. At this range the individual strands were distinct, bronze, sculpted, like a painting. Together they were compact, thick, heavy, parted with a dead giveaway seam. Whether or not anyone was meant to be fooled I couldn't tell. Around the rim the real Lionel blended unconvincingly, soft pink against the hard orange with the odd wisp of grey.

'Who did you speak to, exactly?' I shifted in my chair, intent but nonchalant.

'Your Irish friend, O'Mahoney, the one who pinched the Formby Five from me.' Lionel's eyes of cloudless blue were on me now, unflinching. I'd been wondering about that, ever since the shock of fitting the face to the name.

'Did he? Oh, dear.'

'As if you didn't know. Don't come the innocent with me. I know why you're here. But you can't run this place without me, you see. Even O'Mahoney knows that!'

'Two heads can be better than one sometimes, you know.' I stared doubtfully at the rug.

'Too many crooks spoil the broth, more like.'

It was a relief when Woody knocked and entered all in the same breath – 'Ayeaye!'

'What is it now, wretched boy!' Lionel ejaculated through teeth clenched on a long cigarette-holder. They were unnaturally white and sepulchral.

'Holy hairpieces, Lionel!' Woody stood dramatically just inside the room, his knees slightly flexed. He looked at me. 'Come on. It's time fer the Caped Crusader!'

It was, perhaps, time for a natural break. By following Woody to what he called the Batcave I soon found myself back in the Grapes.

A telly stood over the bar. A small knot of patrons was staring at it expectantly. There was still time to get one in, Woody said, which he obligingly did.

I brooded on the reflective surface of my drink. 'Nobody bothered to tell me there already was a manager, of course.'

'Not to woorry. All yer gorrer do is coom up with some fookin' superb fookin' notion tharr'l knock ev'rybody's socks off.'

I brooded a bit more. I thought I already had. 'I could always be Daytime Manager, I suppose.'

'Sounds a bit naff that, Daytime Manager. Know warrer mean, like Latrine Co-ordinator or some fookin' thing like that. Anyway, I'm the daytime bloke.'

'It's not the real solution, I must say.'

'What you need's a real role, mate.'

I hardly had time to reflect on this sobering fact when the Dynamic Duo jumped on to the screen. I hadn't seen them before and was soon able to lose my own problems in their absorbing war against the supercriminals of Gotham City.

'Holy Gobi Deserts!' exclaimed Woody when it was over, 'me glass is empty an' I'm dyin' o' thirst!'

'To the Bat bar!' I cried, leaping to my feet. 'Hold on Batman, you can leave this one to me!'

'That's it!' A few rounds later we both saw the light. 'Knockout!'

'It's fookin' brilliant!'

'What about Lionel though?' A moment of uncharacteristic doubt in the Batbosom. Not so Woody. 'Yer can leave that old poove to me!'

'A penguin!' Lionel appeared outraged at the suggestion, 'I don't look anything like a penguin!'

'Not joost any penguin, Lionel' – Woody stroked the managerial feathers with an experienced hand – 'the Penguin. You know, from the series. The Penguin's a real star.'

'I don't know what you're talking about.'

'The resemblance is pretty striking, I must say,' I said. 'No offence, of course.'

The Batman and Robin act was a big hit in the club right from the start. We got it going a few days later, just as soon as we could get our costumes together. Woody was Batman and I was Robin.

Attracted as he was by our instant success, Lionel in the end remained aloof. He continued to introduce what he called 'the Talent' while we kept the customers satisfied in between acts. If anybody thought he was The Penguin all well and good. The natural resemblance was not denied. But when it came to embellishing it with a top hat and silly spats Lionel drew the line. He was after all a legend in Liverpool as it was. A sudden change of image now could only confuse people.

When a group concluded its routine and shambled off, the lights went down. Now came the tricky part for me. Provided one of the foregoing musicians hadn't trampled it, I had to chuck a match with deadly accuracy on to a small pile of gunpowder. When I scored a direct hit (it sometimes took a few shots) a puff of smoke reminiscent of the entry of the Demon King enveloped the stage. The lights went up and – hey presto! – we were on.

'Gerroff yer fookin' fairies!' They loved it. We pranced about, capes akimbo, dodging missiles. In between ad libbing popular bat-repartee with the mob we played discs on a DJ deck and mimed to them.

Behind us the next group set up. What had been a boring two minutes had become a highlight. When they were ready they twanged a warning note or two. Reactions to this could be mixed. Two minutes was about my limit but sometimes the crowd thirsted for more. Lionel stalked on stage if things needed really sorting out.

'Now then, now then,' Lionel describing a languid arc in the air with the holder. The hall full of hisses.

'Holy Homos!'

'Is it a berd? Is it a plane?'

'It's a fookin' hairship!'

In very extreme circumstances I would join the group for their opening number and treat the rabble to a sample of my Mick Jagger dancing.

In the daytime I set aside my Robin outfit as being unsuited to my managerial image. I was pushing ahead relentlessly with my masterplan. Lionel and I had reached a sort of working arrangement which did not as yet extend to my using his office but which was otherwise amicable. I had installed a telephone in the embryonic woodwork of my coffee-bar. Lionel had no interest in my vision of daytime expansion. He was a night person.

'God made the daytime for sleeping!' he declared grandly one day.

'I don't know how you work that out,' I said. It was hardly work-ethic talk.

'He made the night-time for having fun, didn't he?' I couldn't deny it. Promo from the ship was making the club the hottest place in town. Woody couldn't deny it either, and didn't. Nor was he a work-ethic-er at heart. But in the daytime, while Lionel slept, he took off his Batman suit and became the chief and only instrument of my ambitions. Even the boutique, which I knew he still viewed with the greatest scepticism, came gradually to life under his hand. While I buzzed about making managerial noises, Woody, his belt festooned with tools, his mouth full of nails, worked. Men and materials assembled at his command. All winter we toiled towards the Grand Opening Day of the Shrine.

The boutique came into its own at the Grand Opening. We had been pushed for a really big attraction. The Tribe, not much to my surprise, couldn't make it. Liam and John, from their Isle of Man headquarters, could turn on the airtime but not the stars. Memos arrived from Douglas with news of various pull-outs. The last one let me know that they themselves would be occupied on the big day. I was on my own.

The fashion show was Woody's idea.

'It'd work in perfect with the Batman and Robin Parade.'

'What Batman and Robin Parade?'

'The one where we fill the Batmobile full o' berds wearin' all that daft lookin' gear.' My stock had been ariving by the boxload from London.

'What bloody Batmobile?'

'The one we're gonna buy fer the parade!'

'Be a fookin' traffic-stopper this, you wait!' We were blasting excitedly through the tunnel to Birkenhead in Woody's clapped-out Mini. Fear of breaking down either mechanically or mentally held me half breathing in my rattling seat. Woody kept his Cuban heel hard down on the floor. He lived life from moment to moment. It kept his spirits high most of the time. Only when drunk would he sometimes descend into Celtic gloom. Right now they were higher than ever.

When talked about in a pub over a large whiskey the 1959 Cadillac is an exciting enough thing. In the salty glare of that New Brighton afternoon the Sedan de Ville surpassed all expectations. It was white with red upholstery. The red hide rag top had been folded down.

'It's a four-door, know-what-I-mean?' Woody's mate Kevin stood, head down non-committally, fists deep in his pockets, rocking on his heels.

'Yeah.' Woody and I, equally non-committal, nodded.

'Not like the Eldorado.'

Woody shook his head. 'No way.'

I said, 'What's the Eldorado like, then?'

Kevin removed the cigarette butt from his lower lip and ground it under the toe of his winkle-picker. 'Eldorado's a fookin' two-door. Nothin' but trouble, the Eldorado.' His black hair was arranged in a DA which required constant combing.

The night before – thanks to heavy plugging from the ship – had been a big one. The featured group was Billy J. Kramer and the Dakotas. Woody held the takings from the show. He ran his thumb thoughtfully along the furled edge of the wad. The chrome on the triple tail fins glinted.

'What's on the clock?'

'Twenty thou, honest.'

'Fookin' bollocks!'

'Swear ter God, Woody, no lie.'

Woody moodily kicked a tyre. 'If this heap's had a fookin' herr cut it's concrete boots fer you, Kevin.'

'Genuine mileage, Woody, honest. Look at the fookin' condition. It's bin nowhere this motor.'

'Let's go somewhere in it now, then. Give it a try-out.'

We wound away into North Wales. Woody and I both took a turn at the power-assisted wheel. At a place called Ffynnongroyw the deal was struck. The Batmobile was ours.

*

The impact of the Batmobile on the Liverpool traffic was as Woody had foretold. Everything ground to a halt. Behind the car came the Batparade: a lengthy crocodile of birds with banners announcing the Grand Opening of the Shrine. Each was clad daringly in the latest gear from the boutique. Blouses were see-thru, body stockings slinked seductively under metallic mesh dresses, leather skirts were little wider than belts. The police arrived but we had Bessie Braddock in the Batmobile. She was more than just a local MP. She was a living Liverbird, a walking monument, an even bigger legend than Lionel Prewitt. It was Lionel who at the eleventh hour had produced her, our only real celebrity.

Pink-faced coppers were quickly dragooned by Bessie into a highly effective force. They directed the traffic while we cruised the town. Kevin drove the car. He was the only one who understood the 'cruise control'. Lionel sat next to him, flicking ash on the multitude, making like the Penguin. Batman, Robin and Bessie stood in the back of the car, gathering support for the Shrine. The Pied Piper of Hamelin could have done no better.

At lunchtime we arrived at the club. Most of Merseyside was now behind us. The Batparade flowed from Button Street to the city centre. A fringe of fairground lightbulbs flickered rhythmically around our new Dayglo sign. A champagne buffet had been laid on in the coffee-bar, but only for the few. I didn't want anyone chucking anything at my sign. Then I spotted Frank's brother Pat filling the doorway. He was flanked by two back-up heavies. The sight of them was reassuring. A couple of our coppers were chatting to them and they looked like puppies frisking at elephants.

Apart from local celebrities and dignitaries like Lionel, Bessie Braddock and Roger McGough, the few included the press. When we got inside most of them were already there. The Formica surfaces of my American-style Espresso Juke Box Lounge (featuring Shrinedog'n'Fries) were enhanced for the occasion with festive matter. Cocktail sausages shone greasily in the neon glare. The term 'champagne' had been stretched to embrace an extensive mix of drinks.

'And now, ladies and gentlemen! For your further entertainment, the moment we've all been waiting for . . .' Lionel mounted the makeshift catwalk and spread his hands as only he knew how. Rather him than me, I thought. My morning's work had taken its toll. Woody knew a good champagne drink involving a dash of most things, poured over a sugar lump soaked in Cointreau. I was enjoying my fifth or sixth of these in the company of one of our models. Her name was Samantha. She said she liked my Robin costume. I liked hers too. When the fluid reached my knees she didn't mind propping me up on her daringly exposed shoulders.

'. . . it gives me great pleasure to introduce to you now . . .' Samantha fancied a job in the boutique. It was her life's ambition, actually, she said.

'. . . my esteemed friend and colleague, Mr Paul Shaw!'

'What!? What was that?' Surely my ears were deceiving me. Beaming Lionel was clapping and nodding in my direction. All eyes turned to follow his.

'That's you, isn't it?' Samantha looked impressed.

'Yes, but . . . there's no way, I mean . . .'

'He will present the very latest fashions from London. Come along, Paul.'

Samantha had to come with me. 'Just say you're Catwoman,' I hissed. At that moment I couldn't imagine being without her, wasn't prepared to risk standing up alone in front of all these local VIPs. She needed no persuasion. It was her big moment and I knew she knew it as she wrestled me up into the unwelcome limelight.

My mind was in a fog but I knew there must be some joke connecting Catwoman with catwalk. 'Er . . .'

'Sock it to 'em, Robin. Fookin' A!' I spotted Woody leering at me from the solid refuge between two of Samantha's girlfriends. It was all right for some.

'I must say I . . . yes, yes, what is it?' Another hand on my shoulder now, much bigger than Samantha's.

'There's a berd on the door insists on bein' admitted.'

'Really, Pat, can't you see I'm . . .'

'Very insistent. Say's she's from the *Echo*.'

'That's all right then, isn't it? This is a Press Show.'

'That's what they all say though, know what I mean? No ID.'

'Well tell her to fuck off then.'

'Bit risky that, know what I mean? Very insistent she is on seeing the manager.'

'Well what does Lionel say?'

'Lionel says in the daytime that's you.'

'Shit! Look, Pat, surely you can see I'm . . . Excuse me ladies and gentlemen, one moment . . . What's she like, you know?'

'Right oop your street I'd say.' Pat's huge face ogled blandly.

'Oh really?'

'Talks with a mouth fuller marbles, know what I mean?'

I glanced at Samantha. Her attention was entirely taken up with the audience.

'Better put her in the front row then, eh, Pat?'

Everyone suddenly started clapping. I clutched my mike, just managing not to fall off the edge of the catwalk. 'Holy Hotpants!'

A smirking band of mannequins surged around me, walking as if on tightropes, overdoing it heavily on the protruding hips. For the next few minutes I tried to decipher what they were all wearing from my sheet and describe it in suitable salonese to the audience. Samantha kept pointing and saying, much too loudly and too near the mike, 'Look, there, silly, there!' then smiling hugely at her adoring fans.

'Stephanie, as you can see, is dressed ideally for a date with the whole of Everton Football Club . . .' It was going down well. I was getting into my stride. There was a mild upheaval at the front of the house, right below me. Pat had dislodged a couple of protesting females with notepads in favour of a small neat girl in a smart blue minicoat with brass buttons. I looked at her curiously. Short chestnut hair, big dark eyes. I looked again. Jolly banter died on my lips. I thanked God that Robin wore a mask. The clothes were not the same. The hair was not the same. But the girl was unmistakably Natasha.

I got through the rest somehow. I kept glancing at her, my concentration undermined by a mixture of disbelief, apprehension, curiosity and lust. My movements within the Robin suit became increasingly stilted. As soon as the show was over I legged it for the green room. What could she possibly be doing here? I got rid of Samantha as gallantly as I could, pointing out how much better off she would be with Woody. He was at the centre of a gaggle of Swinging Mersey Men, who were about to go on, and this convinced her.

Alone, I ripped off the Robin gear and pulled on my own.

I gave myself a cold look in the mirror, lowered the eyelids, sucked hard on the lips. Trying desperately for indifferent thoughts I bolted through the door.

The throng had swelled but there was no sign of Natasha. Ben E. King sang 'Stand By Me'. People pumped up and down unconsciously as they munched and swigged and laughed.

'Hey, Paul, you were great.'

'The mask was a big improvement.'

'Oh, yeah, right. Ha! You haven't seen a . . . er, hang on, back in a minute . . .' I was up on the toes of my desert boots, neck waving like a tortoise. I worked my way all the way to the vestibule without any luck. Here the crowd was thinner. Pat stood massively near the exit sign.

'Pat, I say, I don't suppose you've seen that, you know, that bird, have you?'

'You mean the snotty one? Fancied 'er, did you? Said yer would.'

'You haven't seen her, have you?'

'Not recently.' He called to his henchmen in stentorian tones, 'Lads, 'ave yis seen a skinny bint with a voice like Lady Barnett? Robin 'ere fancies 'is chances.' They shook their heads impassively. Baffled and disconsolate I turned away. Three feet from me the Ladies' Room door swung open. She was busy buttoning up her coat and didn't see me. The thought of Woody's spy-hole flashed through my mind. I felt better.

'Natasha.'

She looked up, was motionless for a moment. I seemed to have limitless leisure in which to study her. Her hands held a button halfway through a buttonhole.

'Paul, God . . .'

'Didn't you realise it was me?' I blurted.

'How do you mean? What are you doing here?'

'I work here.' I turned furtively to look at Pat and lowered my voice. 'I run this place, you know.'

'God. They told me the manager was a man named Prewitt.'

'Yes, no, I mean, it's a bit complicated, you know . . .'

'I was just leaving. I didn't see you in there.'

'I was Robin.'

'Robin?'

'You know, introducing it all.'

'What, you mean . . . Oh, God, yes, of course . . .'

'The voice? Something about the voice? Couldn't quite place it?'

'That's right, Paul, there you go. Moan moan moan.'

'I must say, Natasha, it's awfully good to see you.'

'I might've known that was you in that ridiculous outfit.' Natasha nibbled at the edge of a poppadam. We sat in the warm curried air of the Star of India near Central Station. She had to catch a train to Southport.

'I still can't believe you didn't.'

'I was concentrating on the clothes. That's my job.' A pimply youth in a turban brought my bottle of Taj Mahal beer. Natasha had a Coke.

'What exactly is your job?'

'Cub reporter. On the *Liverpool Echo*.'

'I still don't understand.'

'I don't see why.' Natasha looked nettled.

'Well, I mean, all the way up here. It's not quite your scene I wouldn't've thought.'

'You're up here.'

'That's different.'

'I don't see why.'

'Look, Natasha, I've got major business commitments here. We've got the ship off the Isle of Man. That Shrine operation is pretty well entirely down to me.'

'Wow.'

'God. I suppose you came up here because of Val.' I felt my eyes hot and angry.

'It's got nothing to do with Val.' Her face looked tense too. 'It was something to do with Ned if you must know.'

'Oh God, Natasha' – I put my fork down hard – 'I can't believe I'm getting into all this shit again.'

'Don't if you don't want to. Nobody's forcing you.'

'Ned Wessex . . .' I shook my head.

'He was really nice to me when Daddy died. The only one.'

'I didn't even know he was . . . I mean . . . God, how awful for you.'

'I wrote to you.'

'Did you? Did you? When?'

'Ages ago.'

'God, Natasha. It's just I thought we were, you know . . .'

'Thought we were what?'

'Well, you know . . . finished. Obviously.'

'That's not exactly very nice, is it?'

'No, I suppose not, but I mean you . . .'

'I remember you once said . . .'

'Yes, yes, I expect there were lots of things I once said . . . What did I once say?'

'You once said' – Natasha crumbled a small piece of nan between economical fingers. She looked up – 'that you'd never stop loving me. Ever.'

'Did I say that? I suppose I did.'

'Anyway Ned was good. He got me this job.'

'I don't see what's so good about that.'

'When Daddy died, apart from anything else, it turned out there wasn't any money.'

'No money! But I thought . . .'

'So did we. It turned out he was insoluble or something when he died.'

'Sounds awful. What does it mean?'

'It means a lot of nasty little men in bowler hats. Mummy still hasn't got over it.'

'God.'

'Ned said he'd marry me, but . . .'

'But what?'

'But I'd rather earn my own living, I decided. Ned knows lots of newspaper barons. So here I am. I'm a different person now.'

'I didn't know there were lots.'

'Lots of what?'

'Newspaper barons.'

'Oh.'

'And do you like it?'

'I don't know. I'm quite good, I think.'

'Why can't you work on a paper in London, if Ned knows all these barons?'

'You have to start, you know . . .'

'At the bottom?'

'In the provinces, if you want to be a proper journalist. I don't want to have strings pulled for me the whole time.'

'Like in the theatre?'

'How d'you mean?'

'You know. On tour. Shows. My brother's an impressario. He's always doing it.'

'I suppose so. God!' Natasha started as if bitten by her own wrist. 'I've got to get going.'

'Same old Natasha.'

'But it's the last train. How else am I going to get home?'

I poured out the remains of my Taj Mahal. It sat dismally at the bottom of the glass, all bubbles gone. Natasha rummaged in her bag. Speaking directly into it she said, 'Why don't you come with me?'

Screaming gulls woke me early next morning in Southport. Natasha slept on. I lay there for a while listening to her even breathing, trying to adjust. We had never spent the whole night together before. All I could see was a swag of hair poking out above the pink mound of blanket. Underneath I knew she had nothing on except a gold medallion round her neck. I tried hard not to think about how she had come by her new veneer of sophistication. The effort galvanised my knees up and out over the edge of the dark wooden frame. I stared at my feet on the worn rug for a minute or two before hauling up cautiously off the creaking springs. I walked stiffly over to the sofa where my jeans lay. We had sat there with our knees together in the darkness whispering before we'd finally kissed. Her dry lips had welcomed me with unexpected warmth. When I couldn't undo her belt buckle, her deft fingers had come to my aid. She was much more flesh and much less porcelain than I remembered.

Pulling back a heavy brocade curtain I could look straight down on the promenade. Beyond the boating lake Southport Pier jutted out into a cloudless expanse of sea. The tracks of a small railway ran to it from just below where I stood. The sun shone on the wheeling seagulls and the motionless rides of an empty funfair. Maroon and cream municipal ironwork fenced an impressive acreage in front. Sky-blue benches gleamed near beds of marigold and tulip.

'What d'you think?' She was sitting up, the sheet round her shoulders.

'This is a great place. Marvellous.'

'You see what I meant now? Much better than the smelly old city.'

'Like being on holiday all the time.'

'Except for having to go to work.'

'I like the look of that pier. It goes out miles.'

'It's the longest in England, and the oldest.'

'My God, you reporters certainly know your stuff.'

'We could have breakfast on it. There's a place, right at the end.'

'What time do you have to get to work?'

'I don't know. What time do you?'

I looked down at the pier. The little train waited with open carriages in the sunny station. 'Can we go on that railway thing at this time of year? Is it running?'

'The pier one? Every twenty minutes all the year round. It's hydraulic.'

'What does that mean?'

'I don't know. It's fun, though.'

'Hmmm. Every twenty minutes.' I studied Natasha behind the sheet. 'D'you think we've got time?'

After breakfast we wandered about the town. We had fish and chips for lunch, and soft Italian ice cream, sitting on one of the sky-blue benches. After lunch we hired a boat for an hour but got bored in about ten minutes. The zoo was better than the boating lake. The animals had an abstracted out-of-season air about them. Equally pleased to see us was the attendant on the one ride working at Pleasureland. Heights gave me vertigo but I couldn't spoil Natasha's fun. Southport looked good from the top of the big wheel. The man with the lever said we could keep on turning as long as we liked. It made the dead funfair look alive. The ground rushed gently up and then receded. I said to Natasha, 'I'm glad there's no third man.'

The movie showing at the Rialto that afternoon was *The King and I*. We sat in the back row of the deserted stalls. 'D'you remember when we went to see *Cleopatra*?' I whispered.

'Oh, no,' she hissed back, 'why on earth would I remember that?'

An usherette with a tray appeared and shone her torch on us. I handed her money guiltily for Kia-Ora and she went away. Outside the cinema it was dark. Bare bulbs twinkled around the mouths of the empty arcades, which belched echoing carousel music out on to the deserted streets. We stood facing each other, in the cold. When I spoke I could see my breath. 'I ought to work tonight at least.'

'Shall I come with you?'

'If you want. I needn't stay for long.'

While I spoke to Woody my eyes were on Natasha. She wore velvet hipsters with a wide belt and a skinny-rib sweater. The small movements she made as she danced with herself in front of a pinball machine made me want to get back to Southport as soon as possible.

'I think I might take a few days off, Woody. I need a rest after all that opening business.'

'Rest, is it?' Woody's eyes followed mine. 'Yer derty booger. I could easily fancy a rest with that one meself. All fookin' night long, mate!'

At the Churchill Hotel Mavis Fanshawe looked deeply disappointed in me.

'I thought you were happy here.'

'It's only for a few days, Mavis.'

Mavis eyed Natasha doubtfully. 'That's what they all say.'

'Sea air, Mavis. A change is as good as a rest.'

Mavis remained unconvinced. 'You won't get a full English breakfast like mine anywhere in Southport.'

We walked together with my bag back to Central Station. We went some way in silence before Natasha said, 'What a ghastly room. How do you stand it?'

'I'm not there much.'

'She didn't want to let me even see it.'

'That's just her rules. Keeps me out of trouble.'

'Oh sure.'

Natasha's flat occupied the first floor of a gothic folly on the promenade. The mullioned windows of its one big room looked straight out to sea. It had a large Victorian bathroom and a tiny kitchen. When we got back it was late and the town was definitely closed. Natasha fiddled with keys and we clumped up the dark stairs. She shut the door behind us and switched on the lights. Old lamps glowed. Natasha had filled the place with books and cushions and plants. A stone cat I had once given her stood in a corner.

I dropped my case near the door and fell into a battered leather armchair.

'God, I'm starving. Aren't you?'

'Pity we can't just pop out to Valentina's.'

'That does seem a long time ago.'

'Maybe Dolly's been. We could cook something.'

'Dolly?'

'You know Dolly. You knew her before I did.'

I shook my head. 'Do I?'

'Dolly's great. She found this place and everything. Sometimes she goes shopping for me and leaves things in the fridge. She worries about me, a bit like you and Mavis.'

'I still don't know who on earth you're talking about.'

'You do, but when I tell you you mustn't get uptight.'

'Why should I get uptight?'

'Dolly is Val's mum.'

'So you're still hung up on him.'

'Of course I'm not. I haven't seen him for ages.'

'But you came up here with him, went to his house and everything . . .'

'Yes.'

'I don't think I can stand this. I think I'm going to go.'

'Come on, Paul. I said don't get heavy.'

'I can't help getting heavy, you bitch. You fucking whore!'

'Please, Paul, don't spoil everything.'

'You spoiled everything, you, when you went off and fucked that fucking guy!'

'No I didn't.'

'You did, you did, you absolute bitch. Why did you have to do it?'

'It wasn't anything. It wasn't that important. I wanted to have fun. You were suffocating me.'

'You were just a disgusting little tart. God!'

'I had to get away from you somehow, don't you see?'

'You just wanted to fuck a pop star. You fancied him, didn't you? Because he was a star, you fucking groupie, you dirty little starfucker!'

'Just fuck off, Paul.'

'What was it like, eh? Go on, tell me what it was like with him.'

'Don't be so crazy. You're being pathetic.'

'I'm going to go, Natasha. That's it.' I got up.

'Good.'

'There's lots of places I can stay in Southport.'

'Lots.'

'That aren't brothels!' I moved resolutely towards my bag.

When I got level to where she was sitting she said, 'Anyway, what about you? What about that awful girl you were living with in Pont Street? She was a real groupie.'

I looked down at her on the sofa. 'That was all your fault, too. Anyway, it was Pavilion Road.'

She looked up into my face. 'God, Paul, I can't stand you. I really can't.'

I sat down next to her. 'Is that why you had to get away from me?'

'Yes.'

The tiny hairs on her sweater felt surprisingly prickly. 'I can't stand you either, Natasha, you know that, don't you?'

'Yes,' she said, 'yes . . .'

In the morning it was sunny again. We woke up late. The bed was warm. Natasha said, 'I suppose I could ring them up and say I was ill.'

I was fiddling with the bedside radio, trying to get Camelot. 'What's wrong with this bloody thing?'

'Nothing's wrong with it. What do you think?'

'About what?'

'About me going to work?'

'I think you should definitely go to work. How else are you going to get to the top?'

'I don't want to get to the top.'

'That's not what you said before.'

'I had to say something to get out of marrying Ned.'

'Why can't I get Camelot? Can you do it?'

'Of course. Here.'

'If I could tune into that at least one of us would be working.'

'I can't get it either. Something's wrong.'

'I'd've thought a high-powered reporter like you would at least have a decent radio. It's all down to information, you know.'

'Oh fuck off. It's nothing to do with my radio. There's something wrong with your stupid ship.'

'So why didn't you want to marry Ned? He's a pretty cool guy.'

'I just didn't want to, that's all.'

'You'd've been a countess.'

'You're not starting again?'

'No, Natasha, I'm really genuinely curious.'

'I think you're genuinely an absolute bore.'

'I want you to tell me you were saving yourself for me.'

'Don't be silly.'

'How d'you mean, don't be silly?'

'I couldn't possibly marry you.'

'Why not?'

'Mummy'd have an absolute fit!'

'Who cares about that old crow?'

'Anyway think of all the fuss.'

'What fuss?'

'There'd be a ghastly fuss, invitations and Archbishops and things.'

'Would there have to be Archbishops?'

'No, honestly, I'm serious. It'd be a nightmare.'

'So am I serious, I think.'

'You're not, are you?'

'I didn't think I was . . .'

'You really want to marry me?'

'Yes, I do.'

'OK.'

We telephoned my parents but there was no reply. I said, 'Let's go anyway.' I wanted to get it over. In the train Natasha read magazines. I watched the changing countryside flash by. Natasha looked up and said, 'I'm rather dreading it, aren't you?'

I said, 'Oh, they'll be OK. It's your mother I'm dreading.'

'She's bound to be awful.'

'God, don't say that.'

'She'll want to know about your prospects and all sorts of details about money.'

'I should say my prospects are rather fantastic, wouldn't you? I mean, I've really got it together, don't you think?'

'The Shrine is amazing. Who'd've thought it!'

'And the ship.'

'And the ship.' The train had stopped at Crewe. Natasha nibbled a finger and looked out across the endless sidings. 'Mummy prefers banks and things, though. That's the trouble.'

'It'll be OK, I'm sure,' I said.

The taxi ground up the steep hill to the parental lair. The driver was full of local updates but it was hard to take an interest. Natasha and I sat in the back, wrapped in silence. There seemed nothing we could say. Our minds were paralysed by the imminent need for approval. One good thought struck me. I leaned over and shoved her in the shoulder. 'Perhaps they won't be there!'

Down the drive the pool gleamed balefully through the wrought iron. I didn't have my key. I was about to ring the bell when the door was pulled sharply open.

'Where the hell've you been?' My father's hair hung over one ear in unusual disarray.

'Hello, Daddy. This is . . .'

'You bloody little fool! Don't you know what's been going on?'

'Well, I . . .'

'We've been hunting for you everywhere, dear.' My mother's face loomed anxiously in the hallway behind my father.

'I've just been . . . that is . . . this is Natasha, Mummy.'

'How do you do, Natasha. Come in, both of you.'

'Natasha and I want to get married!' Unable to think straight, I just blurted it out.

'Christ!' Complete chaos seemed to have overtaken my father's hair, 'What a boy! What a bloody marvellous boy!'

'Look,' I said, 'what's going on? Why are you all so upset?'

'Really, Paul, your father's been having a dreadful time.'

'At five o'clock this morning' – my father sat grimly in his usual chair — 'while you and your bit of fluff were no doubt enjoying yourselves, your friend Vig Moller towed away both our ships!'

'God . . . !'

'And there isn't a bloody thing we can do about it.'

'Why not? I don't understand.'

'You'll have to ask your friend O'Mahoney about that. Do you realise not a single bill has been paid on the shipping account for nearly a year? Frankly I don't blame that bloody Dutchman.'

I remembered the empty hetrodine on Natasha's bedside radio. Was it really only that morning? 'The trouble is, Daddy, I've been pretty involved with the club, you know. Things are going rather well there.'

'Well you can forget that now. You don't think anybody would ever go to your tuppeny ha'penny dive without all that free advertising. And where d'you think all the money goes, you bloody little fool! D'you think I see any? D'you think the shareholders do? Bunch of bloody crooks you've got me mixed up with. That club's going under the liquidator's hammer with everything else. You mark my words!'

'God, Daddy . . .'

'And here's another thing you can forget all about. You can forget all about any bloody nonsense about getting married. You can't afford to keep yourself, never mind little Miss Hotknickers . . .'

'I say, Daddy, hang on . . .'

'From now on you're going to buckle down to something, you take it from me.'

'It doesn't seem sensible, does it, dear, really, getting married just at the moment . . . ?'

'I'd appreciate it if Daddy would stop calling Natasha names.'

'Considering the mess you've landed your father in,' my mother swallowed hard, 'I think you should be thinking more about helping him get things sorted out, not getting yourself mixed up again with someone who . . .'

'Someone who what?' Natasha had sat down on the very edge of a chair and was now looking intently at my mother. Her face was pale, her eyes huge, her mouth firm.

'Well, I'm bound to say . . . Paul has spoken of you in the past not quite so glowingly as now. The fact is you only seem able to make him thoroughly unhappy and confused. I don't know much about you, I admit. I haven't met you before, but from what I read in the newspapers I'm bound to say, I don't think you'd make a suitable wife for my son.'

'Or anybody else for that matter!' My father ground out his cigarette in the ashtray. Natasha and I looked at each other hard. She was just holding on. I got up. My head was singing, my shouting voice echoed in my ears. 'Right! That's it! I've had about as much as I can take from you two miserable fuckers. I love Natasha and she loves me and that's it. You've never believed in me, you don't understand anything about me. All you ever do is find surrogate sons to believe in and load them on my back. Now you blame me when they fuck up. It's their fault and your fault and nothing to do with me. I never wanted to be a businessman. I never wanted to be taken out of school. I wanted to go to university, but you just assumed I couldn't make it, like you always do. Anything to do with books, anything to do with art, is a lot of bloody nonsense. Anything that can't be put in a balance sheet, that's what you think. Anything I might succeed at that you can't control, that you can't come along and say, Christ you're making an awful mess of that, better let me take over. I never wanted to go to America. I hated America, hated being grateful and cute the whole fucking time. I hated that fucking carwash. You couldn't wait for it to fail, and blame me for it. Now it's the same with the radio station. You want me to feel guilty because you did it all for me, but really you only did it to get me off your hands. D'you think I ever had the slightest influence in anything that went on? Don't you understand why I had to go away and get myself together on a tiny island miles away from you? D'you think I want you to pour out thousands setting up businesses in which I fail so you can blame me as you bail me out? D'you really think I want to live my life like that? Fucking up just to please you? You can stick it, d'you hear me! You can stick your damn bloody molly-coddling and your stocks and shares and your *Sunday Night at the London Palladium*. Stick it up your middle-class arses. The one thing I do want is the one thing you can't buy me, the one thing you can't give me. It's something you can't understand and it's the one thing you don't want me to have. Come on, Natasha. We're getting out of here. For good!'

*

We had to walk back to the station. The sense of freedom made me dance up and down crazily on the pavements. No attempt was made to follow us. In a calm moment I said, 'There's not much point in seeing your mother now.'

Natasha said, 'No, there's not.'

'Oh, well' – I swung round a passing lamp-post – 'every cloud has a silver lining!'

We sat on a sky-blue bench, looking out to sea. Gulls wheeled and hung in the morning sunshine. I said, 'Let's get married anyway.'

Without turning Natasha answered, 'If you want.'

'I do want.'

'Let's then.'

'Good. That's settled then.'

After a while Natasha said, 'How will we live, though, now that your empire's crumbled?'

'There's always your job.'

'Oh sure.'

'No, seriously, I've had rather a brilliant idea about that.' I paused to shift position and put my arm along the bench behind her.

'Come on then, let's hear it.'

'Well, you know the boutique?'

'Yes . . .'

'I've always been keen on the boutique. The fact is that having it inside the club is really a disadvantage. What we need, all we need really, is a shop. Our own shop. It can't be hard to find one, nothing to do with all this mess . . .'

'Great . . .'

'. . . we'll just open up somewhere, anywhere we like. Boutiques are where it's at right now. I mean, God, when you think about it, we'd be crazy not to have a boutique. We'll make an absolute fortune!'

'God, do you really think so?'

'Absolutely!'